"You're going to marry my brother, knowing what's happened?

"You can't keep pretending there's nothing between us, Kate," Nick continued.

"Yes, I can. I mean, there isn't anything between us," Kate corrected hastily. "It was a mistake."

"All of it?" He seemed to loom over her. Kate felt breathless, as if there was too little oxygen. "It's not just what happened two weeks ago, Kate. What about the kiss in the gazebo? And five years ago? Are you just going to pretend that none of that happened?"

"Y-yes."

Kate looked into his eyes, and she saw anger reflected there. She felt overwhelmed by Nick, pulled by the force of his will. For a moment she nearly gave in to his demand, nearly admitted…that she wanted him.

Dallas Schulze is "…a powerhouse of mainstream women's fiction."
—*The Paperback Forum*

DALLAS SCHULZE
HOME TO EDEN

MIRA BOOKS

MIRA

ISBN 1-55166-290-6

HOME TO EDEN

Copyright © 1997 by Dallas Schulze.

MIRA and the star colophon are trademarks of MIRA Books.

Printed in U.S.A.

To my editor, Lucia Macro:
Every writer should be so lucky!

I'd like to thank my agent, Ethan Ellenberg, for smoothing the path many times over the last couple of years. And Dianne Moggy and everyone else at MIRA Books for their support and enthusiasm.

Prologue

The shrill jangle of the phone woke him from an already restless sleep. Nick rolled over, his hand groping for the receiver even before his eyes were open. He didn't know the time, but it had to be late. It had been after midnight when he came to bed and, judging from the tangled sheets, he'd been tossing and turning for awhile. Face half buried in the pillow, he mumbled into the receiver, his voice raspy with sleep.

"Blackthorne."

"Did I wake you?"

"Harry." Not an emergency then. If something had happened to someone in his family, it wouldn't be Harry making the call. Along with relief, he felt a certain resigned irritation. He squeezed his eyes shut and then opened them again, trying to wake up. "What time is it?"

"It's a little after eleven here."

"You're in California. I'm in New York. There's a three-hour time difference. That means it's—" still foggy with sleep, Nick fumbled over the difficult calculation and settled for simplicity "—late. It's late here."

"Figured I could be sure of catching you now," Harry said, sounding disgustingly alert and not at all guilty.

"Couldn't you have called at a normal hour?" Nick rolled over and dragged himself into a semi-upright position, leaning back against the headboard. He rubbed one hand over his face.

"Nothing abnormal about eleven o'clock."

"No, but there's something a little peculiar about two in the morning." He'd managed to focus on the clock long enough to confirm the time.

"I did call earlier. When you didn't answer, I figured, since it's Saturday night, you were probably out on a date."

"Why didn't you leave a message on the machine?" He leaned his head against the wall and closed his eyes. He ignored the comment about the date, knowing it was the old man's not so subtle way of probing into the state of his love life. There was no point in telling him just how little there was to probe into. Nick forced his eyes open with an effort.

Damn, he was tired. He tried to remember the last time he'd had a decent night's sleep. It had been weeks. "The machine did pick up, didn't it?"

"Don't like them," Harry snapped. "I don't like talking to a machine, talking to a piece of tape. Takes all the humanity out of communication. If people spent as much time talking to one another as they do yapping at machines, the world might not be in such a mess."

"Afraid it'll capture your soul, Harry?" Forgetting his irritation over the lateness of the call, Nick grinned into the darkness.

"Might be more truth to that than anybody knows," Harry shot back tartly. "People are all the time inventing things without giving any thought to the impact of what they're doing. Look at cars. Must have seemed like a pretty clever idea—horseless carriage and all that. I bet none of the folks who invented them gave a thought to pollution and noise and traffic jams. Not to mention parking lots covering half the planet's surface."

"Probably not. So, I take it you've quit driving?" Nick asked.

"Hell, no! Why would I do that?"

"Because it's clear that the automobile is a danger to all mankind, maybe even worse than the answering machine."

There was a brief silence and then Harry chuckled.

"Hoist on my own petard, damn you. When are you going to learn some respect for your elders?"

"When they earn it," Nick shot back, still grinning.

He hadn't seen Harry Wallace in five years but he could see him clearly in his mind's eye. His face was lined with the joys and sorrows of seventy-five years of living, and he was tall and lean. With his thick, gray hair falling in untidy waves onto his forehead and his clothes wrinkled and socks that usually didn't match, Harry looked like the epitome of an absent-minded professor. The misleading image had served him well during his years as a highly paid criminal attorney. The rumpled appearance and deliberately vague blue eyes had led more than a few opposing attorneys to dismiss him as a bumbling idiot, much to their ultimate regret.

When Nick met him, Harry had been long retired from practice. The two of them had immediately hit it off, and the more than forty-year difference in their ages had never seemed to have any relevance to their friendship.

"I assume you didn't call just to entertain me with your neo-Luddite theories." Nick hitched himself higher against the headboard and stifled a yawn. "What's up?"

"I've decided to sell the house."

"Your house?" Nick's voice reflected his surprise. Harry's grandfather had built the house during the late Victorian era. It featured more gingerbread and fancy trim than a wedding cake. Harry generally referred to it as a monstrosity. He'd often complained in acid-tongued detail about the cost of upkeep and heat, and the absurdity of a single man occupying a home with seven bedrooms. Still, Nick had always thought Harry's attachment to the place was unbreakable.

"It doesn't seem likely I'd be selling someone else's house, does it?" Harry asked tartly.

"Doesn't sound any less likely than you selling your place. Where are you going to live?"

"They're putting up a block of condos on the north end of town, next to the golf course, advertising it as the ideal place to spend your 'golden' years, although I don't know what the hell is so golden about aching bones and prostate problems," Harry muttered in disgust. "But golden or not, I'm not as young as I used to be and I thought maybe I'd buy a condo and play golf until I get too old to swing a club."

Nick tried to imagine Harry living in a condo and filling his time with golf. The image wouldn't come clear. "I thought you hated golf."

"I can learn to like it, can't I?" Harry snapped irritably. "Maybe I'll play chess or checkers instead."

Checkers? Nick frowned into the darkness of his bedroom. Harry Wallace whiling away his time with checkers? Not likely.

"What's really going on, Harry? And don't give

me a line of bull about golf and checkers. Are you sick?''

The silence on the other end of the line tightened the knot forming in his stomach. If something happened to Harry... When he spoke, his voice was quieter, his words slower. For the first time in Nick's memory, he sounded like an old man.

''I'm not sick, not unless you want to call getting old an illness. I'm getting tired, Nick. Just wearing out a bit. Nothing for you to worry about.'' He sighed, and Nick felt something tighten in his chest. Harry was one of those rare people who had always made age seem truly irrelevant. It was frightening to hear him sounding so old and almost frail.

''Is that why you're selling the house?'' He made an effort to keep the concern out of his voice, knowing it wouldn't be appreciated.

''It's just too damn big,'' Harry said fretfully. ''I've let things slide the last few years, and the place is falling down around my ears. I don't have the energy to fix it up and, even if I did, there's no real point to it. I'm not going to be around long enough to enjoy it.''

''Harry—''

''This house was built for a family,'' he continued, cutting off Nick's protest. ''It needs young people in it—maybe some of those yuppies who are trying to escape the rat race in the city and think living in a town like Eden is going to give their life new meaning.''

Nick didn't doubt that Harry would be able to sell the place, probably to exactly the sort of people he was describing, a young couple looking to escape the smog and traffic in Los Angeles. Eden was small enough to feel intimate but large enough to offer the important things in life—cappuccino, good bagels and decent amateur theater. And, if they wanted a taste of big city life, L.A. was just a little over two hours away. Harry's big old house, oozing with the kind of character that came only with time, wouldn't be hard to sell. But it wasn't possible to imagine someone else living there.

"You didn't call me at two in the morning just to tell me you're thinking about selling your house." Nick kept his tone brisk, concealing his concern. "Cut to the chase."

"The problem with you is that you have no finesse," Harry complained.

"And the problem with you is that you have too much," Nick countered. "Spit it out."

There was a brief silence, as if the other man was choosing his words carefully. Nick reached over and flipped on the sleek black lamp on the bedside table, narrowing his eyes against the soft flood of light. Whatever Harry wanted, Nick had the feeling he wasn't going to like it.

"I want you to come home, help me fix the house up so I can put it on the market."

Nick said nothing, letting the faint hum of the long-distance connection fill the silence while he absorbed the magnitude of his old friend's request.

"I know it's a lot to ask," Harry said finally, his tone more defensive than apologetic.

"It's a hell of a lot," Nick said flatly.

"You're the only one I'd trust to do the job. You know the place."

"You don't have to know a house to patch a few holes in the plaster and slap some paint on the walls. You can afford to hire someone who'll do good work. Talk to Jack Sinclair. He doesn't usually do restorations, but I'll call him and ask him to make an exception."

"I want someone doing the work who actually cares."

It was on the tip of his tongue to say that he didn't care, but Nick couldn't get the words out. He *did* care. He'd always loved the rambling old house with its extravagant layers of trim and air of sweetly pompous dignity. And there was something in Harry's voice that worried him—a vulnerability he didn't like. He shoved his fingers through his dark hair and closed his eyes, feeling as if the walls of the loft were starting to move in on him.

"You're not talking about a weekend job," he

said, martialing his arguments carefully. "I've got a job here. A life."

"Last time we talked, you told me you were sick of Wall Street," Harry countered. "You said you were thinking of quitting, getting out of the city."

"Thinking about it is a long way from doing it." Nick threw the covers back and swung his legs out of bed. "I can't just pick up and leave."

But even as he said it, he knew it wasn't true. There was nothing—no one—holding him in the city. His job would be filled by the time he'd packed up his desk. He'd made few friends in the years he'd lived in New York, a matter of conscious choice as much as chance. He could leave tomorrow and the ripples of his departure would fade before he made it to the New Jersey side of the Lincoln Tunnel.

"Dammit, Harry, there are other people who could do the job. I don't restore houses anymore. I sell stock. Talk to Jack Sinclair. He'll do a good job for you."

He could hear the older man's breathing on the other end of the line. There was something about that shallow sound that made his own breathing feel constricted. He tried to call up an image of Harry the way he'd always been—lean and strong, touched by age but not conquered by it—but somehow, this time, he seemed to see new lines in his face, noticed a faint tremor in hands that had always been rock steady.

"You're right," Harry said at last. "It's too much

to ask. I guess I was just thinking you might be ready to come home. It's been five years, Nick.''

Five years, three months and six days. If he thought about it for a moment, he could come up with the number of hours and minutes since he'd left Eden, left California. He'd been running from the past, running from his memories. Five years later and three thousand miles away, they were both still with him. He thought about the restlessness he'd felt lately, about the sleepless nights, the gray sameness of the days.

Funny that it should take so long to realize he couldn't run away from what he carried inside himself. He felt resignation seeping in around the edges of his refusal.

''Is this part of some misguided attempt to save me from myself, Harry?''

''Do you need saving?''

The automatic denial died in Nick's throat. He glanced around his bedroom, taking in the sleek, modern furnishings. The room was cool and carefully soulless, just like his life for the past five years. Maybe Harry was right. Maybe it was time to go home. Maybe the only way to lay ghosts to rest was to face them on their home ground.

''I've got some vacation time I can take,'' he said slowly. He knew, even as he said it, that, once he left this place, he wouldn't be back. Whether he stayed in Eden or not, he wouldn't be coming back to New

York. He released his breath slowly. "Give me a couple of weeks to get things settled here. I'll come home."

Three thousand miles away, Harry set the receiver in place and hoped he hadn't made a mistake. His blue eyes, faded with age, settled on a framed portrait of a young couple, the woman cradling an infant who looked scarcely more fragile than she did herself. His hand shook a little as he reached out and lifted the picture. He studied the faces for a moment before sliding open a drawer in the end table and setting the picture inside. He slid the drawer shut.

He'd interfered once before, manipulated two lives with the best of intentions, and the results had ultimately been tragic. But this time he was right. He knew he was right.

He'd done the right thing, he told himself. He was sure of it.

Almost.

Chapter One

"If Mrs. Kimmel calls about her *strelitzia reginae*, remind her that they're heavy feeders and that she needs to give them time to get established. They do best when they're a little crowded."

"If you think I'm going to discuss Mrs. Kimmel's striped reggaes with her, you can think again! If she wants to talk about that kind of thing, she can call her hairdresser." Brenda's forehead puckered. "Or maybe her gynecologist," she added uncertainly.

Kate Moran had been frowning at the clipboard she held but she looked up at that, her blue eyes bright with laughter, her slight frown disappearing in a quick smile. "I'm talking about Mrs. Kimmel's bird of paradise plants."

"Why didn't you say so?" Brenda asked, widening her eyes in exaggerated surprise.

"I did. *Strelitzia reginae* is the proper botanical name. You know, the Latin name?"

"Oh, Latin." Brenda lifted one plump shoulder in a dismissive shrug. "I don't know why botanists feel they have to use a dead language. Wouldn't it be easier if they just used plain old English? Why confuse things?"

"The Latin names are intended to make things *less* confusing," Kate pointed out. "When someone tells me they want jasmine, they might mean one of a half dozen likely varieties of *jasminum,* but there's a fairly good chance that they're talking about *trachelospermum jasminoides,* which is an entirely different animal."

Brenda looked mildly disapproving. "I'm not sure, but I think it's against the law to use language like that in public."

Kate laughed again. She let the hand holding the clipboard drop to her side and fixed the other woman with a mock stern look. "I don't see how it's possible for you to own a nursery and still know absolutely nothing about plants."

"Practice," Brenda said with a modest smirk. "Years of practice."

"Don't you want to know more about what you're selling?" Kate asked, gesturing to the greenery that surrounded them.

The two of them were in her office at Wisteria, the nursery that Brenda's late husband had left her. There were windows on two sides of the tiny room. One looked out on a display of houseplants, all lush greens, ranging from palest lime to deepest emerald. Outside the other window were tables of bedding plants, many of them already in bloom—pansies, alyssum and Iceland poppies all nodding at the merest puff of a breeze as if greeting the customers who browsed among them. Kate simply couldn't imagine how anyone could be surrounded by such beauty and remain indifferent to it.

"I know everything I need to know about plants," Brenda said, unmoved by the verdant extravaganza that surrounded her. "The green side goes up. I asked you to manage this place because you know all the gory details of what needs sun and what needs shade and when to spoon-feed the little darlings smelly concoctions of manure and compost and what to do when they get an infestation of really gross bugs."

Kate grinned. "You think all bugs are gross."

"Pretty much," Brenda admitted cheerfully.

"You don't even know enough to make sure I'm not ripping you off."

"I don't have to know plants to know that," Brenda said. "I know I can trust you. Besides, I don't really care whether you're buying rarius extrabiggus or geriatric orthopedus. In the year and a half you've been managing the nursery, business has gone up almost fifty percent. As a businesswoman, the bottom line is my only concern."

Kate's grin widened, her blue eyes laughing. "If you're such a tough businesswoman, you would have fired Jim Miller months ago."

"He's a good worker," Brenda said defensively.

"He's eighty-nine and can only make it in to work two days out of five."

"Well, there's nothing wrong with good part-time help."

"Nothing at all, except when you're paying them to do a full-time job."

"Mr. Miller drove the school bus when I was in elementary. He's a nice old man."

"Very nice," Kate agreed, still grinning.

"And working here helps him retain a sense of self-respect."

"Absolutely."

"The customers like him."

"Yes, they do."

"If I only paid him for the hours he's able to work, he would never be able to make ends meet on the skimpy little pension he gets from the school district."

"And the bottom line that you care about so passionately?" Kate inquired gently.

Brenda glared at her a moment and then laughed. "Screw the bottom line."

"Not a very good attitude for a businesswoman."

"That's why I hired you to manage this place."

Kate shook her head, her smile taking on a rueful

edge. The argument had come full circle, and she knew it would be a waste of time to continue it. Brenda Duncan was more than just her employer. Over the past two years, since the death of Brenda's husband had left her sole owner of the nursery, the two of them had become good friends. Brenda was sweet and funny, kind and generous to a fault. What she was *not* was a good businesswoman. It was probably just as well that she'd also inherited a comfortable trust fund from her maternal grandmother and didn't have to worry about squeezing every penny from her late husband's business.

"I'd just feel better if you knew more about what we're selling," Kate said finally.

"Maybe *you'd* feel better but I wouldn't. I know this is going to sound like blasphemy to you, but I think gardening is about as interesting as watching paint dry." She grinned at her friend's exaggerated wince. "You might as well face the facts, Kate. You're never going to make a plant lover out of me. It's not like *I* bought this place. It was Larry's idea, though why he thought a nursery was going to be his personal road to riches, I don't know. No one gets rich selling plants."

Kate lowered her head and made some meaningless notes on the clipboard. She had her own theories about that. In the year she'd worked for Larry Duncan, his main occupation had been hitting on every moderately attractive woman who set foot in the nursery. In his spare time, he'd occupied himself with issuing various—often conflicting—orders to the small staff just so they wouldn't lose sight of his importance. She didn't think he'd been interested in profits nearly as much as he had been in setting himself up as king of his own little empire, but she could hardly say as much. Not that it would have come as a surprise to his widow. Brenda had been in the process of filing for divorce when he died.

Brenda's thoughts must have been going along the same lines because she glanced around at the display of healthy greenery, the customers browsing among the tables of plants and her wide mouth curved in a smile that held more than a touch of malice. "I take a certain satisfaction in knowing that this place is doing so much better now than it did when he was running it. Running this store isn't quite as much fun as firebombing it would have been, but there aren't as many legal hassles involved."

"Isn't there some quote about revenge being a poor motivation for taking action?"

"If there is, whoever said it would have changed their minds if they'd known Larry," Brenda said flatly.

Kate opened her mouth to protest and then closed it without speaking. She hadn't known Larry Duncan long, but it was long enough to know that he'd been small-minded, tightfisted and lecherous—and *those* were his least objectionable qualities. It was no surprise if Brenda was a less than grieving widow. The only real surprise was that she'd ever married him in the first place.

"I think there's also a quote about revenge tasting sweet," she said with a wry grin.

"I like that one much better." Brenda glanced at the big round clock on the wall above the desk. "You'd better get going if you want to have time to shower and change clothes before having dinner at your in-laws."

"Future in-laws," Kate corrected her. Following Brenda's glance at the clock, she dropped the clipboard onto the cluttered desk. "They won't be my in-laws for another six months."

"One thing about marrying Gareth Blackthorne, you know you're not going to have in-law trouble," Brenda commented. She reached up to push a mass of unruly red curls from her face. The scrunchy band of elastic that was supposed to be holding them in place had gradually yielded to a superior force and dangled forlornly from the ends of her hair. Sighing, she tugged it loose and began the process of trying to capture the heavy mass and force it into some semblance of order.

"In-law trouble is the least of my worries," Kate agreed with a smile. "Sara and Philip are so wonderful that I'd be tempted to marry Gareth just so I could be a part of their family."

"But you're *not*, are you—marrying Gareth because of his family, I mean?'' Brenda's tone made the words half-statement, half-question and Kate gave her a startled look.

"I was just kidding."

"Of course you were." Brenda shook her head, her fair skin flushing. "I know that. I guess I just feel a little responsible, since I'm the one who introduced the two of you."

"Lucky for me you did." Kate pulled open the deep drawer where she kept her purse.

"Lucky for Gareth," Brenda said loyally.

"Thanks." Kate slid the strap of her purse over her shoulder and glanced around the office to see if there was anything she'd forgotten.

"I mean, I know you're marrying Gareth because you love him madly," Brenda said.

"Why else?" Kate asked with a smile.

Sometimes, Kate worried that life might be going *too* well. After spending her entire childhood following her father from one city to another while he chased some dream that only he understood, she'd wanted a home, a place to put down roots. Eden, California, had seemed nearly as idyllic as its name. The town was small enough to feel cozy yet big enough for her to find work. The first couple of years, she'd worked odd jobs—waiting tables, checking groceries, anything she could find to keep body and soul together. In those days she'd gone to school part-time, taking every class on botany and landscape design she could find. It hadn't been easy, but it had all paid off when she was hired to work at a nursery.

Putting up with Larry Duncan's heavy-handed flirtation and pompous posturing had been a small price to pay for the chance to indulge her love of green, growing things. A year after she was hired, Larry, assisted by half a dozen margaritas, managed to wrap his car around a telephone pole, leaving his wife the new and extremely reluctant owner of a fledgling nursery. Brenda had planned to sell the place but Kate had convinced her that it could be turned into a profitable business. So Brenda had given her a chance to prove herself.

Kate treasured her success with Wisteria, but her friendship with Brenda meant even more. Her father's peripatetic life-style had made childhood friendships such fleeting things that she'd soon given up trying to make friends. It hurt too much when each new move broke the fragile ties. Settling in Eden had given her a chance to develop lasting friendships for the first time in her life.

As if that wasn't enough, she was engaged to marry the kindest, most decent man she'd ever met. Gareth Blackthorne was solid, dependable, settled—all the things she wanted in her life. She'd never have to worry about him waking up one morning and deciding it was time to move a thousand miles away because of some wonderful opportunity he'd heard about.

Gareth had been born and raised in Eden. He'd spent four years attending college in Los Angeles, getting an English degree, and then, when he came home, he'd surprised everyone by becoming a cop rather than a teacher. As far as Kate knew, that was the last time he'd done anything completely unpredictable, which was one of the things she liked most about him. She could count on Gareth.

And there was his family. The Blackthornes were the embodiment of her childhood fantasies about what a family was supposed to be. They had welcomed her with open arms, making her feel as if her marriage to Gareth was the best thing they could imagine. Philip Blackthorne was a minister, and his wife, Sara, was a doctor. They had two children living. A third, a son, had died at a tragically young age. Gareth was the eldest at thirty-six, there was another brother a couple of years younger than Gareth. Kate knew little about him beyond the fact that he hadn't been home in several years. When his name came up, it seemed to carry with it an indefinable air of regret and sadness. All she knew about him was that he'd left Eden soon after the death of his wife and son.

Kate assumed there had been some split with the family, and her sympathy for his loss had been diluted by the pain his memory seemed to cause the

Blackthornes. She hadn't asked Gareth for an explanation. She told herself it was because she didn't want to bring up a painful topic, but she was guiltily aware that she didn't really want to know anything that might tarnish her image of the Blackthornes as the perfect family. Whatever had happened between Gareth's brother and his family, it had nothing to do with her. Privately, she labeled him "The Black Sheep" and dismissed him. Anyone who could walk away from a family as special as this wasn't worth thinking about.

"Kate?" The sound of her name startled her and Kate blinked, her eyes meeting Gareth's across the table. The quizzical way he was looking at her made it obvious it wasn't the first time he'd tried to get her attention. She smiled apologetically.

"Sorry. I guess I faded out for a minute."

"I was going to offer you a penny for your thoughts but you looked so absorbed, I figured the price might be higher."

"Not even that much."

"No doubt you were lost in admiration of my chicken casserole," Philip Blackthorne said.

"It's delicious," Kate said sincerely. The Mexican-style casserole, with its layers of cheese, tortillas and chicken, was sharply flavored with jalapeños and the more subtle tang of cilantro.

"I think I did a particularly fine job with it," he said expansively.

"Nobody can reheat a casserole the way you can, dear," Sara told him, her tone dry. "Did Annie write down the microwave instructions or did you manage to remember them this time?"

"I remembered them," Philip said with obvious pride.

Neither of the elder Blackthornes were known for their skill in the kitchen—or household tasks in general. Sara's medical practice kept her busy and Philip's duties with the church were equally demanding. Virtually all of the cooking and a good portion of the housework were done by Mrs. Annie Pickle, a tiny woman with a personality as tart as her name, who seemed to view the care and feeding of the Blackthorne family as an assignment handed down from above. Kate had met her soon after she began dating Gareth and had been thoroughly intimidated by the older woman's sharp, assessing look that seemed to weigh her and find her sorely lacking in qualifications to marry a Blackthorne.

"You let Dad in the kitchen?" Gareth asked, his eyes widening in shock. "After the last time?"

"One small fire, two years ago, and you still haven't let me live it down." Philip looked aggrieved.

"Small fire?" Gareth's brows went up. "The kitchen was gutted."

"It needed to be refurbished anyway," Sara said comfortably.

Gareth looked at Kate, his eyes gleaming with laughter. "Some people hire a contractor to remodel the old kitchen. In my family, we just turn Dad loose and let him burn the old fixtures out."

"I forgot I had something on the stove. Everyone does that from time to time."

"But not everyone manages to set the house on fire while reheating a pan of soup."

"I didn't set the whole house on fire. Merely the kitchen. What's the world coming to when a man can't get any respect in his own household?" Philip demanded.

"I have lots of respect for you, Dad. Particularly when you're armed with a match."

Philip's stern expression was at odds with the laughter in his eyes. "Sara, I'm afraid we've nurtured a viper in the very bosom of our family."

"Probably," she agreed, spreading butter on a roll with no real sign of concern.

Kate listened to the exchange with a mixture of delight and envy. This kind of foolish, teasing conversation was new to her. There had been laughter in her childhood, but it had usually come from outside sources—television and movies. She couldn't imagine either of her parents indulging in the kind of lighthearted teasing that Philip and Sara took for granted. She thought it was a wonderful gift to give your children.

The conversation shifted to a discussion of the

women's shelter that was being built in town. Sara was spearheading the fund-raising efforts. Kate made an occasional contribution to the discussion but, for the most part, she was content to listen. This was another thing that was new—dinner table conversations about issues that went beyond the family.

The conversations she remembered her parents having when she was a child had generally consisted of her mother talking about the small details of her job or household matters. Her father would speculate on where the next building boom was likely to take place and make plans for their next move. If they'd thought about anything beyond the limited reach of their own lives, she'd never seen any evidence of it.

You're not, are you—marrying Gareth because of his family, I mean? Brenda's question drifted through Kate's mind as she looked across the table at her fiancé. As if sensing her gaze, he turned his head and their eyes met. He smiled and Kate felt warm affection well up inside her, banishing the brief moment of question. She was marrying him because he was a kind and wonderfully gentle man, but becoming a member of the Blackthorne family was certainly a lovely bonus.

The roar of a motorcycle cut through the quiet conversation, the sound sharp and intrusive. Philip broke off in the middle of a sentence, his dark brows drawing together in a slight frown as the sound grew louder until it was obvious the bike was not simply passing by on the lightly traveled main road but was coming up the long driveway.

"Who on earth could that be?" he asked, speaking as much to himself as to anyone else.

Kate saw the sweep of a headlight cut across the sheer curtains and the roar grew louder, until the room nearly vibrated. When the engine was cut off, the abrupt cessation of sound was almost as startling as the noise had been.

"I'll go see who it is," Philip said. He set his napkin next to his plate and pushed back from the table.

"Philip, you don't think..." Sara's voice trailed off, the thought unfinished. Kate was startled by the sudden vulnerability in her voice.

Her husband's expression gentled. His hand settled on her shoulder for an instant as he walked past her chair. "Don't get your hopes up, my dear."

Bewildered, Kate glanced at Gareth, her brows raised in question, but he was looking after his father, his expression uncharacteristically stern. As Philip left the room, he shifted his attention to his mother.

"What did he say when he called?" he asked.

"Not much." Sara frowned. "He just said he'd be home soon."

"Is he coming home for good?"

"He didn't say. Just that he was going to be helping Harry fix up the house." Her frown deepened.

"Nick said Harry was going to sell the old place. I can't imagine that."

Gareth and Sara seemed to have momentarily forgotten her presence, so Kate dabbled her fork in the last few bites of her casserole and tried to look invisible. But her thoughts were tumbling over each other. Nick was the mysterious missing brother. Obviously, Sara thought the motorcycle might be his.

Kate shivered a little. It was eerie that she'd been thinking about him just minutes ago and now, here he was, popping up in the conversation—maybe even standing on the doorstep. The coincidence sent a chill down her spine. It seemed odd that Gareth hadn't said anything to her about his younger brother coming home, but the past couple of weeks had been exceptionally busy. Maybe he just hadn't had the chance to tell her.

"He said he'd be home as soon as he could put things in order in New York." Sara shifted her wineglass from one side of her plate to the other and then back again.

The agitated movement surprised Kate. It was the first time she'd seen the other woman less than serene. She looked at Gareth again, her brows raised in question. This time, his eyes met hers and she thought he was about to say something, offer some explanation perhaps, but the sound of the front door opening cut off whatever he might have said.

"Anybody home?" The voice was masculine, low

and a little raspy, as if from too many nights spent in smoke-filled bars.

Kate was looking at Gareth and she saw something flare in his eyes, a quick flash of emotion that was there and gone too quickly for her to read it. Relief? Anger? Happiness? Some impossible combination of the three?

"Nick." Sara spoke quietly but her voice held so much suppressed emotion that the name seemed to echo.

"Nick?" Kate repeated as Sara pushed her chair back and stood up. "Isn't that—"

"My brother," Gareth said, his tone as flat and emotionless as his expression. She might have thought he was indifferent to his brother's sudden arrival if it hadn't been for the tension in his shoulders as he rose stiffly, careless of the scrape of the chair's legs on the polished wooden floor. She'd never seen Gareth anything but calm and in control. It was one of the things she liked most about him, one of the things that made her feel as if she could depend on him not to change, not to go off chasing rainbows. But, just now, there had been that flash of emotion in his eyes, and the hand he rested on the back of his chair was white-knuckled with tension.

Interest vied with uneasiness inside Kate. She wondered what it was about Nick Blackthorne that his arrival should send such powerful ripples through his family. Why hadn't she asked Gareth about him long before this?

"Nick. It's been a long time. Too long." Philip's beautifully modulated voice wavered a little on the last word.

There was a pause, and Kate tried to imagine what was going through his son's mind. Guilt? Affection? Was he moved by his father's welcome? Indifferent to it? She couldn't even hazard a guess.

"I'm home now," was all he said and, try as she might, Kate couldn't read anything from his tone. "Where's Mom?"

"In the dining room. We didn't expect you to make it home so soon."

"Neither did I, but when I looked around, I realized my life wasn't nearly as full of terribly important things to take care of as I'd thought at first." There was a rich note of self-directed amusement in the husky voice. "It was quite a shock to find out how completely dispensable I was."

Philip was chuckling as the two of them entered the dining room.

"Nick." Sara's voice cracked a little on the name. When she stretched out her arms, her slim, elegant hands were not quite steady. "It's so good to see you."

"You make it sound like it's been decades. Or have you already forgotten that I met you in Chicago

last year when you went to that conference?'' The
question was affectionately mocking.

Kate twisted in her chair, anxious for a glimpse of
the mysterious missing brother, but his back was to
her as he bent to gather his mother into his arms. All
she could see was wide shoulders and thick, nearly
black hair worn long enough to brush the collar of
his leather jacket. The faded denim of his jeans
molded his narrow hips and long legs. Involuntarily,
she noted that he had a very nice rear view but she
immediately brushed the thought aside. A motorcycle
and a black leather jacket. Her upper lip quivered in
a faint sneer. It was such a pathetically obvious cos-
tume for the returning rebel.

She dragged her eyes away from the tender meeting between mother and son and looked at Gareth.
How did he feel about his brother's sudden appearance? Whatever he was feeling, he was keeping it to
himself, his expression as still and unreadable as a
blank wall. Of course, she could read all kinds of
things into the controlled way he pushed his chair
back into place before moving around the table to
greet his brother.

Feeling as if she was watching a movie—something obscure and Swedish with subtitles in Japa-
nese—Kate turned her head to watch this first meeting between the two brothers.

It suddenly struck her as incredible that she hadn't
ever asked about the situation between Nick and his

family. She'd simply assumed that there had been a
break and had just as easily assigned the blame to
Nick. But if there had once been some family schism,
there was no sign of it now. Philip and Sara were
obviously thrilled to see their younger son.

And Gareth?

Nick released Sara and his shoulders seemed to
tense when he saw his brother. Kate wished she could
see his face. Was his expression as closed and un-
revealing as Gareth's? The undercurrents that swirled
through the room were completely baffling. Without
knowing the history, she couldn't even begin to guess
at what was happening now. The brothers faced each
other in silence for a moment before Nick spoke.

"Gareth. It's been awhile."

"Five years."

There was another brief silence. If Kate had
thought she was imagining the tension in the room,
one glance at Philip and Sara's anxious faces told her
it was real. Then Nick moved forward, his hand outstretched.

"You're looking good, big brother."

Kate couldn't see his face, but his voice was warm.
The change in the atmosphere was immediate. It was
as if everyone in the room had been holding their
breath and they now released it in one soft sigh of
relief.

"I wish I could say the same about you," Gareth

said, smiling as he took his brother's hand. "You look like hell."

"That's just what every recovering flu victim wants to hear. Nice to see you're just as tactful as ever."

"Good habits are hard to break," Gareth said with a grin.

Nick's laugh was hoarse. Kate realized that the husky quality she'd assumed was evidence of hard living could just as easily be the result of a plain old head cold.

"Did it occur to you that riding all the way across the country on a motorcycle might not have been the smartest thing to do when you were recovering from a flu?" Sara asked tartly. She reached up to lay her hand across her son's forehead.

Though she was a doctor, the gesture was purely maternal, and Kate felt her throat tighten. She could remember her own mother doing the same thing, could remember the love that had flowed from that simple touch. Her mother had been dead for fourteen years but, for an instant, the loss was as fresh as if it had just happened. She looked away, busying herself with folding her napkin neatly before laying it next to her plate.

"I'm fine," Nick was saying. "I had the flu, not pneumonia. Besides, I figured riding the motorcycle was easier than carrying it."

"You're still a smart ass," Gareth said.

"Like you said, good habits are hard to break," Nick said, and Kate didn't have to see his expression to know he was smiling.

She was reluctant to intrude on the unexpected reunion, but the longer she pretended to be invisible, the more awkward it was going to be for everyone when they remembered she was there. Drawing a shallow breath, she pushed back her chair and stood up. The movement drew Gareth's attention and he immediately looked apologetic.

"Kate! We didn't mean to ignore you." He moved toward her, one hand gripping his brother's shoulder for an instant as he walked past. The gesture was revealing. Obviously, whatever the reason Nick had been absent from the family scene, it wasn't because he was unwelcome.

"I didn't feel ignored," she said truthfully. She'd been too busy speculating about what was going on to feel left out.

He slid his arm around her waist and pulled her against his side with gentle affection. "Kate, I want you to meet my little brother, Nick. He made my life a living hell when we were growing up."

"Gee, thanks, big bro." Nick was smiling as he turned.

He had dimples, Kate noticed as she held out her a beautiful matched set that gave his smile a of mischief. She knew that smile, she thought. She knew that mouth and the solid thrust of chin.

"Nick, this is Kate Moran." Gareth's voice was warm and happy as he introduced her. "We're getting married in six months."

Kate's eyes swept up to meet Nick's, reading shocked recognition in the chocolate brown depths of his eyes. She started to jerk her hand back but his fingers closed over hers, warm and strong and horribly familiar.

"Kate." The rasp in his voice seemed more pronounced, as if his cold had taken an abrupt turn for the worse.

And why not? Kate thought wildly. Her own throat felt so tight, it was a struggle to breathe. She tugged on her hand and he released it slowly.

"Nick." She was distantly pleased to hear that her voice sounded completely normal. Inside, she was starting to babble hysterically.

"Are you home to stay, Nick?" Philip asked, coming forward to stand beside his younger son.

With an effort, Nick dragged his eyes away from Kate's. He shrugged, the movement stiff and jerky. "I don't know. Harry didn't say much about the condition of the house but I gather there's quite a bit of work to do. I told him I'd stick around until the job is done. I'm not thinking any further ahead than that right now."

"This is your home," Philip began. He started to say more but a warning glance from his wife had him swallowing the words. Kate noted the interplay with a distant part of her mind, the part that wasn't frantically praying that this would turn out to be a dream from which she'd awaken any minute.

"It's good to have you back," Sara said. She brushed her fingers against Nick's arm as if she had to touch him to be sure he was really there. She glanced at Kate, her smile warm with happiness. "I'm so glad that you and Kate will have a chance to get to know each other before the wedding."

Kate swallowed a hysterical laugh. Oh, God, what was she supposed to do now? Casually mention that, as a matter of fact, she already knew Nick—in the most intimate sense of the word? That she would have mentioned it months ago if only she'd bothered to get his name before she slept with him?

Chapter Two

"You've been quiet tonight," Gareth said as he snapped the lid onto the plastic container of leftover casserole.

"I didn't have much to say." Kate knew he was looking at her but she kept her eyes down, as if rinsing the dishes took all her concentration. She'd avoided looking at him for the past forty-five minutes. She wasn't sure whether it was shame or fear that had her avoiding his eyes. Shame that she'd once slept with a man whose name she didn't even know or fear that Gareth might be able to somehow read the past in her eyes and know that that man had been his younger brother.

She'd persuaded Sara to let her take care of the after dinner cleanup. She'd thought that doing dishes would give her a few minutes of time to herself, time to recover her equilibrium. But Gareth had followed her into the kitchen to help. Usually, she appreciated that he was as comfortable in the kitchen as he was in the squad room. Her father had never moved beyond the idea that the kitchen was a woman's domain. Tonight, she would have been grateful for a touch of good, old-fashioned chauvinism on Gareth's part, she thought ruefully.

"I know things got a little crazy, what with Nick coming home in the middle of dinner."

"If you're worried that I felt neglected, don't be." She glanced in his general direction and forced a smile. "Your parents are obviously thrilled that your brother is home."

"Yeah. I don't think they really believed he was coming home again." He reached for the oval bowl that had held asparagus. Two fat, green spears lay in the bottom. Absently, he picked one up and bit off the bottom.

At another time, Kate might have smiled at his predictability. She'd known Gareth for barely six months, but she already recognized his habits. When he ate asparagus, he always started at the stem and worked his way up to the tip. He ran his car—a pale gray, two-door sedan—through the car wash every Thursday afternoon. He always took his first sip of coffee black and then added three lumps of sugar. One of the things she loved most about him was that he always did just what was expected of him, even in the small things in life. She could count on him to do what he said he'd do, to be there when she needed him.

Unless he found out about what had happened between her and his brother five years ago. Her fingers tightened over the edge of the plate she'd just rinsed. If *that* happened, she might not be able to count on him for anything at all.

"It's strange having Nick back," Gareth said.

"Five years is a long time." *But not nearly long enough*. Kate set the plate in the dishwasher and picked up a handful of silverware.

"A long time," he agreed. Absentmindedly, he finished off the asparagus spear and reached for the one remaining in the bowl. "Things always seemed to happen when Nick was around. Even when he was a kid, he could talk people into doing things they'd never dreamed of doing."

"Hmm." Kate clattered the silverware, hoping to discourage conversation. She didn't need him to tell her about Nick's persuasive powers, she thought bitterly, and then caught herself. Honesty came reluctantly. Much as she would have liked to cast Nick as a villainous seducer, that wasn't the way it had been. She hadn't been an innocent victim five years ago. *More's the pity*. It would have been nice to be able to lay the blame squarely at his feet.

"I should have guessed that Harry would be the one to get him to come home," Gareth said.

"They must be very close. Is Harry a family friend?"

"Not exactly." Gareth finished the asparagus and carried the bowl over to the sink for her to rinse. "Nick's wife was Harry's granddaughter. Her parents died when she was little more than a baby and Harry raised her. Nick met Harry when he was hired to do some work on the guest house at Spider's Walk. He actually introduced Nick and Lisa."

"Spider's Walk?" Kate seized on the least important element of the explanation. She didn't want to be reminded that Nick had been married and widowed before he was thirty. She didn't want to feel sympathy for him.

Gareth grinned. "There's a stained glass window above the door that shows a spider and its web. If I remember the story correctly, Harry's grandmother had the window installed because she admired the industrious nature of the spider. It didn't take long for people to start referring to the place as the spider house, which wasn't exactly what she had in mind. But she figured that, even if she took the window out, the name would probably stick, so she gave it a more elegant twist and started referring to it as Spider's Walk."

Kate smiled. "It's unique."

She loaded the last of the dishes into the dishwasher, closed the door and turned the machine on, then looked around for something else to do. The kitchen was immaculate and, for a moment, she found herself bitterly resentful of Mrs. Pickle's efficiency. Why couldn't the woman have left splatters on the stove or a few fingerprints on the refrigerator?

"Are you sure nothing's wrong?" Gareth asked.

The question forced her to look at him. The concern in his expression made her eyes sting with emotion. If she lived to be a hundred, she would never understand what she'd done to deserve Gareth Blackthorne. He was such a good man, kind and caring. The fact that he loved her seemed little short of miraculous.

"Nothing's wrong," she told him, and was pleased to hear the evenness of her response. "I'm just a little tired, that's all."

"Hard day in the jungles?" he asked.

His crooked grin was one of the things she liked best about him. It always seemed to hold an endearing hint of mischief. Tonight, Kate couldn't help but think that, when he smiled, the resemblance between him and his younger brother was striking. She pushed the thought away as she went into his arms. She didn't want to think about Nick anymore.

She rested her head on Gareth's shoulder and wished with all her heart that Nick hadn't come home. Everything had been so perfect.

"Sorry to interrupt." The words made Kate start. She pulled away from Gareth abruptly and then cursed her guilty reaction when she caught his startled look. "There's a phone call for you," Nick told his brother. "Mom says it's the station house."

Gareth sighed. "Kenny probably locked himself out of his squad car again."

Nick's brows rose. "One of your better officers?"

"Usually, but he has this mental block about keys. He can't seem to hang onto them." Gareth glanced at Kate. "I'll be right back."

She forced a thin smile as she nodded. "Fighting crime takes precedence."

"Yeah." There was a friendly hint of malice in the smile Nick gave his brother. "Wouldn't want to leave one of Eden's finest stranded without wheels. You never know when a crime wave might hit."

"Smart ass," Gareth said, but he was smiling as he went to answer the phone.

He left behind a sharp-edged silence. Nick knew that Kate was hoping he'd follow Gareth out. A wiser man would have done just that. There were things that needed to be said between them, but this was not exactly the best time or place. He was tired, his throat hurt, his head ached and, though he'd only been home a few hours, he could already feel the walls starting to close in on him. He'd expected this home-coming to be difficult. What he hadn't expected was to find his brother engaged to a woman he'd once slept with. A woman he'd never quite managed to forget.

She looked different, he thought. The girl he'd met

five years ago had worn her streaky blond hair tumbling onto her shoulders, and her blue eyes had held a loneliness that had drawn him more than the gentle prettiness of her features. The woman standing in the middle of his mother's kitchen looking as if she'd rather be anywhere else was older, of course, but there were other changes. Her hair was still an intriguing mix of pale gold and honey, but it was confined in a neat twist at the base of her neck. And her eyes were the same smoky blue he remembered, but the vulnerability that had found its way through the wall of pain that had surrounded him then was gone. There was a reserve about her—a control—that hadn't been there five years ago. He wondered if it was just a result of maturity or if something had happened to change her.

"Fancy meeting you here," he said.

Kate lifted her chin and looked directly at him for the first time since that initial moment of shocked recognition. "Obviously, I didn't know you were Gareth's brother."

"Obviously." Nick leaned one shoulder against the doorjamb, making it impossible for her to leave without pushing past him. Something flashed through her eyes, there and gone so quickly that he almost thought he imagined it, but he knew he hadn't. She was afraid of him? For some reason, the idea that she might fear him touched off his temper. He was suddenly—illogically—angry at her.

"Were you seeing him when you slept with me?" he asked conversationally.

Kate sucked in her breath, a quick, sharp sound.

"I'll take that as a no. I have to admit that it's a relief. It may be all the rage on *Geraldo,* but I guess I'm old-fashioned enough to find the idea of my brother and me sleeping with the same woman just a little tacky."

In some distant part of his mind, it occurred to him that he was behaving like a bastard. The knowledge did nothing to soothe the sharp anger that drove him.

"I didn't even know Gareth existed five years ago," she said, sounding both defensive and angry.

"No?" Nick arched one brow in mocking question.

"No," she snapped. "What happened then had nothing to do with him."

"I won't argue with that."

Despite herself, Kate felt a quick rush of relief. If he really meant that, maybe he wouldn't say anything to Gareth. It shouldn't matter one way or another—it wasn't as if she'd been unfaithful. She hadn't even known Gareth when she and Nick had met. Gareth hadn't expected virginity any more than she'd expected it from him. But knowing she'd had other lovers was a far cry from knowing his younger brother had been one of them.

"Did you make it a habit?" Nick asked, still in that conversational tone that put a bitter sting in the

words. "Sleeping with men you didn't know, I
mean?"

Kate felt white-hot anger burn away her fear. How
dare he sit in judgment on her, as if what had happened had been her doing alone? She tilted her head
back and looked at him directly, her eyes challenging.

"Did you? Make it a habit to pick up women in
bars and sleep with them, I mean?" Her tone echoed
his sharp civility.

"Touché." Nick's smile held a rueful edge. She
was right. He had no business casting stones in her
direction—not about that night or anything else, for
that matter. He rubbed his fingers against his aching
forehead. He had to be out of his mind to react like
this. Maybe the flu had affected his brain. He
straightened away from the doorjamb and took a half
step toward her, his expression softening with regret.

"Look, I—"

"Somebody lost some paperwork." Gareth's voice
preceded him by an instant. Afraid of what her expression might reveal, Kate turned away from the
door. She pulled a hand towel off the rack near the
sink and began to needlessly refold it.

"No lost car keys?" Nick asked as Gareth entered
the kitchen.

"Not this time."

Kate felt her fiancé glance at her as she picked up
a sponge and began to wipe down the counters. She

felt grateful when Nick spoke again, drawing Gareth's attention away from her, giving her a moment to regain her balance. Not that he was doing it deliberately, she thought bitterly. Their conversation had been brief, but it had been long enough to make his opinion of her abundantly clear. He'd practically called her a slut. Talk about your double standards.

She listened with half an ear to the conversation going on behind her—something about someone they'd both known when they were growing up. Scraping a corner of the sponge down a line of perfectly clean grout, Kate told herself she didn't care what Nick thought of her, as long as he didn't tell anyone about that night.

Nick chuckled at something Gareth said and Kate found herself remembering that they'd laughed together five years ago. It was one of the things that had made everything seem so special. She'd been so alone and lonely. Finding someone to laugh with had felt like magic. *Magic.* It was as good an explanation as any for the way she'd abandoned her common sense along with her morals and invited him into her bed.

"It's been a long day," she heard Nick say behind her. "I'm going to crash."

Knowing it would look strange if she didn't say goodbye, Kate turned away from the counter. She focused on a point just past his shoulder and forced a thin smile. "Good night."

"Good night, Kate." But he didn't leave, and the knot in Kate's stomach tightened a notch.

What if he'd changed his mind about saying something to Gareth? Fear brought her eyes to his face. She couldn't read his expression, couldn't guess at his thoughts. When he turned and left the kitchen without saying anything more, she felt her knees go momentarily weak with relief.

"He looks tired," Gareth commented, frowning as he looked after his brother.

"Traveling across country *is* tiring," Kate said, and was pleased by the evenness of her voice. She turned and dropped the damp sponge on the counter. "I think I'll head home."

Gareth slid his arms around her waist and drew her back against his chest. "Why don't you come home with me tonight?" he murmured against her hair.

She almost said yes. It would be so nice to go home with him, let him hold her. Kate closed her eyes and leaned against him, feeling the strength of his arms around her. She always felt safe with Gareth. But not tonight. She couldn't go home with him, sleep with him tonight. Not when five-year-old memories were tugging at her. Not when, no matter how ridiculous it was, she felt as if she'd been unfaithful to him.

"I really am beat," she said, pulling away from his hold and turning to give him a genuinely apologetic smile.

"You do look a little tired." He brushed a loose tendril of hair from her forehead, his smile so gentle that Kate felt tears sting her eyes.

"We've been really busy at work."

"I didn't realize Brenda was such a slave driver."

Kate smiled, as he'd intended. He knew that her only complaint about her friend as an employer was that Brenda didn't take *enough* of an interest in the business.

"She hasn't exactly been cracking the whip," she said dryly. "But we've had a lot of new stock arrive for spring, and it seems like half the town decided that this was the week to plant acres of flowers. We've been pretty busy. I think I'm going to go home and take a long, hot shower and then fall into bed."

"I'm good with a washcloth," he said, half joking, half serious.

Kate shook her head, feeling as if the word "guilty" was tattooed in neon across her forehead. "I wouldn't be good company."

He didn't push any further, which only added to her guilt. He was too good for her, she thought as she slid her arms around his waist and pressed her face against his broad chest.

Chapter Three

It was late the next morning when Nick came downstairs. The big old house was quiet around him. It had been fifteen years since he'd lived here, but he was willing to bet that the old patterns hadn't changed. His mother would have been at her office for an hour or more. His father spent mornings in his office at the church, working on Sunday's sermon and making himself available to his parishioners. When he was younger, he'd found that predictability maddening, incomprehensible. Now, he found the familiarity comforting.

Reaching the bottom of the stairs, he followed the scent of coffee toward the kitchen, his mouth curving in a delighted grin when he saw the tiny woman standing in front of the sink.

"Dilly!"

Startled, she turned, her narrow features lighting in a smile of welcome when she saw him. "Nick!"

He crossed the kitchen in two long strides and caught her around the waist, lifting her off her feet and swinging her around. She squeaked in protest.

"Put me down! I'm not a sack of potatoes for you to be slinging around any way you please."

"You're much too pretty to be a sack of potatoes," he said, ignoring her demands long enough to plant a kiss on her thin cheek.

"Ha! Flattery doesn't change the fact that you're a hooligan, Nick Blackthorne." But her cheeks were flushed with pleasure. She smoothed her hands over her iron gray hair and straightened her crisp white apron before fixing him with a stern look. "I can see five years in New York City hasn't done a thing to improve your manners."

"Did you expect it to?" he asked, smiling at her.

"I suppose not. You've been beyond redemption since you were a boy." Her eyes went over him in a quick, searching look. "You've lost weight. I suppose you've been eating a lot of that nouvelle cuisine." She packed a world of contempt into the words.

"I think nouvelle cuisine is out of fashion. Now, they're calling it American light," Nick told her.

"Same difference. An ounce of chicken, two green beans and a pea pod served with a teaspoon of raspberry sauce and decorated with goat cheese.'' She sniffed. ''Not my idea of a decent meal.''

''It wouldn't be fair to hold New York cuisine to your standards, Dilly. The truth is, I haven't had a decent meal since the last time I ate here.''

''You're a shameless flatterer,'' she scolded, but she looked pleased. ''Sit down and I'll fix you some breakfast.''

''I can do it myself,'' Nick protested, but she shooed him out of her way. Knowing that this was her way of welcoming him home, he dragged a stool up to the butcher-block work island and sat down.

His hands around the cup of coffee she set in front of him, Nick felt as if he'd finally come home. Last night, he'd been too conscious of the undercurrents running between him and his family to feel any sense of homecoming. And meeting his brother's fiancée hadn't helped matters any.

But sitting here, in the sunlit kitchen, seeing the familiar efficiency of Dilly's breakfast preparations, he felt at home for the first time. There were never any undercurrents with Dilly. He was willing to bet that if one dared to appear in her kitchen, she'd smack it with a spoon and send it on its way.

He had been four when Annie Pickle came to work for his parents. With the wit possible only in four-year-olds, he and his twin brother had promptly nicknamed her Dilly. Gareth had been ten, old enough to sneer at childish nicknames, but he and Brian had always called her Dilly. Sometimes, he almost forgot she had another name.

She was family, in the same way his parents and his brother were. Well, not exactly the same way, he thought ruefully. In some ways, he was closer to Dilly than he was to the rest of the family. He was certainly more comfortable with her.

"I've missed you, Dilly."

"I've been here right along," she said calmly. "You could have seen me any time you cared to come looking."

"I've been pretty busy." He knew, even as he said it, that it was a thin excuse, and the look she sent him said she felt the same. His smile twisted ruefully. "Cut me some slack, Dilly. It's not as if I didn't keep in touch. I wrote."

"Three letters in five years—not exactly a lengthy correspondence," she said acerbically.

"I sent you Christmas and birthday presents," he offered weakly.

"Ha! Extravagant nonsense. Cashmere scarves and fancy jewelry."

"The scarf was the same blue as your eyes. I thought of you as soon as I saw it."

"Ridiculous," she muttered, but she couldn't prevent the corners of her mouth from curling upward. "Where did you think I'd wear such a thing?"

"Mom told me you wore the scarf and the pin to

church several times this past winter,'' Nick said smugly.

There was a brief silence. She jabbed a piece of bacon with a fork and set it on a folded paper towel to drain. "You'd think she'd have more important things to write about than my wardrobe."

"She knew I'd like to hear that you were wearing my gifts," Nick said, his smile coaxing.

"Well, of course I wore them." She broke two eggs into a pan. "They were ridiculously extravagant but they were much too pretty to leave lying in a drawer." She picked up a spatula and waved it at him. "But pretty gifts aren't the same as a letter or a phone call. It would have been nice to hear from you more often." She turned to the stove and flipped the eggs. "It wouldn't have killed you to take time out from your busy schedule to call now and again."

"No, ma'am."

"Your parents worried about you." She set the bacon on a plate and buttered toast with brisk efficiency, turning to the stove in time to slide the eggs out at exactly the right moment. "As little as we heard from you, you'd think that you were in Outer Mongolia or someplace where they'd never heard of a telephone or decent mail service."

"Yes, ma'am."

She set the plate in front of him with a thump and fixed him with a stern look. "Don't 'ma'am' me,

Nicholas James Blackthorne. You deserve a good scold and you know it.''

"Yes, Dilly." He spoiled the meekness of his response by sliding one arm around her waist and pulling her close enough for him to kiss her cheek again. "I've missed you like hell."

For just an instant, her thin arms hugged him fiercely tight. Then she pulled away, smoothing her hands over her apron. "Don't curse," she told him briskly. "And eat your breakfast before it gets cold."

"Yes, ma'am."

"Wretched boy." The tenderness in her voice made the words a compliment, and she couldn't resist brushing a thick lock of dark hair from his forehead. She returned Nick's smile and then turned away before he could see the foolish brightness in her eyes. "I've got some fresh orange juice."

When she came to work for the Blackthornes, she'd been newly widowed and childless. Gareth had been ten, past the age where he could simply open his heart to every newcomer. But Nick and Brian had been perfectly willing to accept her as one of the family, welcoming her with the easy affection of the very young. She'd loved them both but, in her secret heart, she admitted to loving Nick best.

She'd spent the last thirty years watching him grow from boy to man. She'd watched him lose his brother and a part of himself at the same time. She'd seen him deal with the changes that had come into his life after Brian's death, had worried when he fell in love with a woman as fragile as fine crystal and had grieved for him when he lost both wife and child. She'd understood, better than anyone else, his need to get away. But she'd never thought he'd stay away so long, and she hadn't expected him to come back with the emptiness still in his eyes.

"Your mother said you got home in the middle of dinner last night," she said as she set a glass of orange juice in front of him.

"I planned on being here earlier but I got distracted in Vegas."

"Gambling, I suppose." She tried to look disapproving but then spoiled it by asking if he'd won.

"A bit," he admitted. "But I got back on the road later than I'd intended."

What he didn't mention was that the closer he'd come to the California state line, the more doubts he'd had about coming back here. But then, he wouldn't be surprised if she'd already guessed as much. Dilly had always known him much too well.

"I don't think anyone minded having their dinner interrupted," she said as she poured herself a cup of coffee—her fourth of the day—and added a generous splash of cream. "Your parents were delighted to have you home."

"They said as much." Their open pleasure had made him painfully conscious of his ambivalence. "It was good to see them. And Gareth. I met his fian-cée.''

He wasn't sure what prompted him to add the last comment. His brother's fiancée was the last thing he wanted to discuss with Dilly. But the words were out and couldn't be taken back.

"Miss Moran." Dilly nodded. "She's a pretty young woman."

Nick murmured a bland agreement and concen-trated on his breakfast.

"Pleasant spoken enough," she added. Something in her tone brought his head up. He knew her well enough to read the reservation in her voice.

"You don't like her?"

"I didn't say anything of the kind," she protested, genuinely horrified. "She seems to be a very nice young woman."

"But?"

"But nothing. Gareth seems very happy."

"But?" he prodded again. He couldn't have said why he was pushing the issue. Common sense told him to let it drop. The less he knew about Kate Moran, the better.

"There is no but," Dilly said, then caught his eye and shrugged. "I worry a bit that maybe Gareth loves her a great deal more than she loves him. It's prob-ably my imagination and I know for certain that it's none of my business. Or yours, for that matter."

She was right, of course. It was none of his business, but the comment lingered in his mind. He wondered if she was right. And if so, did Gareth know?

"So, what do you think of Nick?" Brenda's eyes were bright with curiosity.

"Nick?" Kate gave her friend a deliberately blank look.

Brenda clicked her tongue in exasperation. "Nick Blackthorne? About six-one, dark hair, dark eyes, body like a Greek god, face to die for? You know the one I mean?"

"I know who you mean." Kate wished the description had been a little less accurate. It brought his image all too sharply to mind. She moved farther down the aisle between two tables of bedding plants, waving the watering wand over them. Brenda followed, her long floral skirt brushing against the trailing leaves of a fuchsia sitting near the edge of the table.

"Well?" she prompted.

"Well what?" Kate wasn't trying to be deliberately obtuse so much as she was giving herself time to formulate an answer. She'd been expecting this. Eden wasn't a village, but the town was small enough that news traveled fast. Brenda had gone to school with the Blackthornes. Naturally, she'd be interested to hear that Nick had returned. Now that Kate thought about it, it was astonishing that he'd been back for almost a week and Brenda was just now questioning her about him.

"You have met him, right?"

"I was having dinner at his parents' house the night he came home," Kate admitted.

"And you didn't say anything?" Brenda's eyes widened in surprise.

"I didn't think of it." Kate shrugged lightly and then wondered if her nose was going to grow. In the week since Nick's return, she'd thought of little else. She hadn't seen him again but that hadn't prevented him from dominating her thoughts.

"Well?" Brenda prompted.

"Well, what?"

"What did you think of him?"

"What's to think?" Kate shrugged again. "He seems nice enough."

"Nice enough?" Brenda's voice rose in disbelief. "You're talking about the guy that had half the girls in high school panting with lust every time he walked into a classroom and all you can say is he seems *nice enough?*"

"Maybe if I was in high school, I'd be a little more overwhelmed," Kate said. She glanced over her shoulder in time to catch Brenda's disgusted look.

"You don't have to be in high school to appreciate looks like that. You just have to be breathing."

"I am engaged, you know." Kate wished she could find more comfort in the reminder.

"I don't see any reason why an engagement ring should make a woman blind to the wonders of nature," Brenda complained. "Nick Blackthorne is good-looking enough to make a nun take a second look."

"Hmm." Kate made a noncommittal noise in the back of her throat and concentrated on watering a flat of pansies.

"It's not like I'm suggesting you sleep with the guy. Hey!" Brenda jumped back in surprise as Kate's hand jerked and water sprayed into the pathway. "Watch it with that thing. I might melt, you know."

"Sorry." Kate angled the long watering wand over the flats and hoped Brenda couldn't see that her hand was trembling. *Idiot,* she thought. *It was just a casual remark, not an accusation.*

"No harm done." Brenda brushed at the dampness on her skirt. Satisfied that there was no permanent damage, she fixed Kate with a bright, inquiring look. "Now, tell me what you really think of Nick."

Kate indulged in a brief moment of fantasy, picturing herself turning the water onto Brenda full force, drowning out the subject of Nick Blackthorne. But she knew her friend well enough to know that, short of physical violence, there was no way to shut her up. She smothered a sigh and gave in.

"He seems pleasant. And very attractive," she added, catching Brenda's disgusted look. "Philip and Sara were delighted to see him."

"They've always been a close family. I was surprised when Nick moved away but then I figured that, with everything that had happened, maybe there were just too many memories here."

"Maybe." Kate didn't ask for an explanation of what "everything" might have been. Obviously, Brenda assumed she already knew and the last thing she wanted was to prolong the discussion.

"It was bad enough when Brian died."

"Brian?" Despite her determination not to encourage Brenda, Kate glanced at her in question.

"Nick's twin." Brenda looked shocked. "You must know about Brian."

"Of course I do. I just drew a blank for a moment, that's all." Kate scowled at a bright red impatiens. She *had* known about Brian. He was the brother who'd been killed in a car wreck a decade or more ago, but she didn't remember Gareth saying anything about Brian and Nick being twins.

"The accident happened the summer after we graduated from high school," Brenda was saying. "It was such a terrible tragedy." She stopped and frowned. "Did you ever stop to think what a stupid phrase that is? *Terrible tragedy.* Like there's such a thing as a good tragedy? Where do you suppose phrases like that come from?"

Kate was accustomed to Brenda's habit of going off on a conversational tangent and knew that an answer was neither expected nor required. Unfortunately, she rarely lost sight of the original topic.

"Anyway, there was a car crash. Brian was killed and Nick almost died, too. I went to see him in the hospital a couple of weeks after the accident. He looked...I don't know." She absentmindedly pinched a faded pansy from its stem, her forehead creasing. "I remember thinking he looked kind of empty, like a part of him was missing." She dropped the flower and looked up suddenly. "You know how you hear that there's a special bond between twins?"

Kate nodded reluctantly. She didn't want to hear this, didn't want to hear anything that made Nick more real to her, let alone something that roused her sympathy. She knew what it was to lose someone you loved.

"Well, I don't know if that's true but I do know Nick was never really the same after the accident."

"Losing someone you love changes you," Kate said slowly, speaking half to herself. "Losing a brother or sister is sometimes harder than losing a parent because it feels so unnatural. It's not the way life's supposed to go."

"I thought you were an only child," Brenda said, her expression both surprised and curious. "You sound like you're speaking from experience."

Kate gave her a startled smile, though her fingers suddenly ached from the force with which she gripped the water nozzle. "I read about it somewhere. Or maybe I heard some psychiatrist on a talk show. They're all the time delving into that kind of thing. Family dynamics is a hot topic these days.''

"Yeah." Brenda looked at her a moment longer, a trace of doubt lingering in her eyes. She shook her head abruptly. "You're probably right—about losing a sibling, I mean. It's hard to imagine what that would be like.''

"Hmm." Kate moved away a little, focusing her attention on watering every single flat thoroughly.

"Nick was certainly never the same after Brian died," Brenda said, moving after her. "The whole family was devastated, of course.''

"Of course." Kate threw a quick, hopeful look over the nursery, hoping to see a pack of ravening gophers descending on the vegetable seedlings or maybe a customer being attacked by a man-eating delphinium—some crisis that would demand her immediate and complete attention and enable her to put an end to this conversation.

"You know, it makes you think of that old question of why bad things happen to good people," Brenda continued thoughtfully. "I mean, you couldn't find a nicer family than the Blackthornes.''

Kate wasn't lucky enough to sight a major disaster but there was a customer browsing near the perennials. She was pathetically grateful to see her.

"That woman looks like she needs some help," she said, cutting Brenda off. She thrust the watering wand into her friend's unwilling hand. "Finish watering this table, would you? After I'm through with this customer, maybe we could spend some time going over the plant orders for next week."

"Whatever you want to order is fine with me," Brenda said. She held the wand over the table, her expression pained. "Besides, I really should be going. I have tons of stuff tu do this afternoon."

"I could hold the order until tomorrow," Kate offered, ignoring the sharp pinch of her conscience. She knew that being forced to look at long lists of plants was sheer torture to Brenda, and she felt a little guilty for using that knowledge to manipulate the other woman.

But she didn't want to hear any more about Nick Blackthorne—past or present. In fact, if she never had to hear his name or see him again, it would suit her just fine.

Chapter Four

Nick was inspecting the front porch for dry rot when Kate's car pulled up in front of Spider's Walk. He'd known she was coming. Harry had told him about the appointment yesterday. He'd known, even before that, that she would be here, he just hadn't known when.

It struck him as painfully ironic that it had been Gareth's suggestion that brought her here. When Nick had mentioned that Harry wanted to do some work on the landscaping, Gareth had immediately suggested Kate for the job. A year or so ago, she'd begun doing landscape design, working through the nursery she managed. The business was still in the fledgling stage but the initial response had been good and she'd had several referrals from satisfied clients.

Listening to Gareth had brought five-year-old

memories rushing back. And he'd heard Kate's voice, telling him about her desire to create beautiful surroundings for people's homes, how much she hoped she'd be able to fulfill that dream now that she'd settled in Eden. He remembered wishing her luck and offering some platitude about dreams coming true. He hadn't really believed it. At the time, he hadn't believed in much of anything, least of all dreams, but he was glad to see that Kate had fulfilled this particular dream.

She got out of her car and started up the walkway. After enduring a hundred years of earthquakes and subtle attacks from the roots of the ancient sycamore that shaded the front of the house, the once smooth concrete was cracked in so many places it resembled a jigsaw puzzle. Cautious visitors tended to watch their feet as they approached Spider's Walk, but Kate seemed oblivious to the potential danger. All her attention was for the faded remnants of what had once been flower beds and carefully tended shrubbery.

Standing in the shadows of the porch, Nick watched her. She was wearing khaki-colored cotton slacks and a matching camp shirt. The only touch of contrast was the soft purple scarf she'd used to catch her hair from her face and the summer sky blue of her eyes. The austerity of the outfit suited her slender figure and gave her streaky gold hair the tawny look of a lioness.

Five years ago, there had still been traces of the

girl visible beneath the woman. Those traces were gone now. He'd thought she was pretty then, but that prettiness had been refined into something more, something not so easily defined. He frowned as he looked at her. She wasn't beautiful. Her mouth was too wide and her nose was a little too short for true beauty. She was...lovely. The old-fashioned word suited her. There was a certain quiet elegance to it, a sense of control that seemed to fit the woman she'd become.

Nick shut the Swiss army knife he'd been using to probe the wooden posts and slid it in his pocket before starting down the steps toward her. He knew the exact moment she saw him. Her shoulders stiffened, and even at a distance he could see her expression ice over. She hesitated and he wondered if she was going to turn and leave rather than speak to him, but he underestimated her.

"Nick."

He winced at her flat tone. "Hello, Kate."

"I'm here to see Mr. Wallace."

"I know." Nick slid his hands in his pockets and tried a half smile. It was met with a cool stare. Not that he could blame her. He hadn't exactly done anything to endear himself to her the last time they'd met. "Harry's in the house. He probably heard the car so he'll be on his way out."

Kate nodded and looked away, focusing on an overgrown pittosporum. Pride kept her where she was, though every instinct urged her to run. Fight or flight, she thought ruefully. When confronted by danger, the human animal still responded on the most primitive level. The danger Nick represented wasn't physical, but that didn't make it any less real, and her instinct was still to flee.

"This was Gareth's idea," she said abruptly, throwing him a quick, challenging glance.

"Yeah, I know. He said you'd be perfect for the job." Nick's broad shoulders lifted in a shrug. "I told him the decision was Harry's to make. I'll handle the work on the house but, when it comes to the landscaping, I'm completely useless. To tell the truth, I wouldn't know a parsnip from a petunia."

He made the confession with a self-deprecating half smile that, at another time, Kate might have found charming, but her memories of their last conversation were still vivid and she was in no mood to be charmed by him. She returned her attention to the pittosporum.

Nick's smile faded in the face of her chilly silence. He pushed his hands deeper in his pockets and contemplated the difficulty of coming up with an adequate apology.

"Kate, I—"

"Good morning." Harry's greeting preceded him down the steps. Kate and Nick turned toward him. They were both grateful for the interruption though for different reasons. "You must be Kate Moran. According to Gareth, you're the greatest landscape designer in the state of California.''

''He's a little biased,'' she said, smiling as she took his hand. ''It's a pleasure to meet you, Mr. Wallace.''

''The pleasure's mine.'' His handshake was pleasantly firm, his smile warm. ''Call me Harry, please. If you're going to be digging up my yard, I think we should be on first-name terms.''

Before Kate could protest that she hadn't agreed to work for him yet, he turned his faded blue eyes on Nick. ''Don't you have something you're supposed to be doing? I'm not paying you to stand around chatting with every pretty girl that comes along, am I?''

''I wasn't aware you were paying me at all.''

''Some jobs are worth their weight in gold in experience alone.'' Harry's faintly pompous tone was at odds with the twinkle in his eyes.

''You're too good to me, Harry,'' Nick said dryly.

''Yes, I know.'' Harry set his hand under Kate's elbow and led her toward the side of the house. ''Pay no attention to his whining,'' he said in a tone pitched loud enough for Nick to hear. ''He's spent the last five years working on Wall Street, a parasite sucking the life from the common man. I'm probably saving his soul from eternal damnation by providing him with the opportunity to do some honest work.''

Nick's quick bark of laughter was cut off as they turned the corner of the house.

Kate's first impression of Harry Wallace was that he looked like an unmade bed. Everything about him was rumpled. His thick gray hair was a little too long for neatness though not long enough to be a fashion statement. He wore a dark blue shirt that looked as if he'd pulled it out of the dryer and put it on immediately. His faded gray pants looked much the same. Scuffed leather loafers and mismatched socks completed the look of gentle disarray.

But his eyes were at odds with the image. The clear blue had faded a little with time but there was a shrewdness in them that made it clear that age might have slowed Harry's body but it had done nothing to slow his mind.

"I'm not a gardener," he said, leading her past an apple tree that looked as if it hadn't been pruned since the last world war. Seeing her frown, he chuckled. "I guess that's self-evident. My grandmother laid the foundations for the gardens while my grandfather was laying the foundation for the house. My mother took over in her turn. She loved these gardens so much that I've always half suspected her of marrying my father just to get her hands on them. My own wife was honest enough to tell me that, if it hadn't been for the gardens, she'd never have been willing to put up with marrying a man named Wallace."

Catching Kate's startled look of inquiry, he grinned. "Her name was Wanda," he explained, and was pleased by her soft choke of laughter.

"She must have loved you very much," she said solemnly.

"Yes, she did," he said, his smile gentle with memories. He shook himself, and his tone became brisk again. "Unfortunately, she's been gone for more than thirty years now, and I'm afraid the gardens have pretty much gone wild since then. I've hired gardeners over the years but most of them know more about repairing lawn mowers and power blowers than they do about plants. They did manage to keep the place from becoming a complete jungle, but that's about all."

As she looked around the property, Kate could feel her determination to refuse the job fading beneath the wild beauty of the place. The house sat on nearly an acre of land and, from what she'd seen so far, it must have been a showplace at one time. She could make out the outlines of flower beds overgrown with Bermuda grass and withered remains of long dead perennials. The only thing blooming in them now was a healthy population of oxalis, their delicate yellow flowers nodding in the slightest breeze.

"Mother put in the rose garden," Harry said, as he led her down a cracked brick walkway and past an empty fountain. "I was still living at home when she put it in. That was during the thirties. The De-pression was on and money was tight but plants were cheap and I provided free labor.'' He grinned at her. ''Reluctantly, I might add.''

Kate returned the smile absently. Her attention was all for the four formal beds laid out in front of her. Wide grass pathways separated them, and in the center, where the paths met, was a life-size statue of the goddess Diana. At the base of the statue was a rusty wrought-iron bench, a silent invitation to sit and enjoy the view. If she narrowed her eyes just a little, she could see what the garden must have looked like in full bloom. The scent of roses would hang heavy on the summer air and bees would drift from blossom to blossom, gorging themselves on nectar. She sighed faintly as the image faded.

''The roses still bloom,'' Harry said, interrupting her fantasy. ''I thought they were supposed to be fussy but it looks to me like you can't kill 'em with a stick.''

''In this climate, they can tolerate a lot of neglect.''

Kate turned slowly on one heel, eyeing the overgrown hedges and underpruned shrubbery. The place had been shamefully neglected but it wasn't beyond saving. Like a wild, unruly child, all it needed was a firm hand to turn it in the proper direction.

''It needs a lot of work. It's been let go for much too long.''

"I know." Harry looked abashed. "I kept meaning to do something about it but time just slipped by."

"Well, it's not too late," she said grudgingly. She had told herself she wasn't going to take the job, but now that she saw the property, it was difficult to turn away from it.

Nick was working on the house, but by his own admission, he knew nothing about plants so it wasn't like she'd have to work with him. If she was careful, their paths might not even cross.

"It can't be done overnight and it won't be cheap," she warned.

"I guessed as much," he said meekly.

Kate nibbled on her lower lip, common sense struggling against a gut-level hunger to get her hands on Harry's yard. Of course, it would be a good business move. There would be the design fee, which, at Brenda's insistence, was hers alone. There would be the cost of plant material and mulch, all to be ordered through the nursery. And it would also be a good advertisement, both for the nursery and for her abilities as a designer. If she could restore these gardens to their former beauty—and she knew she could— she'd have a wonderful addition to her résumé.

Watching her, Harry found himself hoping that she never tried to lie on the witness stand. Her face was utterly transparent, revealing her shifting emotions with perfect clarity. Her professional demeanor had cracked the moment she saw the gardens, and it had been crumbling ever since. He wouldn't have been surprised if, with a little negotiating, he could have had her offering to pay *him* for the privilege of taking on the job.

"We're really very busy right now," she said, looking longingly toward the back of the property. "Is there a stream back there?"

"A small one," he said casually. "If you don't have time to take it on, I understand." He should probably feel guilty for tugging on the line when he knew she was already hooked, but the urge was irresistible.

"I can work it in," she assured him hastily, and he hid a smile. "I'd like to take the job, if we can work out the details."

Privately, she was determined to work out the details, even if she had to cut her own fee out entirely. She wanted this job more than she'd wanted anything in a very long time. She was going to get it, and to hell with Nick Blackthorne.

Nick was lying on his back under the kitchen sink when he heard the back door open. He tensed, but there was only one set of footsteps, which meant that Kate hadn't come in.

"What are you doing?" Harry asked irritably. "Every time I turn around, you're poking around looking for dry rot or sticking your head under a sink."

"That's why I came back," Nick said as he slid out from under the sink and sat up. He looked at Harry and raised one brow. "You wanted me to put the house in shape to sell. Remember?"

"Of course I remember," the old man said irritably. "But I didn't expect you to spend your every waking moment with your head stuck in dank holes." He waved one hand, cutting off Nick's attempt to point out that most plumbing work involved dank holes. "Never mind that now. I wanted to tell you that we've got ourselves a landscaper."

"She took the job?"

"Sure did. She can't wait to get started. Wouldn't make much of a poker player. I could see she was anxious to get her hands on the place." Pleased with himself, he chuckled. "I'm not sure, but I think she might have me brought up on charges of plant abuse if there was such a thing."

"The landscaping is in pretty bad shape," Nick said absently. He got to his feet and glanced out the window, only to find his view blocked by a nearly solid wall of hibiscus leaves. The shrub had grown up over the window, filtering the sunlight so that the narrow kitchen was always tinted the faint green of a deep jungle.

So, Kate was going to be working on the yard while he was working on the house. He wasn't sure how he felt about that. He was glad that she hadn't turned down the job just to avoid him, but he wasn't all that crazy about the idea of having her underfoot, figuratively speaking. He'd be better off keeping a little distance between himself and his brother's fi-ancée.

"Did she go back to work?" He hadn't heard her car leave, but he probably wouldn't have with his head stuck under the sink.

"Not yet." Harry opened the refrigerator and pulled out a box of Chinese take-out from the night before. He took a fork out of the drawer, then speared a hot pepper directly from the box. Nick winced as he bit down on it.

"Jesus, Harry, I can't believe you actually put those things in your mouth. They're hot enough to strip paint."

"We've got plenty of paint to strip. Maybe I should buy a carload of them." He grinned as he bit into another pepper. "Save a fortune on chemicals."

The phone rang, cutting off Nick's answer, which would probably have been nearly as pungent as the peppers. Carrying the take-out carton with him, Harry went to answer it. Nick hesitated only a moment before pushing open the back door and going outside.

Kate wasn't hard to find. She was on her knees next to one of the roses, studying the tangled canes with an expression that was equal parts adoration and annoyance. Nick thought of Harry's comment about Kate wanting to bring him up on charges and half smiled.

"Need a machete?" he asked.

Kate hadn't heard him approach. She'd told herself that she was assessing the condition of the rose in front of her, but in her heart of hearts, she knew she was engaged in nothing less than nature worship. The idea that this garden was hers—more or less—was so incredible that she could hardly absorb it. She'd felt the need to touch the soil, as if that would make it all real. The sound of Nick's voice shattered the moment like a hammer striking a pane of glass.

He was the single, glaring flaw in the whole arrangement, she thought as she got to her feet. She bent to dust off the knees of her slacks, using the moment to regain control of her expression. Knowing that it was inevitable that she'd see him here was the only thing that kept her from shouting with joy.

"I need to get back to work," she said, glancing at her watch without seeing it. "Excuse me."

"Wait." Nick reached out, catching her arm when she would have walked past him. "I think we should talk."

Kate stared past his shoulder, her expression rigid, her stomach churning with nerves. She was painfully aware of his hand against her arm but refused to give him the satisfaction of pulling away. "I don't think we have anything to say to each other."

"*I* have something to say to you. Please."

The last word drew her eyes to his face. What she saw made her heart thud suddenly and painfully against her rib cage. This was the man she'd met five years ago, the one who, for a little while, had made her feel less alone. She almost thought she'd prefer to see the cold, angry stranger of a few days ago. That seemed safer somehow.

"I really don't have much time." She stepped back so that his hand fell away from her arm.

"I'll try to grovel quickly."

"Grovel?"

"It's the least I owe you. I want to apologize for the things I said and for the way I acted the other night."

"Apologize?" Kate felt like an echo, but she couldn't seem to manage anything original.

"I was way out of line. I don't know what I was thinking, why I reacted the way I did."

"It's an awkward situation," Kate said faintly and then wondered if she was trying to make excuses for him.

"It doesn't have to be." For the first time, Nick hesitated, and when he spoke, it was obvious that he was choosing his words with care. "What happened between us—it was a long time ago. It doesn't have anything to do with...anyone else."

She noticed that he avoided saying Gareth's name and wondered if he felt the way she did—that they'd somehow betrayed his brother, even though the single night they'd spent together had happened long before she and Gareth had met.

"Look, this whole situation is based on a coincidence so bizarre it's like something off daytime television."

"Like *Geraldo?*" she asked softly, and Nick winced, remembering his comment the last time they met.

He gave her a lopsided smile. "Actually, I was thinking of *General Hospital*. This goes way beyond the scope of *Geraldo*."

Despite herself, Kate felt herself softening. He seemed to be honestly trying to smooth things over between them. She wanted to hold on to her anger, she admitted, looking away from him. It was safe to be angry with him.

"You're going to be part of the family," Nick continued. "I don't want any awkwardness between us."

"It's a little late for that, isn't it?" She watched a bright green, long-legged insect step delicately onto a rose leaf and thought that *awkward* didn't really begin to describe the situation.

"We can rewrite history a little—pretend we're meeting for the first time today." His smile was coaxing. "Hell, politicians do it all the time and get away with it."

Kate kept her eyes on the insect, which had settled near the tip of the leaf. She wondered if it was either waiting for some smaller creature to get within reach or contemplating its first bite of rose leaf. If she slid her eyes to the left, she could see Nick's feet. He was wearing scuffed brown work boots and a pair of faded jeans—casual, working clothes. The first time she'd met him, he'd been wearing a similar outfit. Harry had said that he'd spent the last five years working on Wall Street. She had a hard time picturing him in a suit and tie.

Kate shifted her gaze to the insect, which seemed to be basking in the sun. Apparently, the dangers of UV exposure had yet to reach his part of the world. It must be nice to be a bug—lolling in the sun with nothing to worry about but whether you were going to *have* dinner or *be* dinner.

Nick's suggestion seemed good—a chance to wipe the slate clean, pretend past mistakes had never happened. Gareth would never have to know. It was what she'd wanted and more than she'd dared to hope for. But now that it was within reach, she hesitated. Shared secrets were intimate things, she thought uneasily. They created ties, linked those who knew the truth. The last thing she wanted was any kind of a bond with Nick. Then again, maybe it was a little late for that.

"I love my brother," Nick said when she remained silent. "I would never do anything to hurt him."

Reluctantly, Kate looked at him, her eyes searching his. He looked as if he meant what he was saying. She looked away. She didn't want to see Gareth hurt, either. She could argue that something she'd done long before she met him shouldn't cause him pain, but emotions were not always logical. Instinct told her that learning she'd once slept with his brother was not something Gareth would be able to shrug off, no matter when it happened.

"All right."

Nick looked relieved. "It's the best way to handle it."

"I hope so." Kate felt a mixture of relief and guilt. Her engagement was safe, but she couldn't get past the feeling that she was protecting it by lying, at least tacitly, to Gareth.

Nick smiled and held out his hand. "Nice to meet you, Kate Moran."

After an almost imperceptible hesitation, she took his hand. She hoped she wasn't making the mistake of a lifetime. She hoped even more that the spark of awareness she felt when they touched was the product of too much sun and anxiety.

"I'll let you get back to work," Nick said as he released her hand. "Harry's very pleased with himself for hiring you, by the way."

"I hope he'll be pleased when he sees the results." She rubbed the tips of her fingers over her palm, as if to erase the faint tingle she felt there.

"I'm sure he will be. Gareth says you're the best."

She knew he'd mentioned his brother deliberately, an assurance—or reminder?—that the past was no longer relevant. It gave her the courage to ask a question that had been haunting her.

"Wait." He'd already started to walk away but he stopped and half turned toward her, his brows raised in question. "Five years ago, when we...met, were you... I know your wife—" At the sudden bleakness in his eyes, Kate stumbled to a halt but she'd gone too far to stop. "Were you married when we...?"

Nick's face looked as if it had been carved from solid granite. She thought he might turn and walk away, leaving her question unanswered. The silence stretched, along with her nerves.

"No, I wasn't married." He turned and walked away without waiting for a response.

Not that she had a response, Kate thought. What could she say? *I'm so glad to hear that your wife was already dead when we made love?* Not exactly appropriate. She felt guilty for being relieved that she hadn't slept with a married man.

Nick disappeared around the edge of a wildly overgrown hedge of Korean box and Kate released her breath on a sigh. *Forget the past,* he'd said. It would be nice if they truly could. Just pretending to forget was only going to make her remember more. She rubbed her fingertips over her palm again, and tried not to think of the awareness she'd felt when he took her hand.

Looking around the garden, she tried to regain some of her earlier sense of elation. She should be happy. She had a fabulous new job. Her engagement was safe. Everything was going just the way she wanted. Life was practically perfect. There was nothing to worry about. Nothing at all.

Lowering her gaze, she saw that the green bug was still perched on the rose leaf. He was dining on a smaller winged creature, which answered the question of his dietary preferences. As she watched, he tilted his head and she had the distinct impression that he was looking up at her. She couldn't help but think that he looked smugly triumphant.

Chapter Five

Kate suddenly became aware of a prickling sensation along the back of her neck. She'd been on her hands and knees, halfway under a rose bush, scraping her hand through the layers of half-rotted leaves in search of a label that might give her a clue to the plant's identity. But she couldn't escape the feeling that she was being watched. Moving carefully, in deference to the wild tangle of canes that surrounded her, she backed out from under the plant. Turning, she sat down in the grassy path.

A very little girl and a very large dog stood a few feet away, watching her with nearly identical expressions of interest. Kate regarded them both warily. She didn't have much experience with either children or dogs. As far as she knew, one was prone to tears and the other was prone to bite.

"Hello," she said when neither of her visitors showed any inclination to speak.

"Hello." The child offered a friendly smile along with the greeting. The dog simply continued to look at her. They were an odd pair, Kate thought. The little girl was as delicately pretty as a china doll, with big blue eyes and a short cap of wispy blond hair that framed her fragile features. The dog, on the other hand, was not only large, he was, quite possibly, the ugliest animal she'd ever seen in her life. His coat was the exact color of steel wool and looked just about as soft. He was built along the stocky lines of a draft horse and was nearly as large.

"I'm Laura and this is Leroy." The child patted the dog on the head.

"Leroy?" The name seemed improbable.

"Like in the old song. You know, 'bad, bad Leroy Brown. Meaner than a junkyard dog?' Only Leroy isn't mean at all. Are you?"

She leaned against the dog, who supported her weight without effort. Kate was inclined to think he could support a small building without exerting himself. Laura looked at her, her wide blue eyes questioning.

"You're the lady who's going to fix up Harry's yard, aren't you?"

"I'm going to try to." Aware that she hadn't exactly done her part in the introductions, she smiled at the child. "I'm Kate."

"I know. Nick told me your name. He said you were going to make everything pretty but I think it's pretty already." It was evident that she viewed any possible changes with suspicion.

"I think it's pretty, too, but it can be even prettier."

Laura looked politely doubtful and changed the subject. "What were you looking for under the rosebush?"

"I was hoping to find a label that would tell me the plant's name."

Laura looked surprised. "It's a rose," she told Kate kindly.

"Yes, I know that." Kate bit back a smile. "I want to know what *kind* of rose it is."

"You mean whether it's white or red?"

"More or less." This didn't seem the time to go into an explanation of *alba* versus *damascus*. "Are you visiting Harry?" she asked.

"I live next door." Laura waved one small hand toward the north. "Harry lets me come over here to play when I want."

"How long have you and...Leroy lived next door?" Kate couldn't quite shake the feeling that the big dog was eyeing her with dislike.

"I've lived next door forever. Since I was a baby." Laura managed to make it sound like that had been centuries ago. "Leroy isn't my dog. He's Nick's."

"Nick's?" Kate felt the name catch in her throat a little.

"Nick is a friend of Harry's. He's fixing up the house," Laura explained graciously.

"Yes. I know." Kate stood up, dusting her hands against the seat of her pants and then leaning over to brush bits of grass off her knees. "I didn't realize he had a dog."

"Nick found Leroy last week. Somebody hit him with a car and drove off." She threw one thin arm around the dog's massive neck, her voice crackling with indignation. "He was hurt but Nick healed him all up."

"That was very nice of him," Kate said sincerely. "I'm glad the doctor was able to help Leroy."

Laura frowned. "It wasn't a doctor. It was Nick. He—"

"What am I being accused of now?" Nick's voice came from behind Kate. She turned quickly, struggling to keep her expression under control. She hadn't seen him in several days, not since they'd stood in this same garden and decided to forget the past. If only it was that easy.

"Hello." Nick's smile was friendly.

"Hello." The word was little more than a croak, and she cleared her throat before trying again. "Hello. Nick." The name was an afterthought, intended to show that she was perfectly comfortable with him—with the situation. The quick flash of humor in his eyes suggested that she hadn't been particularly successful.

"Kate," he said, his solemn tone inviting her to see the humor in the moment. Reluctantly, Kate's mouth curved in a fleeting smile.

"Hello, Nick." Laura's tone had gone from briskly adult to coyly feminine.

"Hey, short stuff." Nick's shoulder nearly brushed Kate's as he walked past her. He smelled like sunshine and sweat—warm, masculine smells that conjured up images of bare chests and rippling muscles. Kate pushed the images firmly away.

"Don't get too close to me," he warned the little girl when she lifted her arms for a hug. "I'm filthy."

His jeans were covered in a fine layer of dust. Patches of dirt made his T-shirt look like camouflage gear. Even his dark hair was coated with dust, giving Kate a preview of what he would look like when he was older. It hardly seemed fair that gray hair should suit him as much as his natural deep brown.

"I don't mind if I get dirty," Laura said, looking at him with worshipful blue eyes.

"Yeah, but I bet your mom does." He brushed his hand affectionately over her golden curls.

Laura looked as if she might melt on the spot, and Kate was annoyed to realize that she knew just how the little girl felt. Those dimples were hard to resist. Not that they affected *her,* but she couldn't help but notice them. She became aware that she was rubbing her thumb against the band of her engagement ring, as if it was a talisman to protect her against powerful magic.

"You look like you've been rolling in the dirt," she said briskly, relaxing her hand with an effort.

"Crawling in it." Nick bent to scratch Leroy behind his ear, and Kate was half amused, half irritated to see the huge dog turn his ugly face upward with a look of adoration. Really, what was it about the man that turned children and dogs into putty? Not to mention grown women, she added reluctantly, thinking back to the first time they'd met.

"Harry says I'm making too much of a mess in the house, so he's going to move into the guest house. I was just in the crawl space repairing a leak in the plumbing." Leroy shifted position, leaning his not inconsiderable bulk against Nick's leg. Nick braced himself against the weight and grinned at the dog. "You're a lazy bum."

"I was telling Kate 'bout how Leroy was hurted and you made him better," Laura said, looking at him adoringly.

"I didn't do much. Leroy did most of the work himself, didn't you, boy?" He rubbed his knuckles over the top of the dog's head, and Leroy's human-sounding sigh of pleasure surprised a smile from Kate.

Laura frowned. "But his leg was all covered with blood and you put your hands on it and you—"

"It looked a lot worse than it was." Nick cut her off, as if uncomfortable with her admiration.

Modest, too, Kate thought sourly. Good-looking, kind to children and small animals—didn't the guy have a fault?

"Leroy looks very...healthy now," Kate said, directing an uncertain smile at the large animal. "He's rather large, isn't it?"

"Just a healthy, growing boy," Nick said.

"Growing?" Kate's imagination boggled at the idea that the dog might actually get bigger.

"Sure. He's just a puppy, aren't you?" Leroy wagged a tail the size of a broom, his square face creasing in something that might have been a smile.

"He seems friendly," she said doubtfully.

"You're not worried about meeting him when you're alone, are you?" Nick asked. "He wouldn't hurt a fly."

"I'd feel good about that if I was a fly."

Nick laughed out loud, and she did her best to ignore the frisson of awareness that ran up her spine. She did *not* want to be reminded of how attractive he was.

"Come shake hands with him. Leroy would never bite anyone to whom he's been properly introduced. Come on," he urged when she hung back.

"Are you scared?" Laura asked, her sandy brows going up in surprise.

"No," Kate lied promptly. She forced herself to

move forward. "I just don't have much experience with dogs, that's all. Actually, I don't have any real experience with them at all."

"Lean down and hold out your hand," Nick told her.

Feeling as if she might as well be holding out a T-bone steak, Kate did as she was told. Leroy eyed her for a moment, his black eyes unfathomable. She hoped he wasn't trying to decide where to bite first but, conscious of Nick and Laura watching, she held her hand steady. When Leroy lifted one massive paw and plunked it into her palm, she jumped in surprise. Kate dutifully shook his paw and then released it. She straightened, aware of a distinct feeling of accomplishment.

"Didn't you ever have a dog back when you were a little girl?" Laura asked, watching the exchange with curious blue eyes.

"We moved around a lot. It wouldn't have been fair to drag a pet away from its home all the time." She'd heard the words so often as a child that they came to her automatically now.

"Kind of hard on a kid, too," Nick commented, and Kate felt her breath catch at the base of her throat.

She remembered worrying that her parents might decide that constantly moving wasn't any better for her than it would have been for a pet. She'd been afraid they'd leave her behind the next time her father decided that a new town, a new state, would offer better opportunities. When she looked back, it struck her as interesting that it hadn't once occurred to her that they might settle in one place for her benefit—only that they'd leave her behind. Even at a young age, she'd recognized her father's wanderlust as the central, driving force in her family.

"I didn't mind moving." The lie came easily. It had been repeated so often when she was a child that it was engraved on her soul. "We saw a lot of interesting places."

"I don't think I'd like to move," Laura said thoughtfully. "I like it here and, if we moved, I couldn't take my friends with me."

Kate's smile felt as if it was pinned in place. "No, you can't take your friends but you make new friends when you move."

"They wouldn't be the same," the little girl said decisively, and Kate didn't argue. What could she say?

Looking for distraction, she reached out to pet Leroy, who had shifted position and now stood between her and Nick. His fur was softer than it looked, and she smiled as she stroked his head.

"We did have a cat once," she said, memory rushing over her. "He was all black and I named him Spooky."

"What happened to him?" Laura asked, displaying the unerring knack of the very young to ask exactly the question you least wanted to answer.

"When we were moving from Atlanta to Baton Rouge, we stopped to get gas and Spooky got out of the car. He got lost, I guess. We were heartbroken."

"We?" Nick asked. "Do you have brothers or sisters?"

Kate froze for a moment, her hand clenching the dog's thick fur. With an effort, she forced her hand to relax, uncurling each finger individually. "I meant my mother and I. We were both heartbroken when Spooky disappeared."

"What about your father?"

"He was so focused on getting to Baton Rouge that I don't think he registered much of anything else." She gave Leroy one last pat before glancing at her watch. "I've got to get to work or Brenda will have my hide."

"Not unless she's changed a lot," Nick said. "The Brenda I remember would never expend that much energy. Not if she could be taking a nap instead."

The description was so apt that Kate grinned. "She hasn't changed much," she admitted. "I've never known anyone else who considers sleeping a hobby."

"And she's a champion at it. When we were in high school, she'd prop a tall book up on her desk and sleep through study hall."

Kate chuckled. "That sounds like Brenda."

"Nice to know some things don't change."

"Brenda will never change. It would take too much energy."

Nick laughed again and, for just a moment, Kate nearly forgot who he was and what lay between them. She felt easy with him, comfortable, the way she'd felt when she first met him. They'd laughed then, too, she remembered, sobering. It was the first time she'd realized that laughter could be more seductive than wine.

Nick saw her smile fade, saw the sudden distance in her and knew what she was thinking, what she was remembering. He remembered, too. He remembered laughing for the first time since Lisa and Kyle's death months before. He remembered thinking—tentatively—that maybe he hadn't really died with his son, with his wife.

"I really do have to go," Kate said, her smile suddenly thin and without meaning. She said a quick goodbye to Laura, patted Leroy on the head and smiled vaguely in Nick's direction.

Nick turned to watch her walk away. He couldn't help but admire the soft, feminine swing of her hips, and he couldn't help but think that, under other circumstances, they might get along pretty well. It was a shame that one night lay between them.

He ruthlessly squashed the small voice that suggested the real shame was that she was engaged to his brother.

* * *

Nick booted the kickstand into place and leaned the big bike onto its support. Lifting off his helmet he swung his leg over the bike's seat and stood up. In New York, leaving the helmet with the bike was the equivalent of hanging a sign on it that flashed the words *steal me* in bold neon. But he wasn't in New York anymore, he reminded himself, and he left the helmet with the bike.

Following the sound of a power saw, he walked around the side of the Spanish-style home. At first glance, the backyard looked like an obstacle course. Piles of lumber, bags of cement and a couple of battered wheelbarrows were scattered across the remains of a lawn. The earsplitting scream of the saw drowned out the staccato thud of hammers, making the men using them look like mimes in some avant-garde theatrical production. The clean, sharp scent of sawdust filled the air.

Nick walked across the lawn, circling the piles of lumber as he approached the building site. The power saw stopped abruptly. In the wake of its scream, the ragged beat of the hammers sounded almost musical.

"Hey, Nick!" A middle-aged man lifted his hammer in a wave. The sound of his name was echoed from several of the other men as they saw him. Nick returned their greetings.

"Nick! I heard you were back in town." Jack Sinclair jumped off the foundation and strode toward him. "How the hell are you?"

"Not bad. How about you?" Nick took his hand, wincing as Jack slapped him on the shoulder with his free hand.

"I'm better than average. When you didn't get in touch, I figured, after spending time wheeling and dealing on Wall Street, you might be avoiding contact with the hoi polloi."

"I haven't been back all that long."

"Thirteen days," Jack said promptly, his blue eyes sparkling with laughter. "You want me to give you the hours and minutes? You rode into town on a black motorcycle at approximately seven-twenty on Friday evening, wearing a black helmet, black leather jacket and black boots and you went through a yellow light at First and Oak."

Nick gave a disbelieving laugh. "What have they done? Installed video cameras in the traffic lights? Trained a spy satellite on the town?"

Jack grinned, pleased with Nick's surprised reaction. "Better than that. Sam and Esther Martinez were taking their dog for an evening constitutional and saw you. When they got home, Esther called Lucy Redmond, who called old Mr. Willits, who called—"

Nick cut him off with a wave of his hand. "I can take it from there. You don't have to recite the whole list. The grapevine in this town must be the envy of the CIA.''

"It's pretty good," Jack admitted with a grin. "The only fuzzy point was what kind of bike you were riding. Sam thought it was a Honda but Esther was convinced it was a Harley. I figured it had to be a Harley."

"Why?"

"Well, it fits better with the man-in-black image. You know, dark and dangerous, riding into town on one of the last of the great American muscle machines, silhouetted against the setting sunset, an icon to— Hey!" He ducked the mock punch Nick aimed at him. "You're spoiling my imagery."

"I'm going to spoil your teeth if you keep it up." Nick grinned ruefully and shook his head. "I'd almost forgotten how fast gossip moves in this town."

"Too many years in the big city, man. You've gotten soft and out of shape."

"The last time I took this kind of abuse, it was from a New York cabdriver."

While they talked, the two of them had moved to the edge of the big yard, far enough from the construction to reduce the sound of hammering to a tolerable level.

"Looks like pretty much the same crew," Nick said, nodding to the men who were framing in the addition. Five years ago, he and Jack had been partners. When he left Eden, he'd sold his interest in the firm to his friend.

"Pretty much." Jack hooked his thumbs in his back pockets and rocked back on his heels as he looked at the crew. "Juan Padilla retired two years ago. He's got a farm the size of a handkerchief about twenty miles north of here. I didn't think he'd make a go of it but he's growing gourmet vegetables for a couple of upscale restaurants in L.A. and it looks like he may do okay.

"Bill Turnquist's wife left him last summer, said she had to find herself. Two weeks after he signed the divorce papers, he won three million bucks in the lottery. His wife came back so fast, her feet were smoking. Said she'd realized how much she really loved him. He told her to take a hike, gave her his half of the divorce settlement and moved to Montana. Last I heard, he's engaged to marry a cowgirl half his age and is happier than a pig in shit."

Nick laughed. "From what I remember of Bill's wife, he's better off without her, even without the three million."

Jack nodded. "Easy on the eyes but about as warm as a frozen chunk of steel."

"Looks like business is good," Nick said, nodding to the half-framed room.

"We're doing okay. Town's attracting a smattering of escapees from L.A. They move here looking for the 'good life in an unspoiled small town setting,' to quote the chamber of commerce. They all want a 'solidly built home with the character that only comes with age,' to quote the real estate ads. Soon as escrow closes, they scramble to hire someone to put on an addition that doubles the square footage. Naturally, they want to retain the character of age but they don't want to pay for a good design or quality materials.''

He nodded to the construction site. ''These people moved here from L.A. looking for a simpler life. They're putting in a state-of-the-art kitchen, adding a bonus room the size of a football field, enlarging the garage so it will hold three cars, and they've got a satellite dish coming as soon as we're through with the work. Near as I can tell, they've both had cell phones permanently grafted to their ears so they can do business anywhere, anytime.'' Jack shook his head as he pulled a pack of cigarettes out of his shirt pocket. ''Obviously, they're really in tune with small town life.''

Nick laughed. ''Maybe this is their idea of small town life.''

''I guess so.'' Jack used a battered steel lighter to light his cigarette. ''It's good for my business anyway.'' Inhaling smoke, he slanted Nick a questioning glance. ''I hear you're going to restore that old wreck of Harry's.''

''So I'm told.'' Nick slid his hands in his pockets,

bracing his feet a little apart as he watched the crew assembling the frame.

He felt completely relaxed for the first time since coming home to Eden. He and Jack had been friends since grade school. The three of them—Nick, Jack and Brian—had played on the same teams, gotten suspended from the same classes and, on a few occasions, dated the same girls. His friendship with Jack had survived Brian's death, college and marriage. Over the past five years, their only contact had been through Christmas cards and one phone call when Jack's second child was born. Yet they'd simply picked up where they'd left off, as if the intervening years didn't exist.

"I wouldn't mind having a partner again," Jack said, interrupting the comfortable silence between them. "Having a gen-u-ine award-winning architect design their additions would impress the yuppies no end. I could double the price and they wouldn't bat an eye."

"One award in college doesn't exactly make me Frank Lloyd Wright," Nick said, keeping his eyes on the crew.

"They wouldn't know the difference between Frank Lloyd Wright and Frank Zappa," Jack said cynically.

"I think Zappa had more hair."

Nick moved his shoulders restlessly. It had been a long time since he'd given any thought to the profession that had once been his dream. It was just another of the things he'd walked away from five years ago. But now, standing here, listening to the sharp rhythm of the hammers and inhaling the mixed smells of newly cut wood and damp cement, he felt a sudden hunger inside him. He'd always loved the actual building as much as the design work and had been as comfortable with a hammer as he had been with a drafting pencil.

"The offer's open anytime," Jack said. He took one last draw on the cigarette and then dropped the butt into the dirt and ground it out with the toe of his work boot. "We were a good team."

"I'll think about it," Nick said and then was half surprised to realize that he meant it. "I don't exactly know what I'm doing yet."

"Harry twist your arm?"

"I think he's trying to save me from myself," Nick said ruefully.

Jack tapped another cigarette loose. "You can't grieve forever."

"No?" Nick's light tone was at odds with the emptiness in his eyes. Without giving Jack a chance to respond, he changed the subject, asking about a mutual friend. After a moment's hesitation, Jack followed his lead and they talked for a few minutes about people they both knew. The conversation ended when one of the men called Jack over to the building site to look at something.

"You want to come to dinner tonight?" Jack asked as he crushed out his second cigarette. "Susan would love to see you again. You haven't even met Rose, and you won't believe how much Matthew has grown. It's probably leftover spaghetti but you won't mind that."

"I already talked to Susan. She told me where to find you and invited me to dinner tomorrow night. She also said to tell you that, if you brought me home for leftovers, she was going to sue for divorce and take you for every penny she could get."

Jack looked startled for a moment and then grinned sheepishly. "I brought a client and his wife home for dinner a month ago. Like I said, there's always plenty of food, so I figured Susie wouldn't mind. Turned out she was in the middle of doing something to her hair. When the three of us walked in, she had pieces of aluminum foil sticking up all over her head. She looked like an alien visitor from some really cheesy sci-fi movie. Once everyone recovered from the shock, we got a good laugh out of it. It ended up being a pretty nice evening but, after they left, she threatened me with a fate worse than death if I ever brought anyone home again without giving her any warning."

Nick laughed, picturing the scene. "You're lucky she gave you a second chance."

"I'm lucky all around. She's pretty special. I've got to get back to work," he said, glancing over his shoulder at the building site. "I'll see you tomorrow night. Good to have you home again."

Nick watched as Jack loped across the yard. *Home*. He turned away. Eden was home, all right. He just wasn't sure it was *his* home anymore.

And why was it that Jack's mention of how special Susan was had made him think of Kate?

He started his motorcycle. But his half-smile faded immediately, and he was frowning as he pulled away from the curb. He'd come back hoping to finally put the past to rest. It would be ironic if, instead, he managed to screw his life up all over again. Letting himself become attracted to his brother's fiancée definitely fell into the category of major screw-up.

Kate lifted her face to the rising sun and drew a slow, deep breath. The air held the crisp scent of green, growing things and the warm, brown smell of freshly turned earth. The temperature was supposed to climb to eighty today, but at this hour of the morning, it was still pleasantly cool.

It had been nearly a month since she'd taken the job of restoring the gardens at Spider's Walk, and she still couldn't believe her good fortune. Every day, she discovered some new treasure—the outline of a pond hidden under a tangle of ivy, a drift of daffodils, naturalized years before and just coming into bloom. She'd found labels for nearly half the roses and had mapped most of the property, sketching in the main features and noting trees and existing flower beds. She had pages of notes to herself—what needed to be replaced, what needed to be pruned, suggestions for filling in the gaps left by time and neglect.

Kate opened her eyes and looked around, her mouth curving in a soft smile. Silly as it was, she sometimes indulged in the fantasy that this was her garden, that she lived in the ornate old house and was building this garden for herself and her family, for generations yet to come. If she narrowed her eyes, she could almost see a dark-haired little boy digging a trowel into one of the flower beds, hunting earthworms or whatever treasure the earth chose to offer up. He looked up, his eyes sparkling with pleasure, his smile revealing a matched set of dimples, one in each cheek. The image was so real and vivid that she almost spoke to him, almost reached out her hand to draw him close.

Looking out the kitchen window—newly cleared of hibiscus—Nick saw Kate standing in the garden. He'd expected to see her there. As far as he could tell, she came by every morning before going to work. She also came by most evenings and spent a good part of her days off here. He wondered how Gareth felt about her devotion to her job, but he hadn't asked. He didn't much like thinking of her with his brother. And he'd been *very* careful not to explore that feeling any further.

Kate lifted her face, eyes closed, expression rapt, as if asking a blessing from the pale sunlight. Her hair tumbled halfway down her back, a silk curtain of tawny gold. It was the first time he'd seen her with her hair down, and Nick's fingers curled against the urge to touch it, pushing aside the memory of its softness against his skin. With an effort, he turned away from the window and the innocent sensuality of her.

"She's engaged," he muttered out loud. "To your own brother, you jerk."

But she was yours first, a sly voice whispered.

He squashed the thought with ruthless force and pulled open a cupboard to take out a coffee cup. After a moment's hesitation, he took out a second cup and set it on the counter. They were going to be related by marriage. They might as well start getting comfortable with the idea.

Kate watched a scrub jay sifting through the layers of leaves and twigs beneath a lobelia that had taken over most of a flower bed. As he worked, he moved in and out of the patchy sunshine, his rich blue color alternately revealed and hidden by the light.

"Good morning." Nick's greeting startled her out of her absorption.

Her head jerked toward him, her smile fading as her expression turned wary. She'd seen him several times in the last couple of weeks, usually at a distance, which suited her just fine. When they did happen to speak, she made it a point to be on her way somewhere, but she could hardly say that she had a vital appointment at six o'clock in the morning.

"I thought you might like a cup of coffee," he said, holding a sturdy white mug out to her.

"Thank you." She would have refused the coffee but the smell seduced her. If she'd hoped he'd simply hand her the coffee and then disappear, she was doomed to disappointment. He stood next to her, sipping his own coffee.

He was wearing faded jeans and an ancient blue cotton shirt with the sleeves rolled halfway up to his elbows. His dark hair looked as if he'd combed it with his fingers, and there was a tiny nick on his chin where he'd cut himself shaving. The scent of the coffee didn't completely conceal the more subtle, spicy smells of soap and aftershave. He looked solidly masculine and appallingly attractive, and she hated herself for noticing.

"You're here early," she said, anxious to break the silence.

"I'm staying here now." He caught her surprised look and shrugged. "It makes more sense than staying with my parents. Now, if I get the urge to strip paint at two in the morning, I'm in the right place for it."

She smiled faintly and hoped he wouldn't realize just how little she liked the idea of him being here all the time. Not that it should make any difference to her one way or another, she reminded herself. It was just that she'd liked the idea of having the place completely to herself, at least in these early morning hours. Harry was in the guest house, of course, but that was tucked into a back corner of the property, easily ignored. Now that she knew Nick was staying in the house, it wouldn't be the same.

Kate sipped her coffee and groped for something else to say. For some reason, silences with Nick always seemed to hold an element of danger, as if there were things better left unspoken that might escape into any quiet moment. Coming up blank, she focused on the jay, who was still shuffling through the leaves as if in search of buried treasure.

"Why do you do that?" Nick asked abruptly.

Kate gave him a wary look. "Do what?"

"Close up whenever you see me."

"I don't know what you mean." Her fingers tightened around the mug and she felt a sharp spurt of anger. Did he really have to ask why she closed up when she saw him?

"Sure you do." His frown was thoughtful rather than annoyed. "You were enjoying the morning, looking all relaxed and peaceful, and as soon as you saw me, your face got all tight and you looked like you'd just swallowed a peach pit."

Stung, Kate snapped at him. "If you knew you were going to ruin my morning, why did you come out here? Has it ever occurred to you that maybe I just flat don't like you?''

Her words seemed to hang in the air. She stared at him, shocked that she'd let her control over her temper slip that far.

Nick's brows went up in surprise and she held her breath, waiting for him to explode. Instead, his expression became thoughtful, as if he was giving her question serious consideration. After a moment, he shook his head.

''Nah. Everybody likes me. I'm charming.''

There was a startled moment of silence and then Kate found herself giggling helplessly. Damn him for being right.

Chapter Six

Nick shut the Harley's engine off and sighed with pleasure at the sudden silence. Perhaps it was time to replace the big bike with something that made a little less noise and held a lot more stuff. He'd had the motorcycle for three years and he'd enjoyed it, but lately it was losing its appeal.

As he stepped away from the bike, he eyed the small yellow truck that sat next to it—Kate's truck. He'd seen it often enough at Spider's Walk during the past few weeks and lately he'd begun to envy her the simple practicality of the vehicle. A motorcycle was severely limited when it came to hauling lumber.

Momentarily shelving the issue of transportation, he walked across the small parking area and stepped onto the brick walkway. The building in front of him had changed since the last time he'd seen it. An old-fashioned wooden sign hung from the eaves. The Wisteria Place was painted across it in gracefully flowing, deep lavender script.

Other than the sign, the building looked like the comfortably frumpy old farmhouse it had once been. The landscaping reinforced the image. Iceland poppies lined the walkway, their colorful, fragile blossoms nodding on slender stems. Neatly trimmed shrubs softened the foundation.

The deep porch ran the full length of the building and was topped by a sturdy wooden trellis. At this time of year, you had to look twice to see the tangle of vines that covered it, some as thick as your wrist. But Nick knew that in another month the whole trellis would be drenched in soft color. Fat, pendulous clusters of wisteria blossoms would create a magical canopy, and for a little while the chunky little building would rival a Victorian mansion for sheer gaudy beauty. When the flowers faded, the leaves would take over, providing a thick, green canopy that would turn the sharp heat of summer into something cool and inviting.

For as long as Nick could remember, the house had been called the Wisteria Place. He wasn't sure if anyone had ever bothered to find out the name of the elderly couple who'd lived there, and it wouldn't have mattered if they had. The name would have stayed the same. If memory served him, about eight years ago, the couple had died within a few months of each other and the house had been occupied by a succession of renters. The last time he'd seen the place, the house had been sliding into a not-so-gentle decline. The paint had been peeling, the walkway had been a jumble of cracked concrete and a scruffy expanse of half-dead lawn had been the sum total of the landscaping.

The place had now been restored in a way that made it look fresh and new without obliterating the mellow charm that only age could give. He was willing to bet that Kate had had a lot to do with that restoration.

Kate. As Nick started up the walkway, he was uneasily aware of a feeling of anticipation at the thought of seeing her. Since the morning when he'd startled her with a cup of coffee, he'd made it a point to be somewhere else when she was around. Propinquity, he'd told himself. It was just propinquity that made her appealing. With a little distance this—whatever it was he felt—would fade away.

A bell jangled cheerfully as he pushed open the nursery's front door. Okay, so he was attracted to her, but there was no crime in that. Engaged or not, she was an attractive woman. What bothered him was that, when he was with her, it was much too easy to remember their brief history together and easier still to forget that she was engaged to marry his brother.

A teenage girl told him that Kate was going over the inventory and directed him out the back door. As he stepped outside, Nick thought he knew how Dorothy must have felt when she landed in Oz and found herself in a Technicolor world. There were plants everywhere, on tables, hanging from the slats of the lattice roof, in large pots on the ground. It was like stepping into a cool, green jungle. Flowers provided bright accents of color, like accessories on a woman's gown.

Kate wasn't hard to find. Her khaki-colored shirt and pants stood out from the surrounding greenery. The teenager inside had been wearing a similar outfit, and Nick assumed it was a uniform of sorts. Her head was bent over the clipboard she held but she looked up, as if sensing his approach.

"Nick. What are you doing here?" Her smile was pleasant but there was an unmistakable wariness in her eyes. Join the club, he thought ruefully. He felt more than a little wary himself.

"I'm here as Harry's emissary. He said you asked him to look at some trees."

Kate's laugh held a touch of exasperation. "He was supposed to come himself. I want him to have *some* input into what I'm doing. It is his property, after all."

"I don't think Harry's much for gardening," he said apologetically.

"That much is obvious from the condition of the gardens at Spider's Walk."

There was a disapproving edge to her voice and

Nick grinned. "When he hired you, he said that you looked like you'd have him hauled off by the plant police, if you could."

"If there was such a thing, I'd be able to send him up the river for life." She sighed and gave him a questioning look. "Do you *want* to look at trees?"

Nick knew she wouldn't protest if he said no. They might have agreed to forget the past but it was always between them—a faint thread of tension that could be ignored but not erased. Truthfully, his interest in trees was about on a par with his interest in the sex life of South American tree frogs. There was no reason to say yes and some very good arguments for saying no.

"I live to look at trees," he said, and called himself seven kinds of fool.

The large trees, in their wooden boxes, were in the far corner of the nursery, set against one wall of an old barn, which was now used for storage. Kate was acutely aware of Nick as she led the way between the rows of plants. He was wearing the familiar uniform of faded jeans and T-shirt. The fabric of the black T-shirt molded the solid muscles of his shoulders and clung lovingly to the width of his chest, making her vividly aware of his size and sex.

Why was she always so conscious of how big he was? she wondered fretfully. Gareth was nearly as tall and every bit as broad-shouldered. So why did Nick always look so very *large?*

"The place looks great," Nick commented. "When I was a kid, half the town used to come out here every spring to gawk at the wisteria when it bloomed."

"They still do. For the last couple of years, we've had a sale and the PTA sells lemonade and cookies as a fund-raising project. It's done very well for us. Last year, a news crew from L.A. came out to film a segment on it."

"I bet they couldn't resist making a comment about finding 'a little slice of Eden right here in California.'" Kate smiled at his dead-on imitation of a commentator's manufactured enthusiasm.

"They did say something along those lines."

"They always do." He shook his head and one corner of his mouth curved in a sardonic smile. "Anytime something happens here that's big enough to make it into the news, they can't resist making some comment on the town's name. If it's bad news, they look solemn and say something about 'violence striking even in Eden.' If it's good news, they talk about finding Eden right here in California. For a couple of weeks, smog-crazed Los Angelenos drive out here to take a look at the place. They eat at a quaint little café, drive around gawking at the gen-u-ine farms and then scuttle back to the city."

"That's pretty much what happened last year,"

Kate said, smiling at the accuracy of his description. "We did a booming business for a couple of weeks, though."

"It's good for business," Nick agreed. "When I was a kid, the café on the corner down from the library was called Selma Ann's because Selma Ann Carver owned the place. But she changed the name to Eve's because she figured the tourists would love it. She was right."

"Is that why half the items on the menu have apples in them?"

"Yep." Nick nodded. "When I was about twelve, one of the local farmers grew the biggest pumpkin in the state. It must have been a slow week for murder in L.A. because a news crew came out to do a segment on this pumpkin. The dust hadn't even settled behind them before Selma Ann borrowed a typewriter and typed up a new menu. She stuck apples in just about everything on it. Even the burgers came with applesauce on the side. She doubled the prices while she was at it."

"Didn't that upset her regular customers?"

"No, because she kept two sets of menus—one for the tourists and one for the locals."

"Is that legal?" Kate asked, throwing him a startled look.

"I don't think the Better Business Bureau would have approved," Nick said dryly. "But she made enough extra off the tourists that year to spend a week on the beach in Maui, sunbathing and surfing.''

"Surfing? Selma Ann?'' Kate goggled at him. She'd met Selma Ann Carver. The woman was short and bone thin, with leathery skin and a face so full of lines that it looked like a topographical map of the Sierra Nevada. She claimed to be older than dirt and Kate believed her. The image of her sunning and surfing in Hawaii was enough to boggle the mind. "Selma Ann on a surfboard?''

"So she said.'' Nick shrugged. "She's mean enough and tough enough to do just about anything. You know that kid's poem that says something about the goblins will get you if you don't watch out? I always figured whoever wrote it must have known Selma Ann.''

Kate was startled into laughter. "I can believe it. I once saw her harangue a customer for taking too long to order. She told him since he couldn't make up his damned mind, he could damn well eat what she damn well chose to bring him and if didn't like it, he could take his damned indecision to some other damned place. I don't know what she brought him but he ate it without question. I didn't blame him. She scares me to death.''

Nick chuckled. "Sounds like she hasn't changed a bit. She always— What the hell is that?''

He came to a dead stop and stared in disbelief at the structure in front of him.

"It's a barn." Kate's answer was calm but her mouth curved in an understanding smile at his shock.

"Barns are red. Or white. Or maybe a weathered kind of gray." Nick blinked as if to clear his vision but the image didn't change. "That thing is *purple*."

"Wistful Wisteria," she corrected. "That's the name on the paint can. Brenda thought it would be a good idea, sort of in keeping with the general theme of the place, you know."

"Was she drunk at the time?" Nick demanded.

"I don't think so," Kate said a little regretfully. She almost wished her friend had been drunk. It made her uneasy to think that Brenda could make a decision like this while stone-cold sober.

The barn had even fewer pretensions to grandeur than the house. A plain, rectangular building with a peaked roof, it put function way above form and it seemed to Kate that it wore its new coat of paint with a faintly embarrassed air, as if it knew exactly how silly it looked.

"It's certainly...eye-catching," Nick said, groping for something positive to say.

"That's one way of putting it. I've hear more vivid descriptions. Gareth threatened to cite us for breaking some sort of visual pollution law."

"It looks like a menace to society to me. Someone with a weak heart could keel right over if they came upon it unexpectedly."

"Did I hear someone taking my name in vain?"

Kate's giggle ended on a startled gasp and she turned too quickly, nearly overbalancing. Nick's hand came out to steady her as Gareth stepped off the gravel path behind them. She pulled away from that light touch, guilt washing over her. There was no reason to feel guilty, she reminded herself, drawing a deep, calming breath. At least no reason to feel guilty for anything that had happened recently.

"Gareth!" She went to greet him, lifting her face for his kiss, ridiculously conscious that Nick was watching them.

"I didn't expect to find you here," Gareth said, smiling as he looked at his younger brother. He slid his arm around her waist and pulled her against his side.

"I'm standing in for Harry," Nick said easily. His gaze flicked to where his brother's hand rested on her hip and Kate fought the urge to pull away from that familiar touch.

She was engaged to Gareth, not to Nick, she reminded herself. And God help her for needing that reminder.

"Were you admiring Brenda's taste?" Gareth asked, nodding to the barn.

Nick shook his head. "I'm not sure 'admiring' is quite the right word. I've got to admit it's a little awe-inspiring, though."

"It's god-awful," Gareth said bluntly.

"That about sums it up," Nick agreed, smiling a little.

"Did you come by to arrest Brenda for bad taste?" Kate asked. She noticed a yellowed leaf on a young sweet gum tree and reached to pull it off. The move shifted her a little away from Gareth and his hand dropped away from her.

"No such luck," he said, grinning. "Actually, I came by to see if I could persuade you to sneak out for lunch. I've got an hour or so before I have to go back to the station."

"Oh, I wish I could but I just got back from lunch," Kate said, aware that her regret was not as sincere as it might have been.

"You could always come watch me eat," he coaxed. He reached out to brush a strand of hair from her cheek, tucking it behind her ear. The gesture was casually intimate, and she was aware of Nick turning away, focusing his gaze on the pale bark of the sapling closest to him. Kate was annoyed with herself for being so aware of him that she noticed his slightest move.

"I wish I could, but I just sent Jim home for the afternoon because he was looking tired. That just leaves me and Nancy."

"I thought I saw Brenda's car out front," he said.

"You did. Like I said, that just leaves me and Nancy." Kate's tone was dryly affectionate. "You know Brenda prides herself on not knowing the difference between a fern and a cactus.''

Gareth smiled, but he looked disappointed. ''I haven't seen much of you lately.''

''I know.'' For some reason, Kate found her eyes drawn to Nick. He was looking at the trees and seemed oblivious to her conversation with Gareth. With an effort, she pulled her attention back to Gareth. ''You can't blame me for that,'' she said lightly. ''You're the one who's spending so much time in L.A.''

''I know.'' He looked guilty, but only for a moment. ''I think this program can really make a difference, though. Gangs aren't just confined to the big city anymore and I—''

''You don't have to convince me.'' She cut him off with a smile. ''I know what you're doing is important and I'm not complaining.''

He smiled and brushed his knuckles across the curve of her cheek. ''*I'm* the one doing the complaining. Between your job and mine, it doesn't seem like we have much time for each other. I hope we're not going to have to schedule time to see each other after we're married.''

''Me, too.'' She smiled, her gaze darting over his shoulder to where Nick stood, apparently absorbed by the information on the plant care label he held.

''You're sure you can't make lunch?''

''I wish I could.'' Kate hoped her regret didn't

sound as false to him as it did to her. The truth was, she didn't feel like going out to lunch with Gareth today. Not because of any specific thing or person— she simply had too much work to do.

"If you're sure I—" Gareth's beeper went off, interrupting him. He unhooked it from his belt and looked at the number display. "I need to call the station."

"You can use the phone in the office," Kate told him, gesturing toward the main building.

"Unless it's an emergency, I'll be back," he promised.

He left an oddly tense silence behind. Kate folded the yellowed leaf she held and didn't look at Nick.

"What kind of tree am I supposed to be looking at?" he asked, and the prosaic question made her realize how foolish she was being. Why should she feel uncomfortable about Nick seeing her kiss his brother? She dropped the mangled leaf and gave him a bright smile.

"We just got in a couple of bauhinias. I think one of them would look great on the west side of the gazebo."

"The gazebo that's falling down?" Nick asked politely.

"It's not falling down. It just needs a little attention."

"Preferably from a wrecking ball," he murmured as he followed her down the far row of trees.

"It's a wonderful architectural feature, perfectly in keeping with its surroundings."

"You mean it's suffering from years of neglect, just like everything else."

"Well…" Kate slanted him a look that was half reproach, half laughter. "I guess that pretty much sums it up."

Nick grinned. "So, let's see this Bohemian that's going to make the whole place look new again."

"Bauhinia," Kate corrected him. "And I didn't say it was going to work miracles, just that I thought it would look good next to the gazebo. It's a fairly small tree—around twenty feet or so at maturity. It blooms in the spring and the flowers look a little like orchids. This is bauhinia blakeana. The flowers are larger than the ones on the forficatas and the tree itself is more umbrella shaped, which I think would be good for that spot."

Nick looked at the slender sapling next to her. It looked pretty much like every other tree in the place—scrawny trunk, skimpy leaves, no sign of flowers and nothing to indicate any future tendency toward looking like an umbrella. She was looking at him, obviously waiting for him to express an opinion.

"Looks great," he said. To show his sincerity, he reached out to tug at a branch. "Really great."

"That's a pomegranate," she said dryly. She pointed to the tree on her other side. "*This* is the bauhinia."

"Ooops." Nick grinned sheepishly. He shrugged. "They all look great. Who can tell the difference?"

"Let me pull this out so you can get a good look at it. Not that you can really tell all that much, I suppose." She crouched and took hold of one side of the tapered wooden box that held the tree's roots.

"Here. Let me help you." Nick crouched next to her and reached for the box. "This looks heavy."

"I'm used to maneuvering them," Kate said. Uncomfortably aware of his closeness, she grabbed the corner of the box too quickly and then jerked away with a gasp of pain as something tore into the tender flesh at the base of her thumb. "Ouch!"

"Let me see." Nick moved so quickly that she caught only a glimpse of blood welling against her skin before his hands closed over hers, blocking her view.

"It's not bad," she said automatically, though it was already throbbing.

"Let me see," he said again, cupping his hands around hers.

His voice sounded oddly distant, as if he was a long way off. He was looking at her hand but Kate had the feeling that he was seeing something else entirely. Then the thought drifted away and she became aware that her hand felt warm where he was touching her. It was a deep, soothing kind of warmth that rolled over the pain, a part of it even as it soothed it.

Time seemed to hold its breath, slowing the moment so that Kate could count each beat of her pulse, could feel Nick's pulse beating in rhythm with hers. The gentle warmth spread up her arm and crept through her body, sinking into her bones. She felt a sense of contentment, a sense that all was right with the world.

Her breath slipped from her in a soft sigh and she had to force open eyes she hadn't even been aware of closing. Nick lifted his head and looked at her, and Kate thought it just might be possible to lose herself in his eyes. For a moment—less than a heartbeat—she felt as if she saw directly into his soul, just as he saw into hers.

Then he looked away and the moment was gone, leaving her with an indefinable feeling of loss.

"You're right. It isn't that bad," he said, his voice husky.

"What?" Kate blinked and shook her head as if to clear it. She looked at her hand as he released it and felt the sense of unreality deepen. Where there had been a cut was...nothing.

"Barely even a scratch," Nick said as he stood. She thought he swayed a little but she couldn't be sure. At the moment, she felt as if she couldn't be sure of anything. She rose slowly, her eyes still on her hand.

"There was a cut." She looked at him as if demanding confirmation. "I saw blood."

Nick looked surprised, but Gareth's return prevented him from saying anything.

"I'm going to have to go in early," Gareth said as he approached them. "I guess it's just as well you couldn't make lunch." His smile faded as he looked from Kate to Nick. "What's wrong?"

"I...I cut myself," Kate said, holding out her uninjured hand as if offering evidence. "At least, I thought I did."

Gareth's breath hissed between his teeth and his eyes shot to his brother's face. Nick met the look impassively.

"It must have felt worse than it was," he said. His shoulders lifted in a shrug. "Probably a splinter just jabbed against the skin."

"But..." Kate's voice trailed off. What was the point of continuing? She could have sworn she'd cut her hand. She'd seen blood—she knew she had. Except that she obviously hadn't. Because if she'd seen blood, there would be a cut and there was no cut—just a faint pink mark, hardly enough to be called a scratch.

"This tree looks fine," Nick said, nodding to the sapling. "On Harry's behalf, I'll give my approval."

Kate looked at the tree without seeing it. She felt vaguely disoriented, her head spinning, as if she'd just stepped off a merry-go-round.

"I...I'll arrange to have it delivered," she said at last.

"Great." Nick smiled but the expression didn't seem to reach his eyes. "I need to get going. Unless you need something else."

"No. No, that's all." Unless he could explain what had just happened. Except that, obviously, nothing had happened. Just her imagination working overtime, making her see cuts that weren't there, making her think—but she didn't know what to think.

"I'll walk out with you," Gareth said, watching his brother with cool, dark eyes.

Kate turned her head to watch them leave, absently rubbing her fingertips against the cut that wasn't there. Almost...almost she could feel it. Only there was nothing to feel. Nothing except the lingering warmth and the sense that something—something extraordinary—had just happened.

"Why do I feel like a prisoner being marched to the guillotine?" Nick said as he and Gareth stepped out the front door and into the sunlight.

"You want to tell me what happened back there?" Gareth's expression was grim.

"Why should I? You obviously think you already know." Nick headed for the parking lot with long, ground-eating strides.

"Am I wrong?" Gareth kept pace with him easily.

"Aren't you supposed to read me my rights before you interrogate me?"

"Dammit, Nick!" Gareth drew a deep breath and

continued in a calmer tone. "I'm not interrogating you. I'm just concerned about what Kate is thinking right now."

Nick stopped next to the Harley and reached for his helmet. His anger was gone as quickly as it had come, leaving him drained and weary to the bone. He turned and looked at his brother, his eyes carefully emptied of expression.

"Kate isn't thinking anything at all except that she thought she'd hurt herself worse than she did." His mouth twisted in a bitter half smile as he mounted the bike and reached for the key. "You don't have to worry about explaining any skeletons in the family closet."

"I didn't mean it that way," Gareth protested.

"Didn't you?" Nick turned the key, letting the roar of the engine drown out any reply his brother might have made.

Without looking at Gareth again, he put the bike in gear and backed out of the parking space. When he reached the street, he glanced in the rearview mirror and saw his brother standing in the same place, looking after him. His jaw tightened and he gunned the engine, sending the big bike roaring into the street.

"Did I just see Gareth and Nick go through here?" Brenda asked as soon as Kate stepped through the door.

"They just left," Kate agreed absently.

"I was going to say hello but they looked like they were in a hurry. I haven't seen much of Nick since he got back, and it seems like Gareth has been spending most of his free time in L.A." When Kate didn't answer, Brenda prompted her. "Hasn't he?"

"Hasn't who what?"

"Hasn't Gareth been spending a lot of time in L.A.?" Brenda's eyebrows rose in surprise.

"Oh." Kate struggled to put off the lingering sense of disorientation and focus on the conversation. "Yes, he has been. He's very enthused about this program he's working on. Something that's aimed at helping kids stay out of gangs."

"He's always been good with kids," Brenda said. She leaned one hip against the counter. When Kate had sent the elderly Jim Miller home, she'd called Brenda and asked her to come in and run the register, the only task for which Brenda—in her own words—was even marginally qualified. At the moment, there were no customers and Nancy Morgan, the only other employee, was outside somewhere, so they were alone.

"Gareth likes children."

"He'll be a good father," Brenda said. At another time, Kate might have noted the wistfulness in her friend's voice but she was still distracted by whatever had—or hadn't—happened with Nick.

"I'm sure he will be."

Brenda's brows rose again. "You sound like you're talking about someone you hardly know. This is Gareth, the guy you're engaged to marry. Remember him?"

"Of course." Kate forced a smile and raised her left hand, wiggling her ring finger. "I'm not likely to forget, am I?"

"I wouldn't think so, but you sound a bit out of it." Brenda looked concerned. "Are you sure you're okay? You look a little pale."

"I'm fine."

"I wonder if there's some kind of flu going around. Nick looked a little...off when he came through here."

"Did he?" Kate rubbed her fingers across the base of her thumb. Was it her imagination or was there a faint tingling there?

Brenda stretched one hand in front of her and frowned at her fingernails. "You know, I'm not too sure about this nail polish. The color looked good in the bottle but I think it makes my skin look like I'm in the last stages of yellow fever. Maybe I should—"

"Brenda, what happened to his wife?"

It was difficult to say who was most surprised by the question. The last thing Kate wanted to do was talk about—or think about—Nick Blackthorne, but she couldn't call back the words.

"Nick's wife?" Brenda stared at her in surprise.

Kate nodded. Now that she'd asked the question,

she wanted to know the answer. "What happened to her? And to their child? Was there an accident?"

Brenda looked uneasy. "Haven't you asked Gareth about it?"

"The only time he mentioned it, he just said that Nick's wife and child were dead. It was obvious that the subject was painful so I didn't ask for details."

And heaven forgive her, she hadn't cared enough to ask, hadn't wanted to know anything that might spoil her picture-perfect image of the Blackthornes. Besides, Nick hadn't been anything but a name to her. His past—his loss—hadn't seemed significant.

"It's not exactly a secret," Brenda said, still looking uncomfortable. "It was in the papers at the time and, God knows, half the town was talking about it. I always thought that was one of the reasons Nick left—to get away from all the whispers and stares."

She paused, her teeth tugging at her lower lip as she debated with herself. Kate waited, and after a moment she sighed. "She killed herself and the baby."

"What?" Kate felt as if she'd been kicked in the stomach. She reached out and braced her hand on the counter, as if she needed actual, physical support to stay upright. "Nick's wife committed suicide? And she killed— How could she— How could *anyone*—" She stopped and stared at Brenda in shock. "I don't understand."

"I don't think anyone can really understand something like that," Brenda said, shaking her head.

"But...what happened?"

"I don't know exactly. I only met Lisa a few times." Brenda frowned thoughtfully. "She wasn't beautiful but there was a kind of sweetness in her expression that made you think she was prettier than she really was. She seemed...I don't know, fragile somehow. There was something about her that made you think she wasn't very strong." She shrugged. "I guess she really wasn't."

"There are a lot of people who aren't strong," Kate said, thinking of her father. "But that doesn't mean they...do something like that."

"True. I really only know what I read in the paper. I'd just married Larry and was in the throes of early marital bliss." Her mouth twisted ruefully. "I didn't keep in close touch with a lot of my friends so I don't know much. They called it postpartum psychosis. I guess after the baby was born Lisa kind of...flipped out."

"How did she..." Kate let the question trail off, not sure she wanted to know the answer.

"She closed up the garage and turned on the car engine." Brenda's mouth tightened and she swallowed before continuing. "She had the baby with her. Nick...Nick found them."

"Oh, God." Kate turned away, her chest aching. She was sorry she'd asked. Maybe Brenda hadn't told her anything that hadn't been public knowledge at the time but she still felt as if she'd pried into Nick's past and pulled out a very private pain.

She didn't want to *feel* for him like this. It made him too human, too real...too sympathetic. She didn't want to care about what he'd gone through. She didn't want to care about *him*.

Chapter Seven

The sensation of being watched was familiar. Kate's shoulders slumped and she released her breath in a soft sigh. She knew what she'd see if she turned around. Laura and Leroy had become her shadows whenever she worked at Spider's Walk. Though she wouldn't have believed it possible when she first met the pair of them, Leroy had turned out to be friendlier than the little girl who was his constant companion.

As if on cue, the small voice came from behind her. "What are you doing?"

I'm not working for her, Kate reminded herself. She straightened her shoulders and turned to face her small inquisitor.

"Hello, Laura."

"'Lo. What are you doing?" When it came to

changes at Spider's Walk, Laura had a one-track mind.

"I'm planting a tree."

"How come?"

"Because a tree will look nice here. You like trees, don't you?"

"Yes." The admission was grudging, as if Laura hated to concede even that much. "There's already lots of trees around, though."

"But there isn't a tree here." Kate kept her smile in place with an effort. "I think one will look nice here. When it's grown up, it will shade the gazebo. Won't that be nice?"

Laura's narrow shoulders lifted in a shrug as she glanced at the young tree behind Kate. "I suppose it will be okay."

Kate's teeth ground together. "I'm glad I have your permission," she said sweetly and then was ashamed of herself for allowing her temper to override her common sense—getting sarcastic with a six-year-old, for heaven's sake! But Laura took the comment at face value.

"I don't mind if you put a tree there," she said graciously, and Kate's molars scraped together.

She's just a child.

"Don't you have something you need to do at your own house?"

"Nah." Laura threw one arm around Leroy's sturdy neck and looked as if she planned to stay put.

"It looks like it's going to rain soon," Kate said, glancing at the gray clouds that pressed down above them. "Maybe you left some toys out that need to be brought inside?"

"Nope."

"I really need to get this tree planted before it starts raining," Kate hinted.

"Okay." Laura's big blue eyes remained fixed on her.

With a sigh, Kate turned to the tree and tried to put her audience out of her mind. She shouldn't have tried to do this today. Not only had the weather report predicted rain, but Jim Miller's grandson, who worked part-time at the nursery and usually helped with the heavy work, had called in sick. A smart woman would have paid attention to the signs and postponed the job. But this was her first major addition to Spider's Walk and she'd been anxious to see it in place.

If the rain would just hold off a little while longer... As if in answer to her silent plea, a sudden breeze swirled around her, rustling the leaves on the little tree and bringing with it the cool smell of rain. Muttering under her breath, Kate dropped to her knees and leaned forward to take hold of the tree's trunk. As long as Laura insisted on watching her every move, maybe she could make herself useful, she thought.

"Does it look straight?"

"Nope."

Kate waited but Laura didn't add anything.

"Which way should I move it?"

"That way."

That way? Kate rested her forehead against her outstretched arm and wondered if she'd committed a crime in a former life for which she was now being punished.

"Do you know your left and right?" she asked in a voice that strained for patience.

"Yep."

"Do you think you could tell me whether the tree needs to be moved right or left?"

"Kinda left," Laura said thoughtfully. Kate started to shift the tree toward the gazebo only to stop when the child continued. "But a little right, too."

For just a moment, Kate considered beating her forehead on the ground in frustration but she refused to give her small tormentor the satisfaction of seeing her break.

"It can't go left *and* right," she pointed out. "It's got to be one or the other."

"Oh, I don't know," a new voice said. "If you move it left and then right and maybe back and forth a bit, you'll probably get it about right."

Startled, Kate let go of the tree and turned abruptly, her bottom hitting the ground with a jolt.

"Nick!" Laura's voice went from coolly disinterested to coyly feminine in a heartbeat. She tilted her head to look at him with blatant adoration.

"Hey, munchkin." He grinned at her. "How are you doing?"

"Fine." Laura batted her eyes at him. "Do you like my dress, Nick? It's brand-new."

He gave the pink cotton dress with its full skirt and lace-trimmed bodice careful consideration before answering. "I think it's the prettiest dress I've ever seen."

"I wore it just for you." The come-hither look she gave him would have put Mae West to shame. Kate was amused to see color tint his cheekbones.

This was the first time she'd seen him since Brenda told her about how he'd lost his family. Watching him with Laura, she found herself wondering if the little girl made him think of his son, who would have been about the same age if he were alive.

"You look very nice," he said. "I heard your mom calling you a minute ago."

Laura looked deeply put-upon. "I'm s'posed to go see Great-Aunt Edith," she said. Her sigh was worthy of the stage. "She pinches my cheek and calls me cutie pie."

Nick glanced at Kate, his eyes full of laughter, but his expression was suitably solemn when he looked at Laura. "She sounds nice."

"She is mostly." Laura sighed again. She looked

at him from under her lashes. "But I'd rather stay here and talk to you."

Kate bit her lip to hold back a smile. Oh, to be six and too young to worry about hiding your feelings from the object of your adoration.

"I'm not going to leave town while you're gone," he assured the child. "Now, you'd better scoot home before your mom decides you've been eaten by an alligator."

"Okay, but there aren't any alligators here, you know," Laura told him as she turned reluctantly toward home. "They're all in the zoo."

"She always has to have the last word," Kate said as the little girl disappeared in the direction of her home.

"She is a trifle willful," Nick agreed.

Kate could have added suspicious, truculent and generally hard to get along with but decided there was no real point to it. A sudden gust of wind reminded her that she had more important things to do than dwell on the faults of her six-year-old nemesis.

"Would you mind helping me get this tree straight?" she asked him.

"What's wrong with kind of left but a little right?" he asked, looking surprised.

"Just a little more detail would be helpful," she said dryly. "It should only take a couple of minutes."

"I don't have any appointments with destiny that I know of. Takc your timc."

"Thanks." Kate turned and crawled under the tree. She was immediately conscious that he was seeing her from a less than flattering angle. She shoved the thought away. It didn't matter what angle Nick saw her from because she didn't care whether or not he found her attractive, she told herself firmly.

"It needs to come to the right and back a couple of inches," Nick said, and Kate focused gratefully on following his instructions. One or two more adjustments and he pronounced the tree to be standing perfectly straight.

"Thanks," Kate said breathlessly as she began pushing soil in around the root ball.

"You look like you could use some help," Nick said, and before she could protest that she was doing fine, he was on his knees on the other side of the tree, using his hands to push dirt into the hole.

"You don't have to do that. You'll get dirty."

"I wash. Trying to keep all the fun to yourself?" he asked, smiling at her.

Those dimples should be illegal, Kate thought despairingly. How was it possible to pack so much charm into a single smile?

"I didn't know you'd consider this fun," she said, forcing herself to ignore the tingle of awareness in the pit of her stomach.

"Playing in the dirt?" Nick's brows rose. "How

often does your average adult get the chance to do that?''

''I think the dirt is about to become mud,'' Kate said, feeling the first light spattering of rain against her back.

It was a race between them and the storm, with the storm coming out the clear winner. They both pushed dirt into the planting hole and tamped it down as quickly as they could, but they couldn't beat the rain, which increased rapidly from a gentle sprinkle to a downpour.

When the final layer of soil had been pushed into place and tamped down, they both crawled out from under the little tree. The rain was coming down in sheets, but Kate paused long enough to take a satisfied look at the young tree.

''It looks at home, doesn't it?'' she said, raising her voice to be heard over the roar of the storm.

''The only thing that would look at home out here is a goldfish,'' Nick shouted back.

He took hold of her elbow and rushed her toward the steps of the gazebo. Since the roof leaked in several places, it was only marginally dryer inside than out. Rain drummed against the roof, as if trying to beat its way through the old wood.

Breathless from the short run, Kate held her arms out from her sides. They were covered in dirt past the elbow. Her clothes were streaked with dirt and she could feel her hair pulling loose from its pins to fall in a soggy tangle down her back. When she glanced at Nick, she saw that he was just as dirty and wet. Their eyes met and they were both suddenly grinning.

"Still think this is fun?" she asked.

"It beats a poke in the eye with a sharp stick all to hell," he said.

Before she could respond, a soft groan had them both turning their heads. Leroy lay under an ancient three-legged table, completely dry and sound asleep. They looked from the dog—dry, clean and comfortable—to each other—soaked to the skin and covered in dirt. Kate bit her lip, but a moment later, she was giggling.

"Leroy's smarter than both of us," she said.

"It looks that way," Nick agreed, laughing. "He's certainly cleaner."

"That's not saying much. You look like you've been rolling in the dirt."

"You think you look any better? Even your face is dirty." Forgetting his less than pristine condition, he reached out to brush his thumb across her cheekbone and then grimaced as he managed to add to the dirt already on her face. "Oops."

"Oops?" Kate inquired politely. Without giving herself time to change her mind, she reached up and dragged her fingers down his cheek, leaving behind a smear of mud.

Nick's eyes widened in surprise. "I can't believe you did that."

"I can't, either," she admitted but spoiled her regretful look by giggling. "You look like you're wearing camouflage paint."

"You realize, of course, that this means war." He took a step toward her, his muddy hands raised in threat.

Kate backed up a step. "What about turning the other cheek?"

"If I turn my other cheek, you'll probably cover it with mud," he said, moving forward.

She retreated again. "I wouldn't do that. Honest." She widened her eyes and tried to look sincere.

"Liar, liar, pants on fire."

The childish taunt had her dissolving into helpless laughter. She eased back another step. "I never understood what the connection was between telling a lie and having flaming pants," she got out between giggles.

"I think it's symbolic." His tone became deeply pompous. "Probably filled with deep, powerful meaning going back to our most primitive days on the savanna."

"Georgia?" she asked politely.

"Pearls before swine," he said, his sad tone at odds with the laughter in his eyes.

"Sorry." She backed another half step and gave a

startled gasp when her ankle connected with something.

"Careful." Nick's hand shot out, catching her arm and pulling her forward. "This place is a death trap."

"It just needs a few repairs," she said.

"It would be easier to tear this place down and rebuild from the ground up." His thumb moved against her upper arm in an absentminded caress that made her skin tingle.

"But it wouldn't be the same," Kate said breathlessly. She should pull away, she thought. Not that his touch bothered her, because it didn't. Not at all.

"You're right, it wouldn't be the same," Nick said. "It wouldn't be a termite-ridden dump."

Had he moved closer or had she? Kate's vision was suddenly filled with the width of his chest. The damp fabric of his T-shirt clung to every muscle, delineating them like a drawing in an anatomy book. She swallowed.

"I should…"

"You have a smudge of dirt right here." He tilted her head and brushed his fingers over the curve of her cheek.

Kate looked at him helplessly. She knew the air was chill, but she was warmed by a heat that came from within. Standing here with the rain drumming on the roof and forming sheer curtains around the open sides of the gazebo, it seemed as if they were the only two people in the world. The sense of isolation was dangerously seductive.

She grabbed for her self-control, only to have it slip out of reach when Nick's fingertips brushed her cheek again, sliding across her skin with a gossamer touch that woke nerve endings to tingling life. Kate put up one hand in protest—she was sure it was in protest—but somehow her palm was resting against his chest, feeling the warmth of his skin through the damp knit of his T-shirt. He jerked at her touch, and she felt a swift thrill of feminine power. He could make her tremble, but she could do the same to him. There was excitement in that knowledge.

Afterward, she could never be sure who moved first. She wanted to believe it was Nick, wanted to think that she hadn't been so completely lost to reality that she'd stepped closer to him. But it was a moot point, really. He moved—or she did. His hand cupped her cheek, tilting her face up. Her fingers curled into the fabric of his shirt, clinging to him.

And then his mouth came down on hers and the world spun away. There was nothing tentative in the kiss, no hesitant moment of exploration, no gentle coaxing. It was pure hunger and need. His mouth opened over hers, his tongue demanding entrance, demanding surrender. And she gave it to him, meeting his demand with her own hunger, her own needs.

She didn't know how long she stood there, wrapped in his arms, her body curved into his, her hands clinging to his shoulders. It felt so real, so right, that time seemed to stand still, gifting them with a space where the real world had no meaning, where all that mattered was the feel of Nick's hands on her body, the taste of his mouth on hers.

When he lifted his head, she sighed in protest. Her lashes felt weighted as she forced her eyes open and looked at him. His eyes were dark with hunger, and if that hadn't been enough to tell her how much he wanted her, she could feel the taut length of his arousal pressed against the soft curve of her belly. She shifted instinctively against him, driven by a primitive feminine need to get closer to that rigid length.

Nick's breath caught on a groan and his hands dropped to her hips, his fingers biting into her skin as he pulled her close with a quick, convulsive movement that told her just how badly he wanted her. Kate felt a deep, hollow ache inside, a painful hunger that formed a knot in the pit of her stomach. She'd never felt like this before—had never felt so physically empty, as if only this man could fill that emptiness and make her complete. Not even Gareth had ever—

Kate sucked in a sharp breath, her eyes widening in stunned disbelief as she looked at Nick. What was she doing? Gareth. How could she have betrayed him like this?

The hands that had been clinging to Nick's shoulders were suddenly pushing against him, her breath catching on something perilously close to a sob as he released her. She took a quick step back and was immediately—shamefully—aware of a feeling of loss.

"Kate." He stretched out his hand and she backed away as if the touch of it might burn her. And it would, she thought. One touch and she just might tumble into his arms, all sense of right and wrong forgotten in the overwhelming need to be a part of him.

"No." In her mind, the word was a shout, but what came out was little more than a whisper. She backed up another step and said it again, louder this time. "No."

"Kate—"

She didn't wait to hear what he might say. She gave him one last, frightened look and then turned and ran, fleeing into the cool rain as if chased by demons, all the while aware that what she most feared, she carried within her.

Nick took a half step after her and then stopped. Shoving his hands in his pockets, he hunched his shoulders against the chill and watched her out of sight, his expression set, his eyes cold and bleak.

"Rain always makes me hungry," Harry said as he walked into the kitchen. "I was thinking about ordering a pizza for dinner. You want to split it with me?"

"Am I going to have to watch you pour a pound of dried red pepper flakes on it?" Nick asked, reaching for a towel to dry his just washed hands.

"You can close your eyes," Harry offered generously. "You want pepperoni and mushroom?"

"Sounds good." Nick draped the towel carelessly over the piece of wire that was serving as a towel rack until he got around to replacing the old one, which was broken. He went to the refrigerator and pulled out two beers, listening with half an ear as Harry called in their order. He set one of the bottles on the counter for Harry and twisted the top off the other.

"They said it will be here in half an hour," Harry said as he hung up the phone.

Nick wasn't really hungry but eating a pizza with Harry was better than sitting around by himself, brooding about what had happened with Kate this afternoon. He'd already had more than enough of that. He'd spent the afternoon with his thoughts circling endlessly about how good she'd felt in his arms, how right it had felt to hold her, to kiss her.

He took a swallow of beer without tasting it. No matter how many times he reminded himself that she was engaged to marry his brother, he couldn't forget those few moments in the gazebo this afternoon. Kate would probably try to deny it but he knew she'd felt the same thing, the same sense of rightness, of belonging.

For those few minutes, when they had been alone in the storm, she'd been his. There had been no past, no future and the present had been reduced to only that moment, only the two of them. It had felt so good, so *right*.

Only it hadn't been right. Even if she hadn't already been promised to Gareth, the last thing he needed or wanted was to get involved with someone. His fingers tightened around the bottle and his mouth tightened into a grim line. He wasn't ready for that— wasn't sure he'd ever be ready again.

With an effort, he shook himself out of his thoughts and turned to smile at Harry. "So, how is the book going?"

"Not bad. I've been going over old clippings and letters. It's amazing how much you forget." Harry was writing a book about his years as an attorney. *Now's the time,* he'd said, *I haven't gotten so senile that I can't remember, but everyone likely to take a contract out on me or sue me to within an inch of my life is dead.* Nick figured that, if Harry could write a story as well as he could tell it, he was destined for the *New York Times* bestseller list.

"The rain was a nice surprise today," Harry said as he twisted the cap off his beer. "Kind of late in the year for it. I figured we wouldn't see rain again until November or so."

"I guess, even in California, the weather can surprise you." He took a drink of beer and tried to think of a new topic. Talking about the rain made him think of Kate. Not that he needed any reminders to think about her, he admitted reluctantly.

Harry cleared his throat. "I see Kate planted that tree she liked next to the gazebo," he said casually.

Too casually? Nick wondered, his eyes narrowing as he looked at the old man.

"It looks nice there," Harry continued. He turned his beer bottle restlessly between his fingers, keeping his gaze on the movement. "Looks real nice." He shot a quick glance in Nick's direction. "I can see it from the guest house, you know. Good place for a tree."

Nick debated about whether or not to pick up the bait. Obviously, Harry had seen some, if not all, of what had happened between him and Kate this afternoon. Equally obviously, he had something to say about it.

"Spit it out, Harry," he said tiredly.

"I don't want to interfere," Harry protested.

"Who are you kidding?" Nick was ruefully affectionate. "You live to interfere and we both know it."

Harry's smile was perfunctory. "I don't want to see you get hurt, that's all. I wonder if you know what you're doing."

"I'm not doing anything." Nick's fingers tightened around the beer bottle until the knuckles showed white. "What happened this afternoon was an aberration. It doesn't mean a thing."

"Are you sure?"

"Positive," he lied. "Kate's engaged to my brother. End of story."

"I hope you mean that," Harry said, looking only slightly relieved.

Nick hoped he did, too.

"I'd hate to think that my asking you to come back here could end up causing problems for you. I'd feel responsible."

"If I was stupid enough to make a play for another man's fiancée, it would be my responsibility, not yours." Nick watched the almost empty bottle swing like an amber pendulum between his fingers.

"I'm the one who brought you back here," Harry insisted.

"So you did." He lifted his eyes from the hypnotic motion of the bottle and looked at his old friend. "Did you ever have any intention of selling this place, Harry?"

"Of course I did," Harry blustered after a telling moment of silence. "I still do."

"Going to move to a condo and play golf?"

"What's wrong with that? Perfectly acceptable activity for an old codger like myself."

"There's nothing wrong with it," Nick agreed. "Except for the fact that you don't know a nine iron from a tire iron."

"I can learn." Harry took a quick drink of beer

and then coughed as it went down the wrong way. "Lots of men my age take up golf."

"Uh-huh." Nick kept his eyes on the bottle swinging between his fingers.

"Good cardiovascular activity," Harry muttered.

"So I've heard."

"Golf's a civilized game—lots of skill and strategy involved."

"You certainly know a lot about strategy," Nick said.

"Damn right I do." Harry lifted his beer but lowered the bottle without taking a drink. He fixed Nick with a fierce blue gaze. "I'd be good at golf."

"I'm sure you would be," Nick said, sounding mildly surprised that Harry should think it necessary to say as much.

"I'm a lawyer. Lawyers all play golf."

"Seems like it," Nick agreed cheerfully.

"It's practically a part of the bar exam."

"Uh-huh."

"Besides, it's ridiculous for a single man to be living in a house this size," Harry continued, as if Nick had argued with him. "I rattle around here like a pea in a rain barrel."

"It's a big house."

"A condo would be more practical."

"Sure would."

There was a short silence. Nick waited, his mouth

curved in a half smile, his eyes still on the bottle between his fingers.

"No." Harry snarled the single word as if it had been dragged from him. "No, I didn't ever intend to sell the damned place."

"Saving my soul, Harry?" Nick asked, as he had once before. He set the bottle down and looked at the old man, his expression amused and a little exasperated.

"Not your soul. That was never in any danger. But you can't grieve forever, Nick."

"So I've been told." He shook his head. "I'm not sure what it is about me that inspires people to tell me that. I didn't throw myself into the grave with Kyle and Lisa, did I?"

"Not physically, maybe, but you just…stopped living, somehow."

Nick pushed his hands into his pockets and turned to stare out the window at the darkness. When he spoke, his voice was hard with suppressed emotion. "I buried my wife and son, Harry. That's inclined to leave a few scars."

"I know." Harry shook his head. "I worry about you. I don't want to see you end up like me—old and alone. And if you look sympathetic, I'm going to break this bottle over your head," he snapped irritably. "I'm not looking for sympathy, just laying out the facts. You're young enough to think you'll never get old, but trust me, it happens to all of us."

He sounded vaguely indignant, as if he still couldn't believe it had actually happened to *him*. Nick caught back a smile.

"I appreciate your concern, Harry, but I haven't sworn off relationships."

"Maybe not, but you certainly haven't gone out of your way to get involved with anyone, have you?" He caught the irritation that flashed across Nick's face and held up one hand. "I know, I should mind my own business."

"I couldn't have put it better myself," Nick said, less sharply than he might have. "I'm a little past the age where I expect my elders to take an interest in my love life."

"You're right." Harry shook his head. "It's none of my business except I... Well, I always felt as if I was responsible for what happened."

Nick felt his stomach knot as memory washed over him. Blindly, he went to the refrigerator and pulled open the door, ignoring the protesting clank of bottles rattling against each other. He reached in and took out a beer he didn't want. "No one was responsible for what happened, not even Lisa."

"But I'm responsible for introducing the two of you," Harry said. "I always knew Lisa was...fragile, that she'd need someone to take care of her. I pushed her toward you." There was an air of confession about his statement, as if he was unburdening himself of a guilty secret.

"I knew that," Nick said calmly.

"You did?" Harry stared at him in surprise. "How did you know?"

"As a matchmaker, you're about as subtle as an elephant at a tea party, Harry." His smile was genuine. "You all but offered her on a platter."

"I did no such thing!"

"You stopped just short of it. I knew all along what you were up to."

"Then why did you…" Harry's voice trailed off uncertainly.

But Nick answered the unasked question. "Why did I marry her?" He shrugged. "She needed me and I guess I needed to be needed."

Silence followed his words. Harry looked at the beer he'd barely sipped. Nick stared at the clock on the wall above the door, watching the second hand tick off each second with a briskly self-important air. He'd never articulated the reasons for his marriage, never put it quite so plainly, even in his own thoughts. He was uncomfortable with having done so now. The chime of the doorbell provided a welcome interruption.

"I'll get it," Nick said. He set down his unopened beer and left the kitchen without waiting for a response.

Harry looked after him, his expression worried. Whatever Nick said, he knew he was at least partially to blame for what had happened five years ago. He'd manipulated Nick's life, and Lisa's, too, and the results had been tragic. Now, he'd manipulated Nick's life again, bringing him here in the hope that, if he dealt with the past, he'd be able to move on and build a future. His intentions had been the best, but everyone knew where good intentions all too often led.

The scene he'd witnessed this afternoon made him wonder if he hadn't made a huge mistake. If Nick was in love with his brother's fiancée... Harry shuddered. It didn't bear thinking of.

Chapter Eight

"I think getting away for a couple of days is going to be good for both of us," Gareth said, glancing away from the road long enough to smile at Kate.

"It was nice of the Sinclairs to include me in their invitation."

"We're a package deal, remember?"

"How could I forget?" She turned her head to look out the passenger window, pretending to be absorbed in the passing scenery. It was certainly worth seeing. The view ranged from pretty to spectacular, depending on whether the road was clinging to the edge of a cliff or winding upward through the mountains.

Jack and Susan Sinclair had invited the two of them to spend a three-day weekend at their cabin in the mountains. Though she'd never met the other couple, Gareth had been enthused, and it *had* seemed like a nice idea—a chance to get away from Eden and all the problems there. Unfortunately, she'd accepted the invitation before she found out that the problems were joining them at the cabin—or at least her particular problem was joining them. Nick Blackthorne, the one person on earth with whom she least wanted to be trapped in a mountain cabin.

She'd thought about backing out of the invitation but hadn't been able to come up with an excuse that wouldn't raise questions, which was the last thing she wanted. Besides, though Gareth hadn't said as much, she had the feeling that he welcomed a chance to spend time with Nick. Maybe even, God forbid, a chance for his fiancée to get to know his brother. The thought didn't do anything to ease the cold, hard knot of guilt that had taken up permanent residence in her stomach for the past week.

"We don't seem to have had much time together lately," Gareth said, drawing her attention to the present. "I know I've been pretty absorbed in this project—"

"And I've been busy at work," Kate interrupted. She shifted in her seat so she could smile at him. "It hasn't been anybody's fault."

"I guess not, but that doesn't mean I haven't missed you."

"Me, too, you," she said, the words sticking in her throat a little as it suddenly struck her how untrue they were. She hadn't missed him, really—not the way she should have. In fact, it was a bit scary to realize how little she'd thought of him. Except, lately, to feel guilty about betraying him.

"I've missed getting a chance to talk to you," she added, determined to believe that it was the truth.

"Talking isn't all I've missed." The leer he gave her was exaggerated for comical effect but the look in his eyes said that he wasn't entirely joking. Kate felt herself blushing like a schoolgirl.

They'd been lovers since the night he asked her to marry him. Though she certainly hadn't been holding out for a ring, as the old saying went, she had never been inclined to share her bed—and her body—easly. Almost never, she corrected herself, painfully aware of the one time she'd thrown morals and common sense to the winds.

With Gareth, the transition from dating to sleeping together had been as comfortable as everything else about their relationship. He was a gentle, undemanding lover, and she enjoyed the sexual side of their relationship. But she'd barely registered how long it had been since they'd slept together. She plucked nervously at the fabric of her soft floral cotton skirt as she tried not to think about how little it had apparently mattered to her.

Her throat closed against telling him another lie, so she settled for a mysterious smile. It was obviously enough to satisfy Gareth, because he reached out to catch her hand in his. Keeping his eyes on the road, he brought her fingers to his mouth and softly kissed her knuckles. Kate held her breath and waited, hoping desperately to feel the kind of wild arousal she'd felt last week when Nick touched her. This was Gareth. This was the man she was going to marry, the man she loved. Why didn't she feel something more when he touched her? Why didn't her heart pound and her bones melt?

"On second thoughts, maybe this weekend at Jack and Susan's isn't such a hot idea," Gareth said, his voice huskier than usual. "With them and their two kids and Nick all there, we're not going to have any time alone together."

"Oh, look, is that a deer?" Kate pulled her hand away to point to the side of the road.

Gareth followed her gesture, and his hungry look vanished. "That's a cow. You've obviously been spending way too much time in town."

"I guess so." She linked her hands together in her lap. "Tell me about these friends of yours."

"You'll like Jack and Susan," Gareth said, accepting her change of subject without question. "They're good people. And their kids are terrific. Jack spent so much time at the house when we were kids that he was practically a member of the family. He and Nick had a business together for a few years, until Nick moved East. I have a feeling he's hoping to talk Nick into starting up the partnership again. I hope he can. I think it would be good for Nick."

"Hmm." Kate made a vague noise of agreement. The last thing she wanted to do was discuss Nick with Gareth.

Just the mention of his name was enough to bring back every detail of those moments in the gazebo. Every time she thought of that kiss, she was consumed with guilt. She still couldn't understand what had happened, how she'd so completely lost control of herself. She was engaged to be married, for God's sake. *Happily* engaged.

As if that wasn't enough, she had reason to know that Nick Blackthorne was trouble. Five years ago, when she'd slept with him, she'd thought it was pure magic that had led them together, fate taking a positive interest in her life. But when she woke to find him gone, the magic had proven to be as ephemeral as a soap bubble—pretty while it lasted but hardly to be depended on in the long run.

Not like Gareth. She could depend on him. She could trust him. Kate twisted her engagement ring back and forth, her jaw tightening with determination. No matter how much she wished otherwise, she couldn't change the fact that, when she married Gareth, Nick was going to become a part of her family. Since there was no changing that, they were just going to have to learn to deal with each other. Maybe this weekend was as good a time as any to start. She needed to prove to herself that those moments in the gazebo had been a bizarre aberration—a product of the storm, like thunder or lightning. With even more potential for destruction, she thought uneasily.

Kate might have found it reassuring to know that Nick's thoughts were running along the same lines.

It bothered him that he'd so nearly betrayed his own brother. He couldn't even console himself with the thought that he'd come to his senses, because he hadn't. *Kate* had been the one to end the embrace. If she hadn't... But he didn't let his thoughts follow that train of thought, especially since it brought equal amounts of relief and regret.

She'd avoided him since then, of course. At least, he assumed she had. It was hard to tell since he'd been careful to keep his distance, too. No matter how much he wanted her—and his gut ached with the wanting—from now on, she was strictly off-limits. If she hadn't been engaged to Gareth, maybe... But she was, and that's all there was to it.

He'd accepted Jack's invitation before he knew that Kate and Gareth were also coming. When he found out, he'd considered backing out, but then had decided not to. He and Kate had to face each other sometime. Maybe it would do him some good to see her with Gareth, to see them as a couple. If the two of them were going to be related by marriage, they had to find a way to deal with each other.

Like Harry, he considered the possibility that the road to hell really was paved with good intentions. He just hoped he wasn't about to add another brick to that particular road.

Why couldn't life be simple? Kate wondered with a touch of despair. In a more just world, when a woman wanted to dislike a man, he'd have the courtesy to be, well, dislikable. But how could you dislike a man who showed endless patience with children? she asked herself as she watched Nick roughhousing with Matthew and Rose Sinclair.

The children had attached themselves to him as soon as he arrived two days ago and had spent nearly every waking moment with him since. When their father had suggested that they were probably driving their uncle Nick crazy, Nick had laughed and said he was enjoying them. He was kind to children, and he even took in stray dogs, she thought, remembering Leroy. She sighed. It just wasn't fair.

"He's good with children," Susan commented, joining Kate on the raised deck and following the direction of her gaze.

"They certainly like him. Thanks." Kate accepted the glass of iced tea the other woman handed her and looked determinedly away from the tall, dark-haired man playing so comfortably with the two kids.

"They adore him," Susan corrected. She settled into a deck chair next to Kate. The two women were more or less alone, Jack and Gareth having taken a boat out onto the lake to try to catch some fish for dinner. "He's always been good with kids, even when he was little more than a kid himself."

"Have you known the Blackthornes long?" Kate asked, carefully including the rest of the family in the question. She sipped her iced tea and kept her eyes on her hostess, determinedly ignoring the childish shouts of laughter.

"Most of my life," Susan said, smiling. "I was a couple of years behind Nick and Jack in school. And Brian, of course."

"It seems like everyone in Eden grew up with everyone else," Kate said, openly envious. "You've all known each other forever. I don't even know anyone from my high school graduating class, let alone someone I went to grade school with. It must be nice to have so many ties."

"It has its downside. Everyone tends to think they have a natural right to stick their nose into your business," Susan said with a smile. "But I like it—we both do. That's why we've stayed in Eden, so the children can have that kind of stability."

"It sounds wonderful." Kate rubbed her engagement ring like a talisman. A shriek of laughter from little Rose drew her attention and she couldn't help but smile when she saw Nick holding the four-year-old over his head, dipping her in a mock threat to drop her. He grinned at her, all the shadows gone from his face. He looked younger and happier than Kate had ever seen him.

"He should have a houseful of kids by now," Susan said sadly. "He has so much to give to a family. He's had so much loss in his life."

"Were he and his twin a great deal alike?" Kate heard herself ask and then immediately wished the words unsaid. She didn't want to talk about Nick. She didn't want to *think* about him.

"In some ways." Susan frowned, her round face thoughtful. "They were identical, but you could usually tell them apart. Nick always had a kind of sparkle in his eyes, like he was about to do something wonderfully wicked. Brian was quieter. More cerebral, I guess. He was going to go into the ministry, you know, like his father."

"I didn't know that." Kate tried to picture Nick standing at a pulpit, preaching on a Sunday morning, but the picture wouldn't come clear. There was something too restless about him, too questioning. He lacked the calm sense of purpose she saw in his father.

"I'm sure Brian would have made a good minister," Susan said, "but, in a funny way, I always thought he was too perfect for it. I mean, how can you preach against temptation if you don't really know what temptation is?"

"Brian was never tempted?" Kate asked, finding it even harder to connect the image to Nick. She

knew, from personal experience, that Nick understood temptation.

"Oh, I wouldn't say never. Just not very often and
not very seriously. He was genuinely nice but he was
so...so good that it could be a little unnerving at
times. He just never seemed to be quite of this world.
And it was always Nick who brought home stray animals and spent weeks finding homes for them. When
I was about ten, he conned my parents into letting
me have the most hideously ugly cat you've ever
seen in your life. He turned out to be a wonderful
pet and I wept buckets when Blackie eventually died
of advanced old age, but honestly, you wouldn't have
believed how *ugly* he was."

"I think I have some idea," Kate murmured,
thinking of the Shetland pony size mutt Nick had
rescued and adopted.

"At one time or another, I think half the town
ended up with one of Nick's charity cases. He—
Blast that phone," Susan muttered as a shrill jangle
drifted from the house, interrupting her. "I told Jack
it was a mistake to have one put in here."

Kate smiled in sympathy as her hostess got up and
hurried in the direction of the demanding ring. On
the grassy slope below the deck, Nick and Matthew
had their heads together over an interesting piece of
bark. Though he seemed to be concentrating completely on whatever the boy was saying, at the same
time, Rose had hold of one of his hands and was

leaning on her heels and swinging back and forth like a pendulum.

It wasn't necessary to actually *dislike* him, Kate told herself. In fact, it probably wasn't even possible, she admitted with a sigh. What was important was to bury this completely inappropriate attraction—bury it so deep that it would never see the light of day again.

She was fairly sure that Nick agreed with her. In the two days they'd been here, he hadn't given any sign that he even remembered those moments in the gazebo when he'd held her so close it seemed as if he was trying to absorb her into himself. He'd greeted her with exactly the right note of casual friendliness, as if their only connection was her engagement to his brother, and Kate had had to squash a momentary feeling of pique that he'd apparently succeeded in doing what she wanted him to—forget what had happened between them.

Jack and Gareth returned empty-handed from their fishing trip. They endured the inevitable teasing with good-natured stoicism and vowed that tomorrow was another day.

"Another day without fish, you mean," Susan said dryly.

"Oh, ye of little faith." Jack gave her a reproachful look.

"Oh, ye of vast experience," she shot back. "The

only fish we've ever eaten up here come already breaded and shaped in neat little sticks.''

Nick laughed out loud, and even Gareth's mouth twitched into a smile.

Jack sighed. ''You're striking at the very heart of my manhood,'' he said mournfully.

''Last time somebody struck at the heart of my manhood, I threw up and couldn't walk for days,'' Nick offered in a conversational tone.

Susan snickered. Jack struggled to maintain his air of injured dignity. ''A man's ability to feed his family is at the very core of what makes him a man. It's what drives him to strive for greatness, to reach for success, to—''

''I've heard this before,'' Susan said helpfully. ''Is this where you do the part about dreaming the impossible dream and striving with unbearable sorrow and all that stuff? I love that part.''

''You do not appreciate me,'' Jack said, his dignity somewhat spoiled by the laughter of his friends.

''Sure I do, honey.'' She slid her arm around his waist and hugged him. ''If you want to provide sustenance for your family, why don't you start by getting the barbecue ready? I got out some steaks earlier and a couple of burgers for the kids. It takes a big, strong man with lots of heart to his manhood to get a grill going.''

''As long as you appreciate me,'' he said in a petulant tone that made Kate giggle.

The girlish sound brought Nick's gaze to her. For the past couple of days, he'd tried not to look at her if he could avoid it. It hadn't been easy. There was something about her that drew his eyes like a magnet. No matter how often he told himself that she was strictly hands off, he couldn't stop himself from looking at her—wanting her.

He'd been lying when he told himself that he could forget how she'd felt in his arms, how her mouth had tasted under his. He had only to look at her and the memories came rushing back.

He wanted her. It was that simple. And that impossibly complicated.

Nick glanced at his brother. Gareth straddled a redwood lounger, his feet braced on the floor on either side of it. Kate sat on the end of the same lounger, her feet curled under her. They were close but not touching—a pattern he'd noticed more than once in the past two days. Maybe it was his imagination, but he didn't see any signs of a great passion between his brother and his fiancée. There was affection, warmth, but not the kind of intimacy he would have expected between two people who planned to spend their lives together. They seemed more like good friends and comfortable companions than lovers.

Wishful thinking, he told himself. Of course, they were lovers. The thought had him turning away, squinting against the late afternoon sun reflected off the lake. He knew exactly what was tying his stomach in knots. Jealousy. He was jealous of his own brother. Not just envious of his happiness but absolutely green with jealousy. He didn't look at Gareth and wish he had a woman of his own. He wanted the woman his brother had. He wanted Kate, with her tawny hair and eyes that looked blue in sunlight and then turned all smoky gray with passion. He wanted her in his arms, in his bed.

He was fiercely glad that the cabin had only three bedrooms, which meant that Kate shared a room with Rose, while he and Gareth bunked with Matthew. It was bad enough watching Kate and Gareth together, seeing him touch her without having to imagine the two of them in bed together each night.

I'm in big trouble, he thought, his hand clenching on the deck railing. It had been a mistake to come to the cabin. In fact, he was more than ever convinced that it had been a big mistake to come back to Eden at all. It was ironic that he'd been worried about dealing with the past. As it turned out, the present offered more than enough worries of its own.

He'd had plenty of time to think this past week, and he'd just about decided that, once the work on Spider's Walk was finished, he was going to fold his tent and steal away into the night. There was nothing here for him anymore, and he sure as hell didn't want to stay around to dance at his brother's wedding.

"Does anyone know where the kids are?" Susan asked as she came out of the house.

Nick turned to see her walking across the deck. Jack was behind her, carrying a sack of charcoal toward the grill.

"I haven't seen them in quite awhile," Gareth said, and Kate nodded agreement.

"They were together last time I saw them," Nick offered. "I don't think Matt would let Rose wander off."

"No, he's real good about looking after her," Susan agreed. She smiled, but her eyes remained anxious. "It's silly, I guess, but I always get nervous when they're quiet. That's when they're most likely to be getting into trouble."

"I'll go find them," Nick said. "Considering the amount of energy they expended today, they're probably both asleep."

"Children do not run out of energy," Jack said as he poured charcoal briquettes into the grill. "They come with an eternally charged battery pack. Trust me, they can run any adult into the—"

A shrill scream sliced across the air, cutting his words off instantly. The bag crashed to the deck, scattering charcoal across the redwood planks. A second scream came hard on the heels of the first. By the time it ended, Jack was off the deck and running toward the sound with Nick a half step behind him.

There was a third scream and then another, each running into the next, shrill, panicked sounds that inspired a matching terror. Nick rounded the corner of the house and saw Rose standing in the middle of a clearing, her small body absolutely rigid, her mouth a round O of terror. Her brother sat on the ground beside her, his hands clutching his left leg, which was stretched out straight before him. Blood seeped between his fingers and trickled down his leg to sink into the dirt beneath him.

"Jesus God." Jack's words were more prayer than profanity as he hit the ground beside his son. "What happened?"

"I'm sorry, Dad." Matt's young voice quivered with strain, but there was no sign of tears. Shock, Nick thought, taking in his pallor. He probably wasn't feeling any pain. Yet.

"It's okay," Jack said automatically. He reached to pull Matt's hands away from the wound.

Rose was still screaming, those terrible thin sounds of fear. Nick turned toward her, but Susan was already there, scooping the little girl up in her arms and pressing her face into the curve of her neck, murmuring softly, even as her frightened eyes locked on her son. Rose clung to her mother, her small form shaking with sobs. Kate and Gareth stood just behind her.

"I'm sorry, Mom. I know I shouldn't have done it." Matt's eyes looked painfully blue in his stark white face. "I was showing off. You told me not to but I wanted to show Rosie. It looked so easy when you did it." He looked pleadingly at his father, as if afraid that Jack was going to punish him for being disobedient. "I'm sorry."

"It's okay," Jack said soothingly. "Let me see."

He pulled the boy's hands gently away from the wound and stared, appalled, as blood welled up from a deep gash that sliced across Matt's lower leg.

"Oh, God!" He put his hand over the injury, but not before Nick caught the white gleam of bone. "God." Jack sucked in a ragged breath. His face was nearly as white as his son's, but he struggled to call up a reassuring smile for the boy. "It's okay. You're going to be okay."

"I just wanted to show Rosie that I could chop wood," Matt said.

Nick saw the ax laying in the dirt next to the boy and felt bile rise in his throat. Behind him, he heard Susan give a deep, ragged sob and turned to see her face pressed into her daughter's golden hair, her arms rigid around the child.

"Oh, God." Jack pressed harder on the wound, but the blood continued to well between his fingers, dribbling down Matt's leg to soak into the dirt beneath.

"He needs a tourniquet," Gareth said, coming forward.

"A tourniquet." Jack grabbed at the word as if it were a lifeline. "We need something to tie around his leg."

"Here." Kate reached up and pulled loose the silk

scarf she'd used to hold her hair back. Gareth took it from her and came to kneel across from Jack.

"You did quite a number on yourself, Matt," he said as he deftly wrapped the tourniquet around the boy's leg. He took the stick Nick handed him and used it to tighten the knot.

"I'm sorry," Matt said again, but his voice was thin with shock and loss of blood.

"We'll get you fixed up," Gareth said, his eyes on the injury. Gradually, the bleeding slowed until it was no longer welling up between Jack's fingers. "It's pretty well stopped."

Susan drew a shaky breath. Kate went to her, setting her hand on her shoulder in a gesture meant to offer both sympathy and support.

"We can't leave this on very long," Gareth said, his eyes meeting Jack's over the boy's body. "He needs to get to a hospital as quickly as possible."

"The nearest hospital is at least two hours away," Jack said.

"What about a helicopter?" Kate asked, tightening her hand on Susan's shoulder.

"It might be hard to find a clearing big enough for one to land," Nick said, nodding to the woods that pressed in around the cabin.

"We have to do something," Susan burst out, her voice ragged. Hearing the fear in her mother's voice, Rose began to sob louder.

"Is Matt going to die?" she wailed.

"No!" Jack's denial was immediate and fierce, as if he was prepared to hold off death with his bare hands. "He's going to be fine." He started to stroke his son's hair from his face but stopped when he saw the blood that coated his fingers. He stared at them a moment and then slowly lifted his head and looked at Nick.

Nick saw the look in his eyes and shook his head, his expression nearly as agonized as his friend's. "God, Jack, don't ask me."

Bewildered, Kate looked from one man to the other. What on earth was happening? Why weren't they rushing Matt to a car or trying to get a helicopter to him? What was it Nick didn't want Jack to ask him? She looked at Gareth, seeking an explanation. His eyes met hers for a moment and then he looked away, his expression grim.

"He could die," Jack said simply, as if that answered Nick's protest. And perhaps it did.

Nick looked from him to the boy. Gareth had eased Matt back so that he lay on the ground. His eyes were closed, his face chalky. He looked alarmingly small and so fragile it was difficult to remember that, just a little while ago, he'd been running and playing, full of the pure joy of life. Nick looked at him and then lifted his eyes to Jack's face again. His expression was suddenly as still and calm as a photograph. Whatever turmoil he'd felt a moment ago, it seemed to be gone. Or hidden away somewhere inside.

"I can't promise anything."

"I'm not asking for promises," Jack said, hope blazing suddenly—startlingly—in his face.

Gareth rose as Nick moved forward. Their eyes met for a moment, but Kate was too far away to see what, if anything, passed between them. Then Gareth stepped back and Nick sank to his knees next to Matt. He reached out, his hands hovering over the gash, from which blood oozed with sullen malevolence. The gesture made Kate think of a blind man, judging by touch rather than sight. And then his hands settled gently on the wound.

"Take off the tourniquet," he said.

Susan sucked in a quick breath as if to protest, but Jack was already loosening the scarf around his son's leg. Blood gushed between Nick's fingers with frightening speed, and Susan started forward, her mouth open in denial. Acting on instinct, Kate tightened her hand on the other woman's shoulder, holding her back.

"Don't."

Susan turned her head, her eyes asking for an explanation Kate couldn't give. She didn't know what was happening, didn't know anything except that it suddenly seemed important that Nick not be disturbed. Whether Susan felt the same thing or was simply too frightened and confused to argue with her, she stayed where she was, Rose still sobbing softly in her arms. She rubbed her hand up and down her daughter's narrow back and kept her eyes on her son.

Nick was oblivious to the byplay. He didn't seem aware of anything but the boy who lay so still beneath his hands. His fingers rested lightly on the wound, too lightly to stem the flow of blood. Yet it seemed to be slowing.

Kate became aware of an odd feeling of energy filling the air, almost a warmth. Her scalp tingled with it, and she could feel the hair on her arms lifting. Her fingers curled into her palms, and she rubbed them across the base of her thumb, remembering those odd moments at the nursery when she'd felt a similar warmth, a sense that time no longer existed in quite the same way it always had. This was much stronger, and it kept building until the air seemed to crackle with it, until she could almost reach out and touch it. She knew, without questioning how, that Nick was at the center of that energy, that it flowed from him.

His hands hovered over Matt's leg, barely touching the torn flesh, and yet the bleeding was definitely slowing. With an effort, Kate dragged her eyes from his hands and looked at his face. In profile, his features seemed finely drawn, stripped of humanity, as if what was left was the pure core of life. He didn't look at his hands. He looked straight ahead, but his eyes were blind, turned inward to something only he could see.

Kate realized that blood no longer oozed over Nick's fingers. She looked at Matt. He seemed almost to be dozing, his face relaxed, all the fear drained away.

Time seemed to stand still, as if the world held its breath. Waiting. Watching.

Nick moved suddenly, startling her. He drew a deep, shuddering breath, the air rasping in his throat. He was still for a moment, as if gathering the strength to move, and then his hands slowly lifted away from Matt's leg.

And where there had been a gaping wound was— nothing.

Kate stared in disbelief. Matt's leg was whole, the flesh knit cleanly together. The only sign of the life-threatening gash was a thin pink line, like a scar from a long-healed injury.

Jack's breath exploded from him in a sob. He reached for his son, gathering the boy into his arms and holding him painfully tight. Matt seemed groggy, as if he'd been half asleep. Jack looked at Nick over his head.

"Thank you. Thank you." His voice was thick with emotion, his eyes wet with tears.

Nick's nod was slow and heavy, as if the gesture took a great deal of effort.

Susan recovered from her shock and rushed forward, dropping to her knees next to her husband and son and setting Rose on the ground. "Matt! Oh,

God." Tears ran down her pale cheeks. She threw her arm around her son and dragged him close. "Look, Rosie, Matt's okay. He's okay. Oh, God, he's okay."

Nick stood, his movements slow and stiff. All the color had leached from his face, making his eyes and hair look black against his skin. He seemed almost to sway, and Gareth took a quick step forward, one hand outstretched as if to offer support, but Nick's hand moved in a sharp gesture of rejection and his brother stopped as if he'd run into a brick wall.

Nick turned his head slightly and his eyes locked on Kate's. For an instant, she felt as if she looked straight into his soul and saw the loneliness of the man, the hunger that ate at him. Her heart twisted painfully and she swayed toward him as if drawn by an invisible force. She understood his loneliness, knew what it was to be hungry. And then he looked away and the moment was gone.

He glanced at Jack and Susan, holding onto their children as if they'd never let them go. His expression was utterly passive, completely unreadable. Without saying a word to anyone, he turned and walked away. Watching him, Kate thought she'd never seen anyone more alone.

Chapter Nine

It's a fact that life's most significant moments are rarely recognized at the time they occur. It's only hindsight that reveals the instant at which your world rearranged itself. Like Carl Sandburg's fog, change often came on little cat feet, unnoticed, unsuspected. But stealth made it no less powerful. Of course, some events are so powerful you know immediately that life will never be the same.

For Kate, the death of her mother when she was twelve had been such a moment. In an instant, everything had changed. But even then, it had been months before she'd realized the extent of the change, before she'd been forced to face—and accept—her father's inherent weakness. That had been the moment when she'd left the greater portion of childhood behind.

Years later, she'd made a conscious decision to rearrange her life when she chose to settle in Eden and put down roots for the first time in her life.

If she'd thought about it, she might have been vaguely disturbed to realize that accepting Gareth's proposal did not seem to be a profoundly life-altering moment. It seemed too much of a natural progression, as if it was part of a carefully guided pattern.

But those immeasurable seconds when she'd watched Nick heal a child's wound with nothing more than his bare hands were not part of any pattern Kate understood. Nor could Gareth offer any clear explanation.

"It's something that appeared a few months after Brian was killed," he said when she finally gathered her thoughts together enough to ask just what it was she'd witnessed. "Nick was in the car with him when a tire blew. Brian lost control. He...he never regained consciousness."

He stopped, his throat working as he stared intently out the windshield. Kate remained silent, allowing him time to deal with the memories.

They were parked in front of her apartment building, and her hesitant question about what had happened was nearly the first thing either of them had said since they left the cabin. The drive out of the mountains had been almost totally silent, both of them too drained by the events of the afternoon to discuss them.

Nick had walked away from the scene in the clearing, gotten on the Harley and left without bothering to gather his things from the house, without saying anything to anyone. Jack and Susan were still shaken by the knowledge that they'd nearly lost their son, and both children had been exhausted. No one had protested when Kate suggested cutting the visit short.

"For awhile, it looked like we might lose Nick, too," Gareth said finally. He kept his eyes on the darkness outside the car. "He actually died on the operating table and was gone for a couple of minutes before they managed to get his heart going again. Who knows, maybe that was what gave him this...this ability." He lifted one shoulder. "I've heard all kinds of weird claims from people who died and then were revived."

"But this...whatever it is...this isn't a claim," Kate said. "I saw it happen. I saw Nick lay his hands on Matt's leg and...and heal him. It's real."

"It's real," Gareth agreed. The words sounded as if they were dragged from him. "It's not predictable, though. It works sometimes but not others, and he doesn't know which it will be at any given moment."

"It worked today." Her voice was husky with remembered awe. "Matt probably would have died without him. It was like...like watching a miracle. I don't understand why you've never mentioned this," she said, shaking her head in bewilderment. "It's so incredible."

"That's why I didn't mention it." He shifted rest-lessly in his seat, muttering a curse when he banged his elbow against the steering wheel. "When we—my parents and I—realized that Nick had this...this gift, we decided that we should do everything we could to keep it in the family. We didn't want the media getting hold of this and treating him like some kind of freak. You know what they would do with something like this."

The thought made her shudder. "I can imagine. But I still don't understand why you didn't tell me. You can't think I'd call a press conference about it."

"No, of course not!" He reached out and caught her hand. "It wasn't a matter of trust. I guess it was partly habit. It's not something we talk about much, not even amongst ourselves. I did start to tell you once or twice but it's... Well, it's kind of hard to explain. This is my younger brother, Nick, and by the way, he works miracles?"

His effort to lighten the moment drew only a half-hearted smile, and he sighed and squeezed her hand before releasing it. "I guess it didn't seem all that relevant," he admitted. "Nick wasn't even home. No one knew if he'd ever come home again. And it isn't like he goes around healing people left and right. It's never been a regular part of our lives. It's just some-thing that happens now and again."

"I understand," Kate said, but she didn't, really. Oh, she understood why Gareth hadn't told her about

Nick's abilities. She could hardly blame him for keeping secrets. God knew, she had more than a few of her own, some of them involving his brother. What she didn't understand was what she'd seen today. She couldn't quite shake the feeling that she'd witnessed an honest-to-God miracle, and the idea of that left her feeling restless and unsettled.

The feeling lingered long after she'd given Gareth a chaste kiss good-night and gone into her apartment. He didn't suggest spending the night, and she didn't ask him to come in. She needed to be alone, needed to sort through the day's events and try to make sense of them.

But long after he was gone, she was still pacing her small apartment, moving restlessly from room to room, unable to settle in one place for more than a moment. She kept thinking about Nick. What was he feeling now? Was he exultant that he'd saved Matt's life?

Thinking of that instant when their eyes had met and she'd felt almost as if she was seeing into his soul increased Kate's restlessness. He'd looked so alone when he walked away. So lonely. Had he sought out Harry's company when he got home to Spider's Walk? Or was he all alone in that big house? Or had he gone somewhere else entirely?

"It's none of your business," she muttered, but she couldn't shake the memory of those few seconds when it had seemed as if they'd communicated, not as one human to another or even as man to woman but as soul to soul.

"Forget it," she told herself. "Just forget it."

It was crazy to come here, Kate thought. Crazy to be standing on Nick's doorstep at almost midnight. He was probably asleep. She could see a light behind the living room curtains, but that didn't mean anything.

And even if he was still awake, she had no business being here. So what if she thought she'd seen pain in his eyes in that last moment before he'd turned away? It wasn't her place to soothe that pain. She wasn't his mother, his wife or even his lover.

Kate stared at the cracked paint on the door. She didn't know why she'd come here, didn't even really remember making the decision. One minute she'd been staring at the pages of a book, the next she'd been getting in her truck. She hadn't really thought about what she was doing until now. If she was honest, she'd have to admit that she'd been careful *not* to think. It wasn't until she was standing on the sagging front porch, face-to-face with the fanciful carvings on the door Nick had yet to refinish, that a small voice of reason made itself heard.

Hadn't she decided that Nick was a threat to everything she'd worked to build these last few years, to everything she wanted in her life? She should turn around and go straight home, forget she'd ever come here. She'd forget everything she knew about the losses Nick had suffered, forget the power that had radiated from him when he'd set his hands on Matthew's leg this afternoon. And most of all, she'd forget the aching emptiness she'd seen in his eyes just before he'd turned and walked away.

But as if from somewhere outside herself, Kate saw her hand come up and watched her finger press the doorbell. She heard the two-tone chime of the bell inside the house. There was still time to turn and walk away, she thought, feeling her heart suddenly beating much too quickly. Time to go home, where she should have stayed in the first place.

But then the door was opening, and there was no time after all.

Nick stood in the open doorway, looking at her. He was wearing the same clothes he'd had on at the cabin—faded blue jeans and an old gray T-shirt. Kate remembered how guilty she'd felt for noticing the way the fabric clung to the solid muscles of his shoulders and chest. Now, looking at the rusty smears of blood streaked across the worn denim, she felt her throat tighten with emotion.

''Kate.'' He said only her name, his voice flat and empty, offering no clue to his thoughts.

She forced her eyes upward, looking at him. His hair tumbled onto his forehead in thick, dark waves, as if he'd run his fingers through it again and again.

His expression was as unreadable as his voice, drained of emotion, closed and unwelcoming.

"How are you?" The banal words seemed to hang on the warm night air and she felt herself flushing even before she saw Nick's brows go up.

"I'm fine. And you?" The studied politeness mocked her concern.

Obviously, he wasn't anxious for visitors. She shouldn't have come but, now that she was here, she couldn't go without trying to tell him how she felt.

"I wanted to tell you that what happened today was—"

"Came to see if I knew any other parlor tricks, did you?" he interrupted, his voice sharp and mocking. "Are you wondering if I read tea leaves or hoping to see me bend a spoon with the force of my mind? Sorry, Kate. I don't particularly like tea, and the only interesting trick I can do with a spoon is balance it on the end of my nose. I'm afraid you'll have to take my word on that, though, because I'm not really in the mood to demonstrate."

He started to shut the door, started to close her out and close himself in alone. Kate was shocked to feel the flat of her hand braced against the solid panel, preventing him from closing it. Her eyes were on Nick's face, and for an instant she saw emotion flicker in his eyes, as if he was as surprised as she was by her action.

"I'd like to come in," she said quietly.

"I'm not good company right now."

"Please."

His fingers tightened over the edge of the door, the knuckles showing white. She thought he might shut the door in her face but then he seemed to change his mind, not as if he welcomed her company but as if it wasn't worth the effort to fight her.

"Have it your way," he said with a shrug and then turned and walked away, leaving her to follow him or not.

Kate hesitated, aware of a small voice that warned her to turn and walk away before it was too late. *Too late for what?* she wondered, but there was no answer and she stepped across the threshold and pushed the door shut behind her.

The tiled entryway was empty. Nick hadn't bothered to see if she followed him. He'd gone into the front parlor. The room must have been elegant once. Faded flowers peaked out from the wallpaper and were still faintly visible on the long drapes. The finish on the floor was worn, but the beauty of the red oak boards showed through that wear. Nick had apparently designated this room as a storage area while he worked on the rest of the house. Cans of paint were stacked neatly along one wall. A pile of lumber stood next to the paint. Plastic drop cloths were tossed carelessly beside a battered tool chest.

Kate ignored the organized clutter, her attention focused on the man standing next to the empty fireplace. He was watching her, his expression unreadable in the light from the single floor lamp next to an aged sofa upholstered in faded blue linen. A bottle of Chivas Regal and an old-fashioned glass sat on an upended packing crate. The base of a red clay flowerpot sat beside them, overflowing with half-smoked cigarettes. The room reeked of smoke.

"I didn't know you smoked." It was the first thing that popped into her head.

"Only when I'm celebrating."

"It's bad for you," she said and felt color creep up her neck at the astounding obviousness of her words.

"No kidding!" Nick raised his brows in amazement. "I hadn't heard that." He lifted a cigarette to his mouth and took a deep, deliberate drag on it. He exhaled slowly, the mockery fading, his eyes suddenly watchful through the curtain of smoke. "What are you doing here, Kate?"

The question of the hour. Too bad she didn't have a good answer. She tried to smile, but her face felt stiff and uncooperative. She slid her hands into the pockets of her soft cotton slacks and looked away from him.

"I don't know exactly why I came," she admitted slowly. "I keep thinking about what happened today, about what you did."

"Don't think about it," Nick said, his tone so sharp her eyes were drawn to him. He stubbed the cigarette out. He half turned away from her, reaching for the bottle of Chivas. He splashed some into the glass, his hands not quite steady "I've already forgotten it."

"I don't believe that." She shook her head, groping for the words to explain what she was feeling, why she'd felt compelled to come here. "What I saw was extraordinary. I've never seen...never imagined anything like it."

A harsh laugh cut across her words, startling her. Nick turned and lifted his drink in a mocking toast. "Ladies and gentlemen, come see the amazing Blackthorne. He walks, he talks, he crawls on his belly like a reptile."

"Nick—"

He ignored her, continuing in the same mocking, singsong tone. "Bring him your lame, your poor, your huddled masses yearning to be cured. But the management makes no promises, ladies and gentlemen. No promises whatsoever. The amazing Blackthorne can never tell whether his astounding powers will be in the mood to work at any given moment. But why worry? It's only life or death. Step right up, put a quarter in the hat and take your chances."

The derisive sound of his laughter cut straight through to Kate's heart. He tilted his head and tossed off the shot glass of Scotch. He turned and reached for the bottle again but she was suddenly beside him, her hand closing over his.

"Don't. It's not going to help."

"How the hell do you know?" he snarled, but he didn't pull away.

"Because if it helped, you'd be drunk by now," she said quietly. She lifted the bottle from the end table and screwed the lid in place. Nick watched her in silence, his eyes shadowed, his expression shuttered and unreadable. Kate set the bottle down and looked at him. "You saved a child's life today. That's a wonderful thing. You should be happy."

"What makes you think I'm not?" he asked, lifting one dark brow in mocking inquiry. "Maybe this is how I like to celebrate—a good smoke, a few drinks, some time to contemplate just how wonderful everything is. Time *alone*."

Kate ignored his deliberate emphasis of the last word. "Gareth says this...ability showed up after your accident."

"*My* accident." Nick repeated the words as if tasting them, weighing them. "Is that how the family refers to it? Funny, I don't remember applying for ownership." He caught Kate's worried look and sighed sharply before half turning away from her.

"I was dead, you know," he said suddenly, his tone almost conversational. "When they got...us to the emergency room, we were both dead. It was just the way they describe it in those new-age books about near-death experiences, the ones where the authors wear flowing robes and beads and look terribly serene. There was the white light, the feeling of peace, every cliché in the book.''

Lost in memory, he looked past her at things she couldn't see. "I wasn't afraid. I felt safe. I could feel Brian there, as if he was standing beside me. When I felt him moving toward the light, it seemed good. Right." He looked at his glass, at the thin film of Scotch. "And then I woke up in the hospital. Alone. Brian was gone."

Kate's heart ached for the pain she heard in his voice. She knew what it was to be alone, knew what it was to lose people you loved, knew the emptiness he'd felt inside, the emptiness he still felt. Her hand came up, lifting toward him, but Nick spun away abruptly, as if her touch might burn. He brushed past her and picked up the bottle of Scotch. He flashed her a quick smile, a shadow of the wickedly attractive grin that had haunted her guilty dreams these past weeks.

"Sorry, Kate. Telling my life story always makes me thirsty."

He splashed Scotch into the glass and set the bottle down without bothering to screw the lid on. But when he picked up the glass, he didn't drink from it. Instead, he cradled it between his palms and stared into it, apparently fascinated by the play of light dancing in the amber liquid.

The silence stretched. Kate told herself that she should go. She'd said what she'd come to say. It was time to go home, time to walk away before her life became even more inextricably intertwined with his. But she couldn't quite bring herself to leave him alone.

"Do you know what it's like to have a gift like mine?" Nick asked abruptly, startling her. He continued without waiting for an answer. "It's like nothing you've ever imagined. To know that you have this ability to touch someone and heal them, to take away their pain with just your hands—it's heady stuff."

"The dog—Laura said he was bleeding and you put your hands on him and made him better."

Nick lifted his glass in acknowledgement. "An equal opportunity healer, that's me."

"A couple of weeks ago, at the nursery, when I cut my finger—I really *did* cut my finger, didn't I?" It had been in the back of her mind since she'd seen what he did for Matthew.

His mouth twisted in a rueful half smile. "I overreacted on that one."

"I was so sure I'd cut myself, but then, when it was gone, I thought I'd imagined it."

"People usually do." He took a swallow of Scotch and then lowered the glass and glanced at her. "Matthew probably won't remember much of what happened. Rosie will have a few nightmares, and then the memory will fade away. Even Susan will eventually start to half-believe she imagined the whole thing, that the cut wasn't as bad as it seemed. Jack knows, though. He knew today, and that's why he asked me to help Matthew.''

"You don't regret helping him, do you?"

"No." He shook his head impatiently. "No, of course not. I'm just grateful I *could* help." In his eyes was a reflection of the fear he had felt when Jack turned to him. "I'm never quite sure. And even when it does work... It's scary as hell, if you want to know the truth. Each time, it's like feeling the breath of God."

"A miracle," Kate said softly.

"Yeah." Nick's agreement was flat and emotionless. "It's a certifiable miracle, all right. But it came too late to save my brother." He set his glass down and thrust his hands in his pockets, hunching his shoulders a little, as if he felt cold. "It wasn't enough to let me help my wife. It wasn't enough to keep her or my son alive."

The cool facade was gone, revealing such stark pain that Kate's chest ached with the impact of it. She had no answers to give him. There was nothing anyone could say that could take away his pain. Acting on instinct, she did the only thing she could think of—she put her arms around him, offering the primal comfort of touch.

She felt him stiffen and knew she'd made a mistake. Despite all that had happened between them, they were still little more than intimately acquainted strangers. She wanted him to know that he wasn't alone, that she could share it with him. Feeling suddenly awkward and self-conscious, as if she'd intruded on his pain rather than eased it, Kate started to ease back.

Feeling her withdrawal, Nick moved abruptly, his arms coming around her and pulling her against him, his hold almost painfully tight.

"Don't," he muttered, his voice thick and guttural.

Kate froze in surprise, but only for a moment. Her heart aching, she relaxed in his hold. Her slender arms tightened around his waist and she held him as tightly as he was holding her, offering the only comfort she could.

She had no idea how long they stood there. Time had no meaning. She didn't question her need to comfort him. It felt too right to allow questioning. When Nick's fingers slid into her hair, tilting her head so his mouth could find hers, that felt right, too. The kiss was part of the moment—more comfort than hunger—and Kate accepted it as such. Comfort, that's all it was.

Nick's mouth left hers slowly. Kate forced her eyes open and looked at him. His eyes had darkened to almost black, until pupil and iris blended together. She could fall into his eyes, she thought. Sink into them and never surface again, swallowed completely by the hunger in them.

His hand shifted on her back, sliding along the

sensitive ridge of her spine. His other hand still cupped her skull, and she felt his fingers move against her scalp. Around them, the big old house was quiet, adding to the sense of isolation. Nick's hand settled at the base of her spine, his fingers splayed across the gentle inward curve.

Did he move? Did she? It was impossible to know and it didn't matter anyway. All that mattered was that his mouth was on hers and he was kissing her, holding her, as if he'd never let her go.

Abrupt as it was, the shift from comfort to passion seemed inevitable. Hunger—always there, seldom acknowledged—rolled over them in a single, overpowering wave, leaving no room for thoughts of past or future, right or wrong. Only the moment existed. Only the moment mattered.

Need hammered in Nick. He had to touch her, had to feel her skin beneath his hands. He reached for the front of her shirt, his fingers impatient as he struggled to slide buttons open. He felt one tear loose, heard the faint ping as it hit the floor and the edges of fabric finally fell free. She was wearing a flesh-colored bra. The lacy fabric barely covered her breasts, but even that was too much. Ignoring the front clasp, he slid his hands inside the cups. Kate moaned and the sound tore away the last of his control.

If his hands were impatient with her clothing, hers were equally so with his. She tore at the buttons on his jeans, frantic to touch him. The zipper on her slacks yielded with a faint raspy sound just as her fingers closed around him. She felt him shudder and felt a wild surge of power that her touch could affect him so powerfully. He was silk and steel in her hand, heat and hunger, need and lust. Kate felt a deep yearning in the pit of her stomach, a throbbing ache that made her skin feel heated and almost painfully sensitive. She tightened her fingers around him.

An inarticulate growl sounded deep in his throat and then his hands were sliding inside her pants, stripping slacks and panties down with one impatient tug. The world spun dizzily around her and she felt the worn upholstery of the sofa against her back. And then Nick loomed over her, his face hard and intent in the dim light. His jeans wrenched apart, his shirt hanging open, his body quivering with tension, he mounted her.

She felt the warm, seeking brush of him against the delicate folds of her most secret femininity. Reaching between their bodies, she held him, guided him to her. There was a moment of testing, a heartbeat of waiting and then his hips flexed and he sheathed himself within her, filling her emptiness with one powerful thrust.

Kate's body arched, a low, keening cry torn from her throat as she took him into her body, feeling herself completed, fulfilled, the long, endless wait over at last. But instead of easing, her hunger took on a new edge, sharp and painful in its intensity. She whimpered with frustration, but Nick was already moving within her.

It was fast and hard, hot and earthy. This was no gentle give-and-take, accompanied by soft sighs and warm kisses. This was a struggle, a primal battle between man and woman. Nick took her like a conqueror, his powerful body driving into hers, stamping her as his.

Kate was no less hungry. She arched to take his every thrust, demanding more and still more. Her heels dug into the worn sofa cushion, her nails biting into the hard muscles of his hips, pulling him to her, her need every bit as ferocious as his.

Tension spiraled within her, tight and hard. She sobbed with it, her body struggling to escape the painful intensity of it, even as she fought to draw him deeper into her. Nick had been bracing his weight on his elbows but he shifted, letting the weight of his chest anchor her as his hands caught her hips, fingers digging into the soft flesh of her bottom, controlling her movements, working her on his invading shaft.

It was enough to shatter the coiled spring of tension. Kate arched wildly beneath him, her breath leaving her in a thin, breathless cry as all her senses exploded in one dazzling burst of pleasure. Her inner muscles tightened around him, relaxed then tightened again. Nick shuddered and thrust heavily into her, giving himself over to the hunger. A harsh, guttural sound tore from his throat as he pulsed within her, flooding her with his release.

For a long time, the only noise in the room was the ragged sound of their breathing. Nick's weight pinned her to the sofa, making breathing an effort, but she didn't care. Kate welcomed the rasp of his chest hair against her breasts, the warmth of his skin against hers, the sense of fullness where he was still nestled inside her.

It wasn't enough, Nick thought despairingly. The aftershocks of his climax were still rippling through him and he already wanted her again. He moved, thrusting gently, and felt her shudder of response as he began to swell within her. It could never be enough. No matter how many times he had her, he'd still want her. The force of his hunger sparked an anger in him.

Ignoring Kate's whimper of protest as he withdrew, he settled on his knees. His hands were hard as he caught her by the shoulders and dragged her up with him so they knelt face-to-face on the cushions. There was a drugged look of pleasure in her eyes when she looked at him.

"I want to see you," he muttered, shoving her shirt off her arms and throwing it to the floor. Lacking the patience to deal with the plastic clasp on her bra, he tugged it off over her head. Her breasts spilled into his hands, all soft creamy curves and rosy nipples. He bent to taste them, first one and then the other, laving them gently with his tongue and then drawing each one into his mouth and sucking strongly. He felt himself swell with lust as Kate's back arched when she offered herself to him.

He wanted to make this time last forever, wanted to savor every step of the way. But he was already so hard that it hurt and the hunger was tearing at his self-control, demanding release.

"I can't wait," he muttered as he dragged his mouth from her breasts.

"Who asked you to?" she whispered, her fingers closing around him, stroking and teasing.

Her touch burned away the last of his patience. Shuddering, he pulled away and stood up, stripping his shirt from his shoulders and shoving his jeans and briefs the rest of the way off. Kate lay back on the sofa, watching him undress, her eyes heavy-lidded with desire. The sight of her stretched out before him, her tawny hair splayed across the faded cushions, her slender body soft and pliant, was almost more than Nick could stand.

She lifted her arms and he came to her. It was like coming home, fulfilling a destiny. They belonged together. He'd never known anything as surely as he knew that.

Kate came awake slowly, aware of a pleasant feeling of lassitude that permeated her entire body. She had no idea how long she'd been asleep, but she felt deeply rested, sated. She could lie here forever, she thought sleepily. Except her back was cold. Had she kicked off the covers? No, because there were no covers.

Reality began to sneak in around the edges of her contentment. There were no covers because she wasn't in bed. Reluctantly, she opened her eyes. The first thing she saw was a broad expanse of furred male chest. Her hand was nestled in a mat of crisp curls, looking feminine and almost fragile in contrast. The light was subdued but it was enough to reflect off the small diamond in her engagement ring. Kate stared at that soft gleam for several seconds. Reality no longer nibbled at her consciousness, it crashed in wearing hobnailed boots.

Nick. Oh, God. Nick. And Gareth. What had she done?

She scrambled off the sofa with an inarticulate whimper of distress.

"Kate?" Startled awake, Nick sat up and reached for her.

"Don't!" She backed away as if his touch might burn. On her face was such a look of loathing that Nick felt as if he'd been struck. He let his hand drop, his face going cold and still.

The loathing Kate felt was for herself. How could she have done this? She fell to her knees and began scrambling through the tangled heap of clothing on the floor. Oh, God, what had she done? Gareth. How could she have done this to him? He was everything she'd ever wanted and she'd betrayed him in the most fundamental way possible. Not only had she slept with another man. She'd slept with his own brother. He'd never be able to forgive her.

Pain lanced through her chest and she curled into it for an instant, her slender body drawn into something approaching a fetal position as she rocked with the impact of her own actions.

Nick responded to her pain. "Don't tear yourself up like this," he said, reaching out to touch her shoulder.

"Don't!" She jerked away from his touch. "Don't you ever touch me again."

Nick pulled away as if burned. "I didn't exactly drag you kicking and screaming," he pointed out sharply.

"No. No, you didn't."

She'd finally managed to sort out most of her clothing. Beyond caring that he was looking at her, she stepped into her slacks and jerked them up around her hips, fastening them with shaking fingers. She pulled on her shirt but her hands were trembling too much for her to slide the buttons through the buttonholes. With a frustrated whimper, she tied the tails in a knot at her waist instead.

"Don't you think we should talk?" Nick asked. He stood up, magnificently unconcerned with his nudity.

"We have nothing to say," she muttered, kicking aside his jeans in search of her shoes. One of them had been lying next to a paint can but the other one eluded her. She found her panties instead, and her cheeks flamed as she snatched them up and stuffed them in her pocket.

"What about Gareth?"

She spun to face him, her eyes bright with anger. "Don't you dare tell him about this!"

Nick's head jerked back as if she'd slapped him. Stung, he struck back. "What do you think I'm going to do? Announce it over breakfast? Pass the toast and, by the way, bro, your fiancée is a hell of a lay?"

Kate turned white, her eyes huge and dark with distress. With a curse, Nick bent and scooped up her shoe from the floor next to the sofa. He tossed it to her, and she caught it automatically. "Don't worry, Kate, your dirty little secret is safe with me. I'll just add it to the rest of them."

"I think I hate you," she whispered hoarsely.

Nick gave her a sharp smile. "Is that why I have your fingernail marks on my back?"

She stared at him an instant longer and then turned and ran, barefoot, from the room. Nick stayed where he was, listening to the solid thud as the door shut behind her. A moment later, he heard her truck pull away from the house, and then there was only silence.

He was alone again.

Chapter Ten

Hollow-eyed and pale, Kate watched the sun creep through a crack in the curtains and slice a pale gold path across the bedroom carpet. When the thin blade of light slid across the foot of her bed, she stirred sluggishly and crawled out of bed with movements as stiff and slow as an old woman's.

She went into the bathroom and followed her morning routine as if on autopilot, washing her face and brushing her teeth without once looking at herself in the mirror. It wasn't until she was pulling her hair from her face that she caught a glimpse of her reflection. Meeting her own eyes, she felt her fingers start to tremble and she jerked the elastic-covered band into place, ignoring the stinging pain when it pulled at her scalp. She looked away quickly, afraid that the past twenty-four hours might have left visible changes.

In her bedroom, she dressed carelessly, pulling on sweatpants and a worn gray sweatshirt. Though she knew the chill she felt came from inside, not out, she pulled on a sweater, tugging it close around her as she went into the kitchen.

She measured coffee into the filter and pushed the button to start the water heating, then moved automatically to check the plants that filled the bump-out window behind the kitchen sink. The window had been one of the reasons she'd chosen to rent the small apartment. She pinched off a few faded leaves and tipped a little water into one or two pots, soothed by the simple tasks.

She'd be able to have a *real* garden after she and Gareth—

The tenuous calm vanished in an instant. Kate dropped her hand to the counter, her fingers curling into a fist. Gareth. The thought of him sent a lancing pain through her heart. How could she have betrayed him so completely? Guilt twisted her stomach into knots, and she closed her eyes against the burning ache of tears. It was too late for tears. They couldn't change what she'd done. What she and Nick had done.

Nick. His name triggered a flood of memories— him kneeling beside Matthew, power flowing from him. The pain in his eyes when he spoke of his wife and child. The taste of his mouth, the feel of his hands—

Kate's eyes snapped open. Her hand was shaking as she took a mug from the cabinet and filled it with coffee. She wasn't going to think about *that* ever again. Or about *him*.

Sitting at the table, she wrapped her hands around the mug, trying to absorb its warmth into her. But the chill she felt was bone deep and it spread throughout her body in a slow, icy tide. Trembling, she pushed the cup away, folded her arms on the table and let her head drop to them as the tears began to fall.

What had she done?

As far as Nick could see, the one immutable law was that life went on. No matter what happened—good, bad or indifferent—the sun still rose every morning and the world kept on turning. Win the lottery? Fine. But there was still laundry to be done and the dog to feed. Sleep with your brother's fiancée? Too bad. You might as well scrape the paint off the crown molding.

Standing on a ladder in the formal dining room, he ran a scraper along a strip of molding, peeling away a hundred years worth of paint. It was backbreaking, miserable work and he'd chosen to start the job today because it fit his mood. And maybe he'd chosen it as

a kind of penance, he admitted to himself. As if physical discomfort could somehow absolve him of guilt.

A boom box sat on the floor, and he'd turned the
sound up to a level guaranteed to have him wearing
a hearing aid by the time he was forty. At the moment, the Beach Boys were trying to talk Rhonda into
helping them get over a lost love. The driving rhythm
echoed in the big room but it wasn't enough to drown
out his thoughts.

Nick doubted if anything short of a two-by-four up
alongside his head could have kept him from thinking
about Kate—the way she'd tasted, the sweet warmth
of her in his arms, the incredible feel of her body
yielding to his. He ground his teeth together as he
used the corner of the scraper to tease bits of paint
from the edges of the crown molding. What kind of
a prize bastard was he to keep thinking of how good
it had felt to make love to her? He'd do better to
think about the way she'd looked at him afterward,
as if the sight of him might turn her to stone. Or he
could think about the way he'd betrayed his brother.

He and Gareth had never been exceptionally close.
The five-year gap in their ages had seemed enormous
when they were children, and the bond he and Brian
had shared hadn't left much room for anyone else.
Even after Brian was killed, Nick and Gareth had
never really seemed to connect.

But that hardly excused him. He'd never been one

to poach on another man's territory. He had nothing but contempt for married people who had affairs. And while Kate wasn't married—yet—she wore another man's ring on her finger, which put her off-limits. Yet all he'd had to do was touch her, hold her, and his scruples had disappeared. He hadn't thought of anything but the need to have her.

"I could hear this thing three blocks away!"

The shouted comment startled Nick into jerking halfway around, barely avoiding a fall as he grabbed the top of the ladder. He nearly fell the rest of the way down when he saw Gareth leaning over the boom box, apparently looking for the volume control. When it wasn't immediately apparent, he punched the button to stop the tape, cutting Brian Wilson off in mid-word. The abrupt silence seemed louder than the music had been.

"I rang the bell but no one answered," he said as he straightened. "I guess I'm not surprised, considering how far up you've cranked the volume. If you're not careful, you're going to be deaf before you're fifty."

"I figured I'd be lucky to make it to forty." Nick's response came automatically. His brother's sudden appearance had his mind reeling.

"I could cite you for noise pollution, you know."

"It would never stand up in court. Not in California. Not when it's the Beach Boys."

Gareth grinned crookedly. "You could be right."

Outside the open window, Nick could hear Laura's mother calling her. He wondered if the little girl had hidden herself somewhere in Harry's gardens. She had a knack for finding spaces just the right size for her and Leroy and then developing a convenient deafness to her mother's voice. For a moment, he was tempted to escape by saying that he had to go find the girl.

Gareth watched Nick pull a rag from his back pocket and begin wiping off the blade of the scraper he'd been using. He pushed his hands in his pockets, his carefully planned little speech suddenly vanishing into thin air. Why was it always so damned hard to talk to Nick? he wondered, exasperated with himself.

Even when they were boys, he hadn't known how to talk to Nick. It hadn't been that way with Brian. Brian had been quiet. Focused. With Brian, there were no hidden corners, no surprises. He'd understood Brian. But not Nick. As a boy, Nick had been like quicksilver—changeable, unpredictable. Easy to love but impossible to grab hold of—impossible to really know.

"Have you got a minute?" he asked finally. Nick's head came up, his eyes wary. He nodded.

"I've got two, if you need them." He came the rest of the way down the ladder. "Why don't we go someplace where the fumes are less likely to cause a toxic reaction?"

Gareth followed him across the foyer and into the

living room. "Looks like you've got every room in the place torn apart," he commented, looking around.

"Pretty close. I suppose, if I were more organized, I'd do it one room at a time but it's less boring this way, and with Harry hiding out in the guest house, I'm not driving anyone crazy but me."

He took a pack of cigarettes from the mantel and tapped one loose. Gareth's brows rose as he put it in his mouth.

"I didn't know you were smoking again."

"I'm not." Nick struck a match and held it to the cigarette's tip. "I picked up a pack on the way out of the mountains yesterday. Two packs, actually." He gave a half shrug and grinned a little. "When they're gone, I'll quit again."

"Oh, yeah?" Gareth looked doubtful.

"I've done it before. I figure I can do it again. Most things get easier with practice, right?"

"I'm not sure this falls into that category." But he hadn't come here to lecture on the evils of nicotine. "I brought your clothes over. I dropped them on the table in the foyer. You left them at the cabin yesterday."

"Thanks."

"My pleasure." Gareth looked away for a moment, debating the wisdom of continuing. But there were things he wanted to get off his chest and this was as good a time as any to do it. "I wanted to talk to you about what happened yesterday,'' he said slowly.

Nick inhaled too quickly and coughed as the smoke burned his throat.

"You okay?" Gareth asked, concerned.

"Fine. I'm fine." Nick turned to stub the barely touched cigarette out. "Maybe I'll quit before I finish both packs," he muttered. He shoved his hands in the pockets of his jeans and looked at his brother again, his dark eyes shuttered and unreadable. "What about yesterday?"

"The thing with Matthew. It was incredible."

"Yeah, that's me. Incredible as hell." Nick's mouth twisted in a self-mocking smile. Oddly enough, he seemed to relax a little. "Miracles to order—that's my stock in trade."

"I know you don't want to talk about it," Gareth said doggedly, ignoring the sharp humor. "But there's something I want to tell you, something I should have said a long time ago."

Nick shifted uncomfortably. "I have an awful feeling you're about to break the Guy Code."

"The Guy Code?"

"You know, the one that says we don't talk to each other about anything but sports and food. So, what do you think of the Rams' chances at the Super Bowl this next year?"

"I think they've moved to St. Louis." Gareth was

torn between exasperation and amusement. The conversation was going in a typically Nick-like direction.

"I forgot." Nick frowned. "Are the Dodgers still around?"

"Yeah. And, if you really want to, we can analyze whether or not they're going to make it to the World Series, but I'm still going to say what I came here to say."

"You always did have a nasty dogged streak in you." Nick sounded resigned.

"I'll take that as a compliment." Gareth took a moment to set his thoughts in order. "A while ago, when Kate cut her finger at the nursery and...you—"

"I waved my magic wand," Nick finished for him, his voice edgy with temper. "I remember. What about it?"

Gareth cursed his own clumsiness. He was blowing it, but it was too late to back down now. He had to plow ahead and hope he didn't make a bigger mess of it. "You said some things that made it sound like you thought I was ashamed of your...gift."

"Did I?" Nick shifted restlessly, the old oak floorboards creaking under him. "It doesn't really matter one way or the other, does it?"

"It matters to me if you think that." Gareth hunched his shoulders. "What you can do—" He broke off and shook his head. "People use the word miracle to describe everything from a football upset to a sale on toilet paper, but what you did yester-day—that was the real thing.''

"But you didn't want me to do it, did you?'' Nick said more sharply than he'd intended.

"I've seen what it does to you when you suc-ceed—and when you don't,'' Gareth said simply.

Memories suddenly lay between them, as vivid and sharp as a film strip. Gareth pulling him away from the car, away from Lisa and the baby. Gareth telling him it was too late, that he couldn't help them, that no one but God could help them now. He'd finally had to knock Nick unconscious to get him out of the garage.

"That was...a long time ago,'' Nick said, his voice rough with emotion.

"I guess it was,'' Gareth said. "I didn't mean to dredge up old memories. I just wanted you to know that... Well, I guess I wanted you to know that, when I saw what you did yesterday, I was very...proud.'' He shrugged, uncomfortable with the emotional di-rection the conversation had taken. "I just wanted to tell you that.''

"Thanks. I... It means a lot to me to know that.''

"Yeah, well. I thought it ought to be said.'' Gareth pushed his hands in his pockets and then pulled them out again. Wanting to end the sudden, uncomfortable silence, he looked at Nick and grinned. "How the hell are those Dodgers, anyway?''

Nick laughed, but the shadows remained in his

eyes. Gareth wondered if those shadows would ever fade completely, if he'd ever be able to put the past behind him and move on with his life.

"The Guy Code is always there when you need it," Nick said.

"Nice to know there's something you can count on." Gareth nodded to the stack of lumber and paint cans. "You think Harry's really going to sell this place?"

"I doubt it." Nick caught his questioning look and shrugged, smiling ruefully. "He thought I needed to be saved from the evils of Wall Street so he drummed up the idea of selling the house and hit me with a major guilt trip to get me back here. I've got to hand it to him, he put on a hell of a performance."

"He must have been hell on wheels in a courtroom," Gareth said, careful not to make any comment about whether or not Nick might have been in need of saving. There was a limit to the amount of emotional baggage he wanted to shed in one day.

"It would serve him right if I made him sell the damned place when I'm done with it," Nick said, but there was no real force behind the threat.

"It's a great old house." Gareth looked around the room, seeing past the shabby surface to the quality beneath. "They really built to last in those days."

"Labor and materials were a lot cheaper." Nick reached for a cigarette and then changed his mind. He pushed his hands into his pockets instead and watched as Gareth crossed to one of the windows and ran his hand over the woodwork.

"Makes my place look like it's put together with spit and bailing wire." He looked out the window. "Kate's crazy about this yard. She says it could be a real showpiece."

"Harry likes what she's doing with it," Nick said neutrally.

"She's done a little work around my place already." Gareth turned from the window and wandered toward the center of the room. "But I have a feeling she wants to make some major changes and is waiting until after we're married to spring them on me."

"She seems to know her stuff when it comes to landscaping."

"She does." Gareth picked up a paintbrush and flicked the bristles back and forth across his palm a few times before setting it down. "It's funny that she should be so into plants since her family was constantly on the move when she was a kid. She doesn't talk much about it, but I gather she hated moving all the time."

"That kind of thing can be hard on a child." Nick could think of no more exquisite punishment for his sins than to have to listen to Gareth talk about Kate.

"I never have figured out why they moved so often. Something to do with her father's job, I guess." Gareth frowned and looked down as he gently bounced the toe of his shoe against the side of a paint can. "Like I said, she doesn't say much about it."

"Maybe she figures it's best to leave it in the past."

"I suppose." Gareth was silent a moment and then he seemed to shake off his contemplative mood. "I'd better let you get back to work. I'm heading into the station. They weren't expecting me back today so I figure I might be able to catch up on some paperwork."

"All work and no play," Nick reminded him, hoping it wasn't obvious that he was anxious to see this visit end.

"Yeah, I know I'm in danger of becoming a workaholic." Gareth grinned ruefully. "I did call Kate to see if she wanted to catch a movie, but she thinks she's coming down with a cold and wants to spend the day popping vitamin C and resting to see if she can head it off."

"I hope she can," Nick said. Guilt was a lead weight in the pit of his stomach.

"Me, too." Gareth turned toward the door and then hesitated, bending to pick something up off the floor near the sofa. He straightened up with a lacy, flesh-toned bra dangling from his finger.

"Something new in house restoration tools?" he asked quizzically.

Nick felt as if he'd just been kicked in the stomach.

His mind went completely blank, and he stared at the lacy garment as if he'd never seen it before.

"The grapevine must be slowing down," Gareth said, filling in the silence. "I haven't heard about anyone you're seeing."

"Some people like their privacy," Nick got out. His muscles felt stiff as he moved forward and took the bra from his brother. Not knowing what else to do with it, he stuffed it in his back pocket.

"Not even Howard Hughes could have kept his privacy in this town." Gareth looked both curious and surprised. "Someone I know?"

"I doubt it."

Gareth waited, as if expecting him to add something to the flat statement, but Nick's powers of invention had been drained dry. The bra felt as if it was burning a hole in his pocket to match the one guilt was burning in his gut. When he didn't say anything more, Gareth frowned, his expression going from curious to concerned.

"You're being careful, aren't you? I mean, these days, there's—"

"I'm a little past the age of having my big brother lecture me about safe sex," Nick pointed out. He was suddenly sharply aware that the warning came too late.

"Sorry." Gareth's smile was a little sheepish. "Old habits die hard, I guess."

"I suppose." Nick started for the door, beyond

caring if Gareth thought there was something odd in his behavior. Five more minutes in his brother's company and he was going to start screaming a confession neither of them wanted to hear.

For several minutes after Gareth was gone, he stood in the entryway, staring at the closed door. Almost with a sense of detachment, he wondered how long it would take for the fallout from last night to cease.

When the phone rang, Kate hesitated before answering. She wasn't in the mood to talk, and she was tempted to let the machine pick it up. But she'd told Gareth she didn't feel good enough to go to a movie. If he was calling to check on her and she didn't answer, he would probably come over. The thought was enough to make her pick up the receiver.

"Hello?"

"Kate?"

Just the one word, but she knew his voice. Her fingers knotted around the receiver, her chest suddenly aching with tension.

"I don't have anything to say to you."

"Then you can just listen while I talk," he said, his polite tone as sharp as a slap. She felt her face flush as anger replaced the turmoil churning in her stomach.

"Maybe I should have phrased it differently," she

said tightly. "You don't have anything to say that I want to hear."

"If you hang up, I'll come over."

The threat caught her as she was pulling the receiver away from her ear. She hesitated, but something told her not to test him.

"I'm listening," she said sullenly.

"I don't know if it's occurred to you yet, but we didn't exactly spend much time discussing some of the more basic realities of sex in the nineties."

They hadn't spent time *discussing* sex at all, Kate thought, remembering the sense of urgency that had her tearing at his clothes. She was ashamed of the way her body reacted to the memory, a tingling awareness flooding over her from head to heels, an unmistakable warmth. She closed her eyes, letting her head fall back against the sofa.

"Kate?" Nick's tone was sharply questioning.

"I'm here."

Though she tried to keep her voice level, she must not have been entirely successful because his tone gentled subtly.

"What I'm trying to say is that I didn't use any protection last night."

She shuddered. He wasn't telling her anything she hadn't already thought of, but it seemed more real somehow when she heard him say it. "I know," she said, helpless to banish the thickness from her voice.

"You don't have to be afraid of getting...

anything,'' he said, all the sharpness gone, leaving only concern. Oddly, that made her eyes burn with tears when his anger hadn't. She breathed through her mouth and fought to get her emotions under control.

"I don't know what the protocol is," Nick continued when she didn't speak. "The truth is, I haven't done much dating since...in the last few years. I just wanted you to know you didn't have to worry, at least not about that."

"Thank you." She drew a shallow breath. "You don't have to worry, either."

"I figured as much." He hesitated. Kate guessed what was coming, and her fingers ached from the pressure of her grip on the phone. "You could be pregnant."

"No." The denial was flat. Inarguable. "You don't have to worry about that, either."

"Are you sure? You don't have to deal with it alone. I'll—"

"I don't have to deal with it at all," she interrupted. "It's not an issue."

"Are you taking—"

"You don't have to worry about it," she said sharply. "Is that all you had to say?"

"I... That's all I called for," he said slowly. "Kate—"

"Goodbye." She hung the phone up and sat staring at it, wondering if he'd call back. But the phone

remained silent. After awhile, she slid down until she
lay curled up on the sofa, her arms wrapped around
her stomach, her forehead resting on her knees.

Chapter Eleven

"**S**houldn't you be home primping for your date tonight?" Brenda stopped a few feet from where Kate was unloading sacks of manure from a truck and stacking them in neat piles next to the purple barn.

"I've got time." Kate hefted another sack to the top of the pile.

"Shouldn't somebody be helping you with that?" Brenda asked, frowning.

"Are you offering?" Kate threw her friend a dry look of inquiry as she reached for the next sack on the truck.

"Ordinarily, I'd like nothing better," Brenda said mendaciously. "But I'm not really dressed for it." She gestured to her trim white slacks and light blue silk blouse. "But I'll go get one of the boys for you."

"Exercise is good for you."

"I've heard that rumor, but I think it's a filthy lie. Shall I get Jerry or Larry?"

"It's John and Don," Kate said, grinning. "And you don't need to call them because I'm almost done."

"Well, I knew they rhymed," Brenda said, shrugging. She narrowed her eyes against the sun. "It's kind of warm out here. You're not going to get sunstroke, are you?"

"Worried about workman's comp?"

"No, I just don't want to have to explain to Gareth how his fiancée came to collapse on the job."

"I'm not going to get sunstroke," Kate assured her.

Every time Brenda mentioned Gareth's name, her conscience pinched viciously. She'd managed to avoid him almost completely for the past two weeks, since that disastrous night with Nick. She'd seen him at church and they'd had one hurried lunch together, but she hadn't spent any real time alone with him.

Sitting beside him in church had been agony. If a lightning bolt had come through the roof and struck her down, it would have seemed no more than she deserved. As she struggled to pay attention to Philip Blackthorne's gentle sermon, she vowed to tell Gareth the truth. He deserved that much from her. If he broke off their engagement... Well, she could hardly expect him to do anything else.

She thought later that she would have told Gareth the truth if he hadn't had to leave right after the service. She hadn't seen him or talked to him for two days, which had given her forty-eight long hours to wonder if telling him was the right thing to do.

Did it serve any purpose to tell him something so hurtful? What if she just kept the truth to herself and did her best to make up to him for the terrible wrong she'd done?

Or was she trying to justify making the easy choice?

The questions spun round and round in her head until she felt dizzy. In the end, she didn't really make a decision so much as she simply took the path of least resistance.

"Are you doing something special tonight?" Brenda asked, breaking into Kate's thoughts.

"Tonight?" Kate tossed the last of the bags of manure on the stack and turned to look at her blankly.

"You and Gareth," Brenda prompted. "Are you doing anything special?"

"I don't know. Dinner or a movie, I guess." She pulled off her leather gloves as she spoke. "It's what we usually do."

Brenda arched her brows. "You sound less than enthused."

"No, I really enjoy our evenings." Kate smiled and hoped the expression reached her eyes. "Some people might get tired of doing the same old thing, but I kind of like it.''

"Gareth *is* a little predictable," Brenda said with rueful affection. "I guess you'd better get used to it, if you're going to marry him."

"Of course I'm going to marry him," Kate said. Brenda's startled look made her realize that she'd spoken too sharply. Guilty conscience at work, she thought, and forced a quick laugh. "I guess that wasn't really a question, was it? Sorry. I'm a little tired. My brain seems to be running in neutral lately."

"You have seemed a little distracted the last couple of weeks." Brenda looked concerned. "Is everything okay?"

For a moment, Kate was tempted to pour out the whole miserable story. She wanted desperately to talk to someone about what had happened. In the back of her mind was the vague idea that maybe, in talking about it, she'd be able to figure out how she'd come to abandon every principle, every moral, every shred of sanity and find herself in bed with her fiancée's brother. Not even in bed, she remembered. They hadn't even made it that far.

"Everything's fine," she lied. Best friend or no, she couldn't tell Brenda about that night with Nick.

"Well, it's not going to stay fine if you don't get home and change," Brenda said, wrinkling her nose as Kate came closer. "You smell a little...earthy."

"Eau de manure?" Kate suggested. "Maybe I can make it all the rage."

"I wouldn't be surprised. If people will embrace navel piercing, they can probably be convinced that smelling like a cow pie is a good thing."

"Maybe we could become filthy rich."

"At least you've already got the filthy part down."

For the first time in two weeks, Kate laughed. The sound made her feel a little better. If she could laugh, maybe there was hope that life, as she knew it, wasn't completely at an end.

"This has been great." Gareth's arm rested lightly around Kate's waist as they walked toward her apartment. "It seems like ages since we spent any time together."

"It has been awhile." She could feel the sharp ridges of her keys digging into her palm and made a conscious effort to loosen her grip. "We've both been pretty busy. You're doing all this volunteer work."

"And you're spending all your spare time at Spider's Walk," he finished.

"Hmm." She made a noncommittal noise in the back of her throat. The truth was, for the past two weeks, she'd spent as little time as she could at the big old house. She'd hired some high school students and showed up in the morning to make sure they knew what needed to be done. Then she'd run from the property. Every second she was there, she was afraid she might turn around and see Nick.

"Nick says Harry is pleased with the work you're doing," Gareth said as they reached her door.

"When did you talk to Nick?" The question came out more sharply than she'd intended.

"A couple of weeks ago," Gareth said, looking mildly surprised.

A couple of weeks ago? Kate felt her mouth go dry. Of course, he'd talked to Nick since that night. Obviously Nick hadn't said anything to him about what had happened. He had no more reason to want the truth to come out than she did. Shaky with relief, she gave Gareth a thin smile.

"I haven't seen much of him lately."

They'd reached her door and Kate slid the key in the lock before turning to face him. "I had a wonderful time tonight."

"So did I." He reached up to brush a strand of hair from her cheek. His hand lingered, his fingers brushing over the curve of her cheek. "I've missed you, Kate."

The look in his eyes made her stomach jump with nerves. Obviously, he thought they were going to be spending the night together—a perfectly natural assumption. He wouldn't insist, of course. She could say that she was tired or that it was a bad time of the month. Gareth was too much of a gentleman to question either excuse. He'd kiss her good-night and leave. For a moment, she was tempted to do just that, but she couldn't put off this moment forever.

She had two choices. She could tell Gareth that she'd been unfaithful and pray he could forgive her, or she could go on as if nothing had happened. And this was the moment in which she had to decide which path to take.

Kate drew a shaky breath and smiled at him. "You're not on duty tonight, are you?"

"Not tonight." His dark eyes smiled even before his mouth curved. "Do you have any plants you need to put to bed?"

"Not tonight." She repeated his response and turned to unlock the door, hoping he wouldn't notice that her hand was shaking.

"What do you want to listen to?" Gareth asked over his shoulder. He was crouched in front of Kate's music system, head tilted as he looked at the row of CDs next to it.

"You choose," Kate said. She set her wineglass on a side table and linked her fingers together in her lap. In the past, she'd appreciated the fact that Gareth didn't head straight for the bedroom as soon as they were alone. When they spent the night together, there was less a sense of urgency than a feeling of comfortable anticipation. They both knew where the evening was going to end, but there was no rush to get there.

Tonight, she wanted to scream at him to get on with it. Not perhaps the best attitude when it came to sex, she thought with a flash of black humor.

"Your taste in music is about thirty years older than you are." Gareth stood up as the mellow tones of Frank Sinatra singing "Only the Lonely" came from the speakers.

"There is no age limit on Sinatra," Kate said automatically. It was an old discussion. He'd been teasing her about her fuddy-duddy taste in music ever since they'd started dating.

"There may not be an age limit on Sinatra, but you're the only person I know under the age of sixty who actually owns an album by the Mills Brothers."

"I like the Mills Brothers."

"So did my grandmother." The sofa cushion dipped as he sat beside her. "You really should update your taste. I'll start you out easy. We'll go for something that came out after the mid-sixties and work our way forward from there. By the time we're married, you might even be ready for something contemporary."

He reached for his wine but Kate caught his hand in hers, stopping him. Startled, he looked at her as she lifted his hand to her mouth and pressed a kiss in the palm.

"You're not really thirsty, are you?" she asked softly.

It took him a moment to adjust his thinking. Kate

was a responsive lover, but she had never been the one to instigate their lovemaking. She'd always seemed content to let him make the first move. This sudden aggression, mild as it was, surprised him. He curved his fingers around hers, feeling desire stir in the pit of his stomach.

"Not particularly," he said, answering her question. He lifted his free hand to her hair, sliding his fingers into the tawny thickness of it. It felt like silk against his skin and he knew that, when he leaned closer, he'd be able to smell the soft floral scent of her shampoo. He curled his fingers around her nape and drew her forward. She bent toward him pliantly but he hesitated, his eyes searching her face. There was something there. Something he sensed rather than saw.

"What is it?" he asked softly.

Kate closed her eyes against the concern in his. She didn't want him to be kind. She wanted him to take her in his arms and make her forget everything but him. She wanted him to sweep her away with passion so that she could only think of this moment, this man.

"I've missed you," she said and leaned forward to touch her mouth to his.

He seemed to hesitate, as if puzzling over her response. Afraid to let him think, Kate took the hand she still held and set it against the soft swell of her breast. He froze for an instant, his fingers stiff, and she thought she'd only made things worse. But then he groaned softly against her mouth. His hand shifted, molding her breast, and Kate knew that, whatever questions he might have, they were forgotten for the moment.

Gratefully, she opened her mouth to his, leaning into his embrace. But instead of the usual warmth she felt when he held her, she felt an odd restlessness, a sense that something was missing. It hadn't been like this with *him*. There hadn't been anything comfortable about *his* kisses. It had been hot and wild and out of control.

Remembered hunger had her shifting restlessly, pressing closer to Gareth. But his touch didn't make her skin burn and his mouth didn't seem to devour her very soul. Panic fluttered in the pit of her stomach. It wasn't fair, she thought despairingly. He was everything she wanted, the kind of man any woman would be grateful to have.

Kate heard his surprised murmur when her fingers began sliding the buttons on his shirt loose. She could make it right again, she thought fiercely. If she tried, she could forget all about *him,* she told herself as she leaned back on the sofa, pulling him down with her. She could make this enough.

Gareth's pager beeped, a shrill demand for attention.

"Dammit!" He jerked up, fumbling at his belt. He

glared at the number displayed. "I'm not on duty tonight."

"It must be urgent," Kate said, struggling to keep the relief from her voice.

"It had better be," he said grimly. He turned and reached for the phone next to the sofa.

Kate took the opportunity to sit up and straighten her clothing. Guiltily, she hoped he'd have to leave. She was shaken by her lack of desire, shaken by the way thoughts of Nick had intruded. This wasn't the way it was supposed to be, she thought. She needed more time, that's all. She wasn't ready for this. She refused to consider the possibility that she might never be ready.

"I've got to go," Gareth said as he hung up the phone.

"What's wrong?" she asked, her relief wavering when she saw his grim expression.

"Nick's been in an accident."

"Nick?" Kate heard her voice, sounding high and thin. "Is he all right?"

"I don't know. But they said he was conscious and arguing with the paramedics. That sounds positive."

"Where is he?"

"At the hospital. They took him to the emergency room." Gareth reached up to peel her fingers from his arm. "You're cutting off the blood supply to my hand," he said, giving her a curious look.

Kate hadn't been aware that she'd grabbed him.

"Sorry." She let her hand drop into her lap, knowing she'd overreacted. As far as Gareth knew, she barely knew his brother. Struggling to keep the appropriate level of concern in her voice, she asked, "Was he…wearing his helmet?"

"God, I hope so." Gareth stood up. "I'll call and let you know how he is."

"I'm going with you," Kate said without thinking. She caught his surprised look but he didn't argue, for which she was grateful, because her powers of invention had run out. She couldn't even come up with a good explanation for herself as to why she so desperately needed to know that Nick was all right. It was certainly beyond her to explain it to him.

Chapter Twelve

There were half a dozen people in the waiting room. A tired-looking woman rocked a fussy toddler, and a middle-aged man stared stoically at the wall, one hand wrapped in a bloodstained rag. Two frightened teenagers had their heads together, talking in low tones. The boy had his arm around the girl, who looked as if she might start crying at any moment. The last occupant was a sweet-faced, elderly woman who sat in a corner, knitting an unidentifiable garment in chocolate-colored yarn. The color made Kate think of Nick's eyes.

"Hey, Gareth." The nurse at the desk smiled when she saw them approaching. "I suppose you're here to spring Nick loose."

"Is he springable?" Gareth asked.

"Should be in a few minutes. The doctor wanted

to keep him overnight in case he has a concussion, but Nick said they'd have to strap him to the bed.''

''Sounds like he's in pretty good shape,'' Gareth said, his relief obvious.

''Not too bad. You can go on back and see for yourself.'' She nodded over her shoulder. ''He's in the third cubicle.''

''Did anyone call my parents?''

''I don't know.'' The phone on the desk rang and she excused herself to answer it.

''I should call my parents and let them know what's happened before they get a garbled report from somebody else,'' Gareth said to Kate. ''Why don't you go on back and I'll be there in a second.''

He turned away without giving her a chance to argue. Not that she *could* have argued, Kate thought, watching him walk toward a bank of pay phones. After insisting on coming to the hospital to see how Nick was, she could hardly announce that she didn't want to actually *see* him.

Reluctantly, she walked past the desk. The curtains were drawn around the cubicle the nurse had indicated. She hesitated a moment before drawing a deep breath and stepping through them. He was Gareth's brother, she reminded herself. That was the only reason she was here.

As soon as she saw Nick, she knew she lied. He was sitting on the edge of the bed, half turned away from her, bare to the waist. Angry-looking friction burns ran down one shoulder, as if he'd slid across the pavement. His left arm was in a sling and the left leg of his jeans was split open to just past the knee, revealing the stark white of a bandage wrapped around his calf.

Though she hadn't made a sound, he must have sensed her presence because he turned abruptly. She saw his eyes widen in surprise and dropped her gaze. But that wasn't such a good idea, she decided, when she found herself staring at the mat of dark curls that covered his chest before tapering into a narrow line that sliced across the taut muscles of his stomach and disappeared into the waistband of his jeans—his unbuttoned jeans, she noticed before jerking her gaze upward.

Their eyes met and she felt her mouth go dry at the look in his. The hunger was blatant and painfully familiar. Her stomach clenched with it, her skin tingled with it. She stared at him helplessly for a moment and then forced herself to look away, aware that her eyes had already revealed far too much.

"Kate."

Before Nick could say anything else, the curtain rattled to announce Gareth's arrival.

"They tell me you're going to live," he said, by way of greeting.

"So they said." Nick's answer was slow. He dragged his eyes from Kate's profile and looked at his brother. The concern behind Gareth's smile grated on his conscience like fingernails on a chalkboard. "They shouldn't have called you. It was a minor accident."

"According to the officer on the scene, you were damned lucky. He says your bike looks like a pretzel."

"I saw it before the damned paramedics stuffed me in an ambulance." Nick slid off the bed, wincing as he put weight on his injured leg.

"What happened?" Gareth asked.

"Are you asking as my brother or as a police officer?" Nick asked dryly.

"Both. There wasn't another vehicle on the scene."

"It left the scene," Nick said. He looked around until he saw his shirt thrown over the back of a chair.

"A hit-and-run?" Gareth asked sharply.

"You could say that." Nick limped to the chair and pulled his shirt free, grimacing at its tattered condition. He glanced at Gareth and started to shrug but changed his mind at the warning twinges of pain. "I swerved to avoid a dog," he admitted. "Damn near killed myself, and the ungrateful beast ran off without even saying thanks."

"I'll put out an APB," Gareth promised, grinning. He came forward and took the shirt from Nick. He started to help him into it but the garment was little better than a rag. What the pavement hadn't demolished, the doctors had. He dropped it on the chair. "Mom and Dad are on their way over."

"Oh, hell." Disgusted, Nick limped to the bed and leaned against it, resting his aching leg. "Is the whole damned town going to show up? Who the hell called them?"

"I did," Gareth said calmly, ignoring his brother's glare. "I thought it would be better if they heard the truth from me, rather than get some garbled report through the grapevine. You know there are no secrets in a small town."

Nick's eyes cut past him to Kate, who was staring at a poster advocating the importance of childhood vaccinations as if her life depended on memorizing every word on it.

"I suppose you're right," he said slowly.

Before Gareth could say anything more, his beeper went off.

"Damn this thing!" he exclaimed, snatching it off his belt. "I'm *supposed* to be off duty. If this isn't a riot alert, I'm going to have somebody's badge."

He pushed through the curtains and Kate was suddenly alone with Nick. Not a good thing, she thought. She cleared her throat. "I'll go watch for your parents," she said without looking at him.

"My mother has worked out of this hospital for almost thirty years. I think she can find her way around."

"But she won't know where you are."

"Afraid to be alone with me?"

Though she hadn't heard him move, his voice came from directly behind her. Against her better judgment, Kate turned, sucking in a quick, startled breath when she saw how close he was. The muscular width of his chest filled her vision. When she breathed in, she could smell him—a combination of sweat, blood and antiseptic.

Though she knew it was a mistake, she couldn't stop herself from looking up. There was an angry red scrape across the top of his left cheekbone, and his hair fell in a thick, tangled black wave onto his forehead. He looked battered, tired and fiercely masculine.

Reluctantly, she met his eyes and felt her heart thud painfully hard against her breastbone at the hunger he didn't even try to hide. Deep inside, an answering hunger stirred. It pooled, hot and urgent, in the pit of her stomach. If she leaned forward just a little—

She caught herself, appalled by how quickly she'd forgotten all her promises to herself. What was it about him that he could so easily make her forget right and wrong and think only of how it felt when he touched her? Breathing quickly, as if with exertion, she took a quick step back and then gasped when Nick's hand shot out and closed around her upper arm.

"You can't keep pretending there's nothing between us, Kate."

"Yes, I can. I mean, there isn't anything between us," she corrected hastily. "It was a mistake."

"All of it?" He seemed to loom over her. Kate felt breathless, as if there was too little oxygen. "It's not just what happened two weeks ago, Kate. What about the kiss in the gazebo? And five years ago? Are you just going to pretend that none of that happened?"

"Y-yes." She lifted her hands to push him away but let them fall before they came into contact with his bare chest. She was afraid to put her hands on him, she admitted to herself.

"You're going to marry my brother, knowing what's between us?" Anger simmered in the question, and when she looked into his eyes, she saw it reflected there. He held her arm with bruising force but she barely registered the pain. She felt overwhelmed by him, pulled by the force of his will. For a moment, she nearly gave in to his demand, nearly admitted...

Admitted what? the small voice of sanity demanded. That she wanted him? So what? Hunger was a fleeting, ephemeral thing. And when it was gone, it left nothing but emptiness behind. She'd seen it often enough as a child. Her father's hunger had been for new places, new opportunities, and he'd spent his whole life following that hunger, dragging his family all over the country in search of some mythical dream. She wasn't going to be like that. What she had with Gareth was good and lasting. She wasn't giving it up to satisfy a few fleeting moments of desire.

She ruthlessly squashed the voice of doubt.

"There isn't anything between us," she said. The words weren't as certain as she would have liked but they were enough to make Nick's eyes flash with rage.

"You're lying." He leaned toward her, his face tight and hard. "You stick in your safe little world, Kate. I won't do anything to damage it. But you might ask yourself one thing. You might ask yourself if my brother doesn't deserve something more than what you're giving him."

"I...I love Gareth," she said waveringly.

"You've got a hell of a way of showing it." He released his grip on her arm and took a step back, as if he no longer wanted to touch her. "Give us five minutes alone and I could have you flat on your back with your skirt around your ears and your legs around my waist."

The contempt in his voice stung her to the core. It hurt all the worse because there was an element of truth in his words. She didn't seem to have much resistance when it came to him.

"You're crude," she said. It was hardly a searing

insult, but she was too shaken to come up with anything better.

"But I'm honest. That's more than you can say."

Before she could think of a response, the curtain scraped open behind her, rings rattling against the metal rod. The sound was as startling—and effective—as a trumpet blast. Kate turned, pinning a false smile on her face when she saw Philip and Sara Blackthorne.

"Oh, good, you found him. I'll go find Gareth and let him know you're here," she said and brushed past them and out of the cubicle without waiting for a response.

Nick watched her go. He wanted to go after her, wanted to apologize for being so harsh. And then he thought of her determination to marry his brother and he wanted to grab her and shake her until her teeth rattled. It was probably just as well that neither was possible, he thought, and made an effort to drag his attention to his parents.

"You don't look too bad," Sara said, her eyes cataloguing his injuries with a professional's skill and a mother's concern.

"I'm fine," Nick assured her. "There was no reason for Gareth to drag the two of you down here in the middle of the night."

"We much prefer getting the news from your brother than getting some garbled version later on," Sara told him.

"That's what he thought."

"Well, he was absolutely right." She picked up his chart and skimmed it. "You were very lucky."

"The dog I missed was even luckier," he said dryly. He stirred restlessly. "Can you do anything to break me out of this place?"

"I'll see what I can do," she promised. She reached up to touch his cheek lightly, her expression both stern and loving. "Don't do this again." She left the cubicle with his chart.

Nick looked at his father. "I didn't want to tell her but I'm going to make a break for it pretty soon, whether she gets permission or not."

"I suspect she knows as much." Philip's dark eyes were worried as he looked at his youngest son. "Is everything all right?"

"You mean other than assorted scrapes and bruises and the fact that my bike is totaled?" Nick asked with a half smile. "Other than that, everything's fine."

"I was thinking of less tangible things," Philip said. "Kate seemed upset when she left."

Nick's smile faded abruptly and he turned away. His father had always had an uncanny knack for picking up on the one thing you least wanted to discuss. It was like he had an internal magnet that led him unerringly to your guiltiest secrets—or so it had seemed when he was a boy.

"Did she?" he asked without looking at Philip.

"It seemed that way." Philip hesitated. Nothing in his son's stance invited him to continue the conversation, but he couldn't bring himself to simply let it drop. "You know, if you ever need to talk, I'm always here for you, Nick."

"Forgive me, Father, for I have sinned?" Nick asked, turning to give his father a humorless smile.

"Wrong church." Philip's worry deepened. "I just want you to know I'm here if you need me."

"Thanks, but there's nothing to worry about. Whatever Kate was upset about, it had nothing to do with me." Nick limped to the chair and picked up his ruined shirt again.

"You know, if you don't want to talk to me, there are other—"

"If you're going to suggest I have a chat with God, forget it." Nick hooked his fingers in the torn fabric and ripped the left sleeve completely off, the sound harsh and grating. "I've tried that."

"Actually, I was going to suggest your mother," Philip said mildly. "But, now that you mention it, it never hurts to go to a higher source."

"No, thanks—to both of them." Nick eased his arm out of the sling, gritting his teeth against the pain as he slid his hand through the ragged edge where the sleeve had been.

"I didn't realize you still carried such anger." Philip resisted the urge to help Nick with the shirt, knowing his assistance wouldn't be appreciated. "There are reasons—"

"No!" Nick left the shirt dangling from one shoulder and turned to face him, his eyes hard. "Don't give me that crap about reasons. There was no reason for Brian to die. Or Lisa. And there sure as hell can't be a reason for a two-month-old baby to die. You explain that to me and maybe I'll find a reason to talk to God again." He jerked the other side of the shirt around and shoved his uninjured arm through the sleeve, ignoring the sharp twinges of protest from his battered body.

"I can't give you an explanation," Philip admitted in a troubled voice. "I can only tell you that I believe, with all my heart, that there is a greater purpose."

Nick forced himself to draw a deep, calming breath. Maybe it was finding himself in a hospital that had his temper stretched thin. The smells of antiseptic and pain brought back too many memories. Or maybe it was the scene with Kate. *That* certainly hadn't done anything to help. But whatever it was, it wasn't fair to take it out on his father.

"I respect your faith, Dad," he said slowly. "But I can't share it. Not anymore."

Fumbling, he fastened a few of the buttons on his shirt. The cubicle suddenly felt small and constricting, as if the curtains had become solid walls that were closing in on him.

"I've got to get out of here," he muttered. He brushed past his father and dragged open the curtain. His mother was on her way in, and she gave him a disapproving look.

"You really should stay overnight," she said.

"Not another minute." He summoned a lopsided smile. "I'm going to blow this joint, with or without your permission."

"In that case, you can come home with your father and me."

He opened his mouth to refuse and then closed it again as he realized that that was exactly what he wanted to do. "Okay."

"You sure you didn't hit your head?" Gareth asked, coming up behind Sara. "I thought for sure you were going to argue."

"And give up a chance to con Dilly out of one of her world-famous breakfasts?" Nick asked lightly. "How dumb do you think I am?"

"I'd better not answer that," Gareth said with a grin.

"Safe bet." Nick looked at Kate, who was standing next to Gareth. Their eyes met for a moment and then she looked away. He ruthlessly quashed a twinge of pain when she slid her hand into Gareth's. That pretty much said it all, he thought. It was ridiculous to feel a sense of loss, because she'd never really been his to start with.

He threw his arm around Sara's shoulders. "Let's go home."

Chapter Thirteen

The graveyard was cool and quiet. Ancient syca-mores cast soft shadows among the gravestones, fil-tering the summer sun and creating a dim oasis from the heat.

Nick walked between the graves, letting his fingers trail along the edges of marble and granite markers. When he was a boy, he and his twin had spent a lot of time here, reading the names and dates on the gravestones, speculating about the lives they marked. It had been at least twenty-five years since he and Brian had sat cross-legged in the grass and spun tales about the people laid to rest here, but many of the names rang bells. It felt a little like meeting old friends after a very long time apart.

He made his way to a single marker set under the outer branches of an ancient oak. It had been five years since he'd been here, but the image had remained clear in his mind. He knew this place as well as if he'd visited it daily. Sun and rain had weathered the stone slightly, giving it a gently settled look. But nothing could soften the short span of years after the first name and the heartbreakingly few number of weeks shown after the second.

It had been almost three weeks since the accident and he was still favoring his injured leg. And his movements were a little stiff as he crouched beside the grave and reached out to brush his fingertips over the cool stone, gently tracing his son's name. For a moment, the pain of loss was a sharp, hard ache in his chest. What kind of a little boy would Kyle have been if he were still alive—rough and tumble or quiet and thoughtful? Would he have hated Brussels sprouts and tried to sneak an extra cookie whenever he could?

"I wondered if you'd come here today."

At the sound of Harry's voice, Nick pulled his hand back and stood up, blinking rapidly. He cleared his throat before speaking, but his voice was still husky.

"It's Lisa's birthday. I haven't forgotten."

"No, I didn't think you would have." Harry came forward and bent to lay a colorful bouquet of mixed flowers at the base of the stone. His movements were stiff with age. "I knew you wouldn't have forgotten. I just didn't know if you'd forgiven."

"There was never anything to forgive," Nick said. He shoved his hands into the pockets of his jeans and hunched his shoulders as if against a chill. "Lisa loved Kyle. She would have given her life to protect him. In a way, that's what she did. She was trying to keep him safe. I can't hate her for that."

A little way off, a mockingbird sang its heart out, running up and down the scales in a way that would have made an opera diva pale with envy. Much farther off, he could hear a dog barking. Both sounds seemed to deepen the silence around them.

"It took me years to forgive her," Harry said suddenly. He kept his eyes on the grave. "I used to come here a couple of times a month, not to grieve but because I was so angry. I just couldn't understand how she could take her own life, let alone her son's. I don't know, I think I was almost coming here to demand answers."

"Did you get any?"

"No." Harry sighed and lifted his head, looking across the rows of markers. "But after a while, I guess I found a kind of acceptance. Not so much of what she'd done but of *why* she'd done it. I knew she'd never have done anything to deliberately hurt anyone, least of all her own son. To do what she did, she must have been very confused."

"Something happened to her after Kyle was born," Nick said. "She was suddenly afraid of everything. She couldn't bear to read the paper or watch the news because she equated every terrible thing she saw with the same thing happening to Kyle. It wasn't just a murder in Los Angeles. It was killers coming after the baby. If there was an earthquake, no matter how small, she was afraid it was a foreshock of the Big One. She was afraid to leave the house for fear something would happen to Kyle. I tried to talk her into seeing a doctor, but the idea upset her so much that I didn't push it. I thought she'd get over it, that she was just a little more anxious than most new mothers."

"You had no way of knowing what was in her head," Harry said, responding to the guilt Nick hadn't quite expressed. He looked at the grave again. "She was always so fragile. I used to wonder if it was because she lost her parents when she was so little or if it was something I'd done to her. She was all I had, and I know I spoiled her."

"If there's one thing I think I'm finally getting through my thick skull, it's that playing 'what if' is a waste of time." Nick pulled one hand out of his pocket and brushed a leaf off the top of the marker, his eyes following it as it fell to the ground. "Some people just aren't tough enough to survive for long in this world. Lisa was one of them."

They stood without speaking for a few minutes, letting the quiet warmth of the afternoon drift around them. It was a good place to sleep, Nick thought. He felt peace slip through him, a kind of acceptance.

There would never be a time when he didn't mourn what he'd lost, but it was time to let go, time to move on. He touched the top of the stone again and said goodbye one last time before turning and limping away.

Harry fell into step with him but neither spoke until they reached the edge of the cemetery. Harry's car was parked next to Nick's new Harley. He opened the driver's door and then set his arm along the top of the window, scowling at the big motorcycle. "I can't believe you bought another one of those death-traps."

"That dog would have run out in front of me if I'd been in a car," Nick said mildly. He'd already survived a thorough scolding from Dilly on his choice of transportation.

"That may be, but if you'd been in a car, you wouldn't have ended up skidding across the road on your face," Harry said tartly.

"Can't argue with that one," Nick admitted. The truth was, he'd bought another motorcycle as a reminder that his time here was strictly limited. A few weeks ago, he'd been thinking about trading the Harley in for a truck, but that was when he'd thought he might be staying in Eden. Before he'd realized how impossible that was.

Harry leaned his arm along the top of the open car door and looked at Nick, his eyes questioning.

"You've been putting in a lot of hours on the

house the last few weeks. The lights are on into the wee hours every night.''

''I figured you'd want to put the place on the market as soon as possible so you could get into that new condo and start playing golf,'' Nick said with bland sarcasm.

Harry shifted uncomfortably, his white brows coming together over his nose. ''I'm in no hurry.''

''Why am I not surprised to hear that?'' Nick murmured.

Harry glared at him. ''Whether I sell or not, there's no reason for you to work yourself to death to put the place in shape. It's been falling apart for years. A few weeks here or there aren't going to make any difference.''

''There's no reason to drag the job out.''

Harry was silent a moment. ''You're leaving when it's done, aren't you?''

''This will always be home, but I don't think it's my home anymore,'' Nick said, answering the question obliquely.

''Will you go back to New York?''

''I haven't decided anything yet.'' Even as he said it, Nick knew it wasn't entirely true. He'd decided to leave Eden. He just didn't know exactly when or exactly where he'd be going.

''Does this have anything to do with Kate Moran?'' Harry asked shrewdly.

The question caught him off guard and Nick's fingers clenched over the keys he held. But his voice was easy when he answered.

"The memoirs must be pretty dull going if you've got time to let your imagination run wild like that, Harry."

"That's no answer." The old man had spent too much time in court to be easily diverted. "You can tell me to mind my own damned business—"

"Mind your own damned business," Nick said pleasantly.

"—but I've noticed she hasn't been around as much lately," Harry continued, ignoring the interruption. "She's doing the job I hired her to do but she skulks around the shrubbery, darting in and out as if there's goblins lurking in the underbrush."

"Considering the underbrush around that place, maybe she's got good reason to be nervous."

"And that's no answer, either," Harry snapped. "If something's happened between the two of you—" He caught the sharp look of warning in Nick's eyes and threw up one hand in quick defense. "Fine. It's none of my business."

"You're slow but you do get there."

"I just don't want to see either of you get hurt," Harry muttered, unable to let the subject drop.

"I think you said that once before." *Not that the warning had done much good.*

"Was I wrong to drag you back here?" Harry

asked, sounding uncharacteristically uncertain. "Are you sorry you came back?"

"No." Nick was surprised to realize that he meant it. He'd needed to come home before he could let go of the past. It was just a pity he couldn't have managed to do that without screwing up the present so thoroughly, but that was another problem. "No, I'm not sorry."

Harry looked relieved. He cleared his throat as if to speak, but Nick didn't want to talk anymore. He tossed his keys in the air and caught them as they fell. "I'm heading back."

He barely waited for Harry's nod before walking away. He pulled on his helmet as he settled onto the Harley's wide seat. Make that the *second* to last thing he wanted to do, he amended as he slid the key into the ignition and gave it a viciously hard twist. The *last* thing he wanted to do was spend the afternoon watching Gareth and Kate together.

He'd barely set eyes on her in the past few weeks. Harry's description of her visits to Spider's Walk had been pretty accurate. When she'd first taken on the task of restoring the grounds, she'd lingered over every small task, savoring her time there. Now, she spent as little time as possible there. Most of the work was being done by a couple of young men who apparently worked for the nursery part-time. Kate's role was largely supervisory.

Not that it was any business of his what she did,

he reminded himself. She'd made it clear that she wanted nothing to do with him. All he wanted was to finish the job at Spider's Walk and leave town the same way he'd come—alone.

"It looks like Nick is already here," Gareth said as he pulled up in front of his parents' house.

Kate felt her stomach roll when she looked at the big bike. It was ridiculous to feel such a sense of shock. The family was gathering to celebrate Gareth's birthday, and she would have expected Nick to be here.

"I can't believe he bought another motorcycle after what happened with the last one," Brenda said from the backseat. "I would have expected him to get something a little more substantial."

"Trust Nick to do exactly the opposite of what you expect." Gareth's exasperation was mixed with a tinge of admiration. He parked behind the bike and shut the engine off.

"Well, I think he's crazy and I'm going to tell him as much," Brenda said as she pushed open her door and got out.

"Not that it will do any good," Gareth murmured to Kate. He looked at her and let his hand drop away from the door handle, his smile fading. "Are you feeling okay?"

"I'm fine." She gave him a quick smile and then

looked down, as if unlatching her seat belt took concentration.

"You sure? You've been pretty quiet and you look a little pale."

"Just what every woman wants to hear—that she looks like hell," she said lightly. The seat belt came loose with a quiet snick and she reached for the door handle, anxious to put some distance between her guilty conscience and the concern in Gareth's eyes.

"I didn't say you looked like hell." He reached out to touch her cheek with gentle fingers. "I said you were pale."

"There's a difference?" she asked, arching her brows. *Why did he have to be so damned nice? It made everything so much worse.* She forced a smile. "I'm fine. Really." He didn't look convinced, and she reached for the easiest excuse. "If I'm pale, it's probably just the lingering effects of the flu."

It wasn't the first time she'd used that particular excuse lately, but this time it had the opposite effect of what she'd intended. Rather than looking reassured, his frown deepened. "This has been hanging around for weeks now. You really should see a doctor."

"I don't need a doctor," she said too quickly, panic catching at her throat. Seeing his startled look, she grabbed for her thinning self-control. God knew, none of this was his fault. She caught his hand in hers and gave it an apologetic squeeze. "I'm fine. Really. Now, stop worrying about me."

She turned and pushed open her door without giving him a chance to say anything else. One more concerned word and she was going to burst into tears and sob out all her worries on his chest—not exactly the best place to go for sympathy with her particular problem.

"I can smell the barbecue from here," Brenda said as Kate got out of the car. She drew a deep breath and released it on a sigh of pleasure. "Mrs. Pickle is the best cook in town—maybe even the best cook on the planet. When I was a kid, I used to follow Brian and Nick home like a lost puppy just so I could get my hands on some of Mrs. Pickle's cookies. Too bad they went straight from hand to thigh," she added ruefully, smoothing one hand over her full hip. "It's a crime that everything that tastes good is bad for the figure."

"There's not a thing wrong with your figure," Gareth said as he joined them. He slid his arm around Brenda's waist and waggled his eyebrows in a dreadful imitation of a pirate's leer. "A tidy armful of femininity."

Brenda laughed, her cheeks warming as she slipped away from Gareth's hold. "Careful. Flattery like that might turn a girl's head."

"And such a pretty head it is, too," he said, grinning at her. For a moment, there was something almost wistful in Brenda's eyes, but it was gone so quickly that Kate thought she'd imagined it.

"Having a birthday seems to have put you in a good mood," Brenda said as the three of them stepped onto the wide front porch. "I thought, after thirty, they were supposed to depress you."

"Not when you've got life going just the way you want it," he said, glancing at Kate. As she returned his smile, she sent up a fervent wish that the ground would simply open up and swallow her whole.

But that mercy was denied her, and she followed Brenda into the cool dimness of the big house. Finding the rest of the family was simply a matter of following the smells through the house and onto the shady patio that extended from the back of the house. Though summer had definitely arrived and the temperature was hovering around ninety, the backyard was shady and cool. A waterfall splashed over lava rock in one corner of the patio, the gentle murmur of the water providing a soothing backdrop.

"We were starting to think we were going to have to eat without you," Philip said, coming forward to greet them.

"You mean you were *hoping,*" Gareth said, returning his father's hug. "More of Dilly's potato salad for you, right?"

"The thought never crossed my mind," Philip protested, his dark eyes twinkling with laughter.

"Don't you believe him," Sara said. "She already had to chase him out of the kitchen twice to keep him from eating everything in sight."

"I simply offered my services as a taster," Philip said with injured dignity.

"With you as a taster, we'd all end up eating at Jack-in-the-Box," Gareth said. He smile widened as he glanced past his father and saw Nick tending the brick barbecue. "Put you to work, did they?"

"It was self-defense," Nick said. "I remember Dad's barbecue skills and I wasn't in the mood for charred ribs."

"Whatever happened to parental respect?" Philip asked plaintively.

"It takes a backseat to Dilly's ribs," Nick said as he brushed barbecue sauce on a rack of sizzling meat. He glanced up to smile at Brenda. "Followed Gareth home this time, did you?"

"I was invited," she informed him with careful dignity. Then she grinned. "But if I hadn't been, I would have hidden in the trunk for a chance at those ribs. I was just telling Kate that Mrs. Pickle is one of the great heroines of my childhood."

Nick looked at Kate and the smile faded from his eyes, though not from his mouth. "Kate."

"Nick." She nodded and aimed a vague smile in

his direction, then turned casually away. Just a few hours, she told herself. She only had to hold it together for a few hours. And then she could lock herself in her apartment and collapse into screaming hysterics.

"I didn't think it was possible, but these ribs taste as good as they smell," Brenda said, closing her eyes in ecstasy as she chewed and swallowed. "Do you think I could talk Mrs. Pickle into giving me the recipe?"

"I imagine so," Sara said. She spooned some potato salad onto her plate before handing the bowl to Kate. "Annie's usually pretty generous with her recipes."

Kate tried not to inhale as she passed the potato salad on to Gareth. The rich scents of barbecue sauce and grilled vegetables already had her stomach sending up warning signals. She swallowed hard and reached for her glass. A few sips of sweet-tart 7-Up eased her discomfort enough that she risked taking a roll when the basket was passed to her.

She listened with half an ear to the comments on the food, the weather and the progress being made on the women's shelter that was Sara's pet project. It was exactly the way she'd always imagined a family get-together—the warmth and affection flowed as easily as the conversation. She'd dreamed of being a part of a family like this, and for a little while, she had been. It was ironic that, by her own actions, she'd put herself outside the circle she'd so desperately wanted to join.

She stole a glance at Nick, who was sitting on the opposite side of the table and down from her. He'd apparently finished eating because his plate was pushed a little back from the edge of the table. He had a half-empty bottle of beer in front of him and was turning it between his fingers, his attention apparently focused on the idle motion. He'd contributed little to the conversation, letting it ebb and flow around him for the most part. It occurred to her that he looked as much apart from the gathering as she felt.

As if sensing her gaze, he looked up suddenly, his eyes locking on hers. His expression was closed, unreadable. Kate thought suddenly of the way his eyes so often smiled even before his mouth moved. The memory of it made her feel very alone, and she looked away. She crumbled a piece of roll between her fingers and wondered what he might have read in her expression.

"You're not eating anything." Gareth's low comment dragged Kate's thoughts from Nick. "Are you okay?"

"I'm just not very hungry." He looked doubtful.

"My stomach's a little upset," she admitted reluctantly.

"This flu has been hanging around too long." He frowned, his eyes worried. "You really need to see a doctor."

"Did I hear someone take the name of my profession in vain?" Sara asked from across the table.

"No."

"Yes." Kate's denial was drowned out by Gareth's response, and Sara's brows went up.

"I'm fine," Kate said firmly. She gave him a warning glance, which he ignored.

"You're not fine." Exasperated, Gareth looked at his mother. "She's been battling some kind of flu bug for weeks now."

"It hasn't been that long." Kate set the half-eaten roll down and pushed her plate away.

"It's been at least a month," Gareth said stubbornly. "And your stomach is still bothering you."

"I'm fine," she said again. Though she didn't look at him, she was aware of Nick's sudden attention, and she put her hands in her lap to conceal their trembling.

"It does seem like this has been hanging around a long time," Brenda said, leaning around Gareth and giving her a concerned look. "You even went home early a couple of days ago. Maybe Gareth's right. Maybe you should see a doctor."

"I do not need to see a doctor." Kate strained for patience. "Now, could we please stop discussing my health?"

"Kate's right," Sara said briskly. "She's smart enough to know whether or not she needs a doctor."

"Thank you," Kate said gratefully.

"Don't thank me yet," Sara warned her with a smile. "Because I'm going to agree with my son to the extent that, if the symptoms hang around much longer, you really should let someone take a look at you."

"I will," Kate lied.

"It's already been hanging around too long," Gareth muttered stubbornly, but to Kate's relief, he let the subject drop.

After a moment, the conversation picked up again. Kate was grateful that she was no longer the center of attention, but her stomach continued to churn with nerves. She was vividly aware of Nick sitting silently across from her. As if compelled by a force outside herself, she looked up. Her heart jolted when she saw him watching her. Their eyes met and held. The indifference was gone, replaced by speculation and sharp question.

Frightened, she jerked her eyes away and stared at her plate, wondering if he'd been able to read the truth in her eyes.

* * *

Nick listened with half an ear to a discussion of the political scandal currently rocking the White House. Leaning back in a redwood deck chair, a half-empty beer bottle cradled against his stomach, he let the conversation drift over and around him. At the moment, his interest was in something considerably nearer to hand than Washington.

From beneath half-closed eyelids, he saw Kate steal a discreet look at her watch for the second time in less than ten minutes. She'd barely said a word since lunch, he thought. And she'd managed to avoid looking at him entirely, not an easy feat in such a small gathering.

He lifted the beer bottle and took a deep swallow as he considered the suspicion that had taken root in his mind. It seemed impossible, and yet... There had been that moment when she'd looked at him and he'd read—or thought he'd read—something in her eyes. Something frightened and maybe—just maybe—a little pleading?

Kate stood, returning Gareth's questioning look with a light smile before moving toward the house. Gareth turned his head to watch her for a moment and then returned his attention to the conversation. Nick took another swallow of beer and watched the door close behind Kate.

This was neither the time nor the place, he reminded himself, even as he got up. "Anybody else need a refill?" he asked. No one else did.

Not here and now, he thought as he walked across the deck and pushed open the door. It could wait. *He* could wait.

Kate was standing at the kitchen sink, holding a damp paper towel to her forehead, the social mask momentarily stripped away. She looked small and fragile, and he was suddenly sure he knew the answer to the question he'd yet to ask. Emotion caught him by the throat—anger and elation, hunger and fear.

Deliberately, he let the door thud shut behind him. She started and turned, the little color that was in her face draining away when she saw him. For an instant, she looked so vulnerable that Nick wanted to pull her into his arms and comfort her. At the same time, he had the urge to grab her and shake her until her teeth rattled. If she really was....

"Feeling warm?" he asked as he moved into the room.

"I—it's hot today." She watched him the way a rabbit would watch a snake, with fear and just a touch of hope that maybe she could escape with her skin intact.

Not this time, Kate. I'm not backing away this time. She flinched at the sharp click of glass against tile as he set the bottle on the counter. He pushed his hands in his pockets, a hedge against the urge to reach for her.

"Something you want to tell me?" he asked.

The tone was almost casual but there was nothing casual about the look in his eyes, Kate thought. She swallowed and looked away.

"I don't know what you mean." Her response wasn't as firm as she would have liked, but it was hard to sound firm when her knees felt as steady as overcooked noodles. She leaned one hand on the counter for support, making an effort to seem natural—an unsuccessful effort, apparently.

"You're trembling," he said. "If you don't know what I'm talking about, why are you trembling?"

"I don't particularly like being here with you," she said, lifting her chin in a futile gesture of bravado.

"Not good enough, Kate." He took a step toward her. "Nausea, tiredness—interesting symptoms."

"Not really. Pretty common for someone with the flu." She edged back a half step.

"Lasting for weeks?" Nick arched one dark brow in question and moved closer.

"It...sometimes it takes a while to kick the flu." The counter was at her back, halting her retreat.

Nick stopped in front of her, much too close for comfort. He loomed over her, his broad shoulders filling her view. She wanted to push him out of the way and run. And she wanted to put her head against his shoulder and feel his arms around her, shutting out the world.

"Are you pregnant?"

The blunt question caught her off guard. She hadn't expected him to bring it out in the open, to voice the word she could hardly even bring herself to think. She stared at him helplessly, her mind emptied of clever answers and evasions. Not that they would have made any difference. He read the answer in her eyes.

His breath hissed out, as if he hadn't really believed it until that moment. The kitchen was utterly still around them. She heard someone laugh outside, but the sound was far off and without meaning.

"My baby," he said. It wasn't a question, but Kate nodded. She closed her eyes against the sharp sting of tears. This was what she'd been dreading, yet now that the moment had arrived, she was almost relieved.

"How long have you known?" he asked hoarsely.

"A little over a week."

"Over a week," he repeated. He shook his head as if trying to clear it. When he looked at her, his eyes were sharp and hard. "Were you going to tell me or were you going to try to pass the baby off as Gareth's?"

Kate whitened. Guilt put a sharper edge to her anger, because for one brief, shameful moment she'd considered that possibility. "I wouldn't do that."

"No?" Nick arched one brow in question. "But you haven't told him the truth, have you? You haven't told him that we slept together. And just when did you plan on telling him that you're carrying my child?"

"She doesn't have to."

Nick heard Kate's horrified gasp as he spun around. Gareth stood in the door, his skin drained of color, his eyes blank with shock.

"She doesn't have to tell me," he repeated. "I already know."

Chapter Fourteen

Nick groped for something to say but his mind was completely empty.

"Dad changed his mind," Gareth said, sounding as dazed as Nick felt. He lifted the bottle he held. "I came in to get him another Coke." His gaze shifted from Kate to Nick and his mouth curved in a thin, humorless smile. "Lousy timing, I guess."

"Gareth." Kate took a shaky half step toward him. "I'm so sorry. I never meant for you to find out like this."

"No?" He turned and set the bottle on the counter, his movements carefully controlled. "Just how did you plan on me finding out?" he asked. When he looked at her again, Kate flinched from the anger in his eyes. "Were you going to tell me over dinner some evening? Or maybe you were going to tell me after we slept together?'' Rage broke through the calm, putting a cutting edge to his voice. ''Did you think I'd take this kind of news better after a good screw?''

''That's enough!'' Nick stepped between them, as if to physically protect Kate from the sharp bite of his words.

''Enough?'' Gareth looked at him, his eyes burning with rage and pain. ''I don't think it's nearly enough.'' He looked past Nick at Kate, who stood white-faced and silent beneath the lash of his anger. ''Is this why you've been keeping me at arm's length?'' he demanded. ''I've been worrying about your health, and the only thing wrong with you is that you're fucking my brother?''

''That's enough,'' Nick said again. ''She's not the one to blame here.''

''How noble of you,'' Gareth snarled. He shifted position so that he faced Nick squarely. ''How the hell long has this been going on? Since you came home?''

''We didn't— It's not that way,'' Kate said, only to shrink back when he turned toward her.

''You're pregnant with another man's baby—my *brother's* baby. How the hell many ways can there be?''

''It only happened once,'' she offered and then winced at the weak stupidity of her words.

''Oh, well, that's all right then,'' Gareth said, his

voice razor sharp and just as deadly. "If it was just once, then I guess I really don't have any reason to be upset, do I?"

"Back off." Nick stepped forward, this time blocking Kate entirely from his sight.

"You back off," Gareth said, his voice rising. "I want some answers."

"You've got a right to answers," Nick agreed. "But I won't let you bully her. Any problems you have are with me. Leave her out of it."

"That's a little hard to do, don't you think?"

"What on earth is going on in here?" Philip asked as he stepped into the kitchen behind Gareth. Sara was with him, her expression worried as she looked between her sons.

"We could hear the two of you clear outside," she said. "What's wrong?"

"Why don't you ask Nick?" Gareth said, gesturing sharply toward his brother. He turned away as if he couldn't bear to look at him another second. "Maybe he'll be able to explain to you how *my* fiancée happens to be carrying *his* baby."

Kate flinched as Sara and Philip looked at her. Shame was a solid lump in her throat, choking her.

"I don't understand," Sara said, bewildered.

"It's simple enough," Gareth snarled. "It seems Kate is pregnant with Nick's child."

"We gathered that much," Philip said, struggling

to retain some control over the situation. "I don't understand how."

"Oh, come on, Dad!" Gareth laughed harshly. "It's simple enough. He's been fucking her."

"That's enough!" Nick said sharply. "This isn't accomplishing anything."

"Please," Kate whispered. "I can't bear for you to argue because of me."

"You should have thought of that before you slept with my brother," Gareth snapped. "Or did you think I'd just give you my blessing when I found out about it?"

His anger was all the more hurtful for being justified. Kate had no defense to offer, no excuses to give. There was nothing she could say that would make up for the pain she'd caused him.

"I'm sorry." Tears burned her eyes and she pressed shaking fingers over her mouth. She looked from Gareth's furious face to Sara and Philip who were staring at her in stunned disbelief. "I'm so sorry."

She turned and ran, fleeing the ruin she'd made of her life.

Nick looked at Gareth, his eyes cold and hard. "I know you've got a right to be angry but if you ever hurt her like that again, I'll forget that you're my brother and do my damndest to take you apart with my bare hands."

He didn't wait for a reply but turned and went after Kate, leaving behind a silence roiling with emotion.

Kate was halfway down the drive before Nick caught up with her. Though she must have heard him coming, she didn't turn or slow down but just continued walking.

"Kate." He caught hold of her arm and pulled her around to face him. "Where are you going?"

"Home." She fixed her gaze on his collarbone.

"On foot?"

"I can't stay here," she said hoarsely.

She turned away from him, as if to keep walking but he didn't let her go. Instead, he wrapped his arms around her and pulled her back against the hard strength of his body. "I'll take you home."

Kate jerked convulsively against his hold. She didn't want him to try and comfort her. She didn't deserve comfort, not after what she'd done. She didn't think she'd ever forget the way Gareth had looked at her; the hurt in his eyes.

"Let me go."

"No." The simple refusal startled her. Nick took advantage of her sudden stillness to gather her closer.

"Don't—"

"It's going to be all right." His breath stirred the hair at her temple. "I'll take care of you." His left hand was splayed across her stomach, his fingers spanning her from hipbone to hipbone, covering his child—their child. "I'll take care of you both."

Kate sagged against him. In some distant corner of her mind, she knew she should protest that she didn't need him to take care of her. She was more than capable of taking care of herself. But it felt so good to lean against his strength. She squeezed her eyes shut, her breath hitching as tears welled up.

"It's okay," Nick crooned. "Everything's going to be okay."

She didn't see how it could be, but she didn't protest when he turned her into his arms. It was just for a little while, she promised herself. She'd only let herself lean on him for a little while. Just until she gathered enough strength to pull away and stand on her own again—just the way she'd always done.

Gareth was halfway through his fourth cup of coffee when the doorbell rang. It was barely ten o'clock in the morning. The only people likely to visit at this time of day were people anxious to proselytize their religion or his parents anxious to offer sympathy. At the moment, he thought he'd prefer the former to the latter. At least he didn't have to be polite to strangers.

He rubbed his fingers over the ache between his eyes. Whoever they were, he wasn't in the mood to deal with them. After yesterday, he wasn't in the mood to deal with anyone. He felt raw and aching. All he wanted to do was crawl into a hole somewhere and pull it in after him. Maybe they'd just go away. The bell rang twice in quick succession, which seemed to pretty much eliminate that hope. He remembered that he'd left the car in the driveway yesterday, which meant it was obvious he was home. If he didn't answer the door and it was his mother and father, they were going to worry.

Cursing, he set his cup on the counter and went to the door. As he flipped the latch on the dead bolt, he tried to arrange his expression into something approaching normal, although who the hell knew what was normal for a man who'd just found out that the woman he'd planned to marry was carrying his brother's child.

He pulled open the door and felt as if he'd been kicked in the chest, all the air forced from his lungs.

"We need to talk," Nick said.

"I don't think I have anything to say to you." Gareth felt the newly familiar mixture of anger and pain twist his gut.

"Well, I have something to say to you." Nick flattened one palm against the door, anticipating his brother's urge to slam it in his face.

Gareth's fingers knotted around the edge of the door until the knuckles whitened from the pressure. For a few seconds, he let himself consider the possibility of slamming his fist into Nick's face, but aside from affording him a momentary satisfaction, it wouldn't accomplish anything. Considering all the time he'd spent counseling gang members that violence wasn't the answer, it was ironic that it should be his first reaction. He dropped his hand and turned and walked away, not saying anything, just leaving the door open.

Nick hesitated. It wasn't exactly an invitation but it was as close as he was likely to get. He stepped inside, shutting the door behind him. It had been five years since he'd been in Gareth's house but it looked much the same as he remembered. The carpet was new but the sofa still sat under the same window with the same two easy chairs at right angles to it. The familiarity was disconcerting. It was as if, in this one place, the last five years had never happened.

"Spit it out." If Gareth's sharp tone hadn't been enough to dispel any feelings of nostalgia, the hard anger in his eyes would have been.

Nick drew a deep breath. On his way here he'd rehearsed a speech, but the carefully chosen words seemed flat and meaningless. He settled for simplicity. "I wanted to tell you that I'm sorry."

Gareth's laugh was sharp and angry. "Is that supposed to make everything better?"

"No. No, I don't expect it to make everything better but I had to say it. I never meant to hurt you— neither of us did."

"How comforting."

Nick thrust the fingers of one hand through his hair and sighed. This was turning out to be even more difficult than he'd expected. Guilt nearly choked him every time he looked at his brother.

"It wasn't something either of us planned. It just... Things got out of control and it...happened."

Gareth shoved his hands in his pockets and half turned away. *Things got out of control.* The words carried a sting he knew Nick hadn't intended. In all the months he and Kate had been lovers, things had never once gotten out of control. She'd never initiated their lovemaking, never given any indication that she particularly missed it when circumstances kept them apart. It hurt to know that it had been different—*she* had been different—with his brother.

"Is that all you have to say?" he asked.

"We need to find a way past this," Nick said quietly.

Gareth's head came up, his eyes black with anger. "Don't tell me what *we* need to do. I don't give a damn what you need. Do you even know what you did?"

"I know exactly what I did." Thin white lines bracketed Nick's mouth but his answer was steady. "I'm not asking you to forgive me."

"Then what the hell do you want?" Gareth asked with a tired kind of anger. "What do you want from me, Nick? Do you want me to say it's okay that you slept with the woman I was going to marry? Am I supposed to feel good about the fact that the two of you couldn't keep your hands off each other? Or how about if I tell you that I think it's just swell that you got her pregnant? Is that what you want?''

The lines around Nick's mouth deepened and a muscle ticked in his jaw. ''We're family—''

''Funny you should be so aware of that now.''

''I can't change what happened and I know it's going to take time—maybe a lot of it—to get past this.''

''There are some things you just can't get past.''

''I hope this isn't one of them,'' Nick said quietly. ''I've lost enough family. I don't want to lose you, too.''

''Maybe you should have thought of that before you got Kate pregnant,'' Gareth said, not giving an inch.

Nick had no answer. What could he say? That he hadn't been able to think of anything beyond the need to have her? The hunger to make her his? Could he even honestly say he'd do anything differently if he was given the chance to live that night over again? He sighed. ''I'll leave you alone.''

He slid one hand in his pocket as he turned toward the door.

''You and Kate—'' The words seemed to be jerked from Gareth. ''Are you— What are you planning to do?''

Nick pulled his hand out of his pocket. His fingers clenched for a moment and then opened slowly. He bent to place Kate's engagement ring on the coffee table. He straightened and met his brother's eyes. "We went to Vegas and got married last night."

He walked out without another word, leaving Gareth alone with the ring and all the dreams it had once represented.

Chapter Fifteen

Kate slid the pruning shears along the rose stem and cut at a slight angle just below a cluster of five leaves before sliding her arm carefully out of the tangle of canes. The faded rose was held neatly in the grasp of the pruning shears. She dropped the blossom into a brown paper bag that was half-full of similar remains. She paused before reaching for the next tattered flower and allowed herself a moment to savor the beauty around her.

In early June, the formal rose garden at Spider's Walk was a riot of bloom—icy white, blood red, soft apricot, butter yellow and every color of pink imaginable, fat blossoms that filled the air with an indescribable perfume. Bees flew from flower to flower, guests at a scented feast. Months ago, she'd tried to picture what the garden would look like when it was in bloom, but her imagination had fallen short of the reality. Aside from some minor cleanup, she hadn't even begun work in the rose garden, but it was already her favorite place on the property and the most beautiful, she admitted ruefully. Nature didn't really need human assistance to put on a spectacular show.

Releasing her breath on a happy sigh, Kate reached for another faded blossom. It was her day off and no one expected her to be anywhere or do anything. The morning sun was warm against her back. She could spend the entire day puttering in the gardens if she wanted. The remains of the perennial border were overrun with weeds. She might—

Sunlight caught on the gold of her wedding band. She stared at the dull gleam, the problems of the perennial border momentarily forgotten. She tilted her hand back and forth, watching the light run across the simple band. It had been almost two months since Nick slid it on her finger, but there were still moments when it surprised her to see it there. Less and less often, though, she admitted as she rubbed her thumb over the inside of the band.

Living with Nick—being married to him—hadn't been as much of an adjustment as she would have expected. She gave most of the credit for that to him. From the beginning, he'd acted as if there was nothing extraordinary in the situation.

After the horrible scene with Gareth at his parents' house, she'd thought her life in ruins. Her mind had been spinning with half-formed thoughts of leaving town with her head bowed in shame, like the heroine in a creaky Victorian novel. But Nick had picked up the pieces of her life and put them together again in a whole new pattern.

"We'll get married," he had said. His tone made the words a statement rather than a question.

Kate had felt the bottom drop out of her stomach as she stared at him. "This is the nineties. No one gets married just because of a baby."

Nick had arched one dark brow. "Can you think of a better reason?"

She'd found herself without an answer.

When she thought about it, it seemed incredible that she'd given in with barely even a token struggle. From the time she was small, one of her primary goals had been to control her life. She didn't ever again want to be at the mercy of someone else's whims or find her life pulled apart by their weakness.

Yet, from the moment Nick had placed his hand over the child she carried and said that he would take care of them both, she'd found her need to be the captain of her fate giving way before the desire to lean on his strength. Maybe her pregnancy had awakened some age-old need to be cared for, to let the male of the species protect her and their unborn child. Or perhaps her reasons were more pragmatic. She was tired—physically, mentally and most of all emotionally. Tired of worrying, tired of making decisions, tired—heaven help her—of being strong.

She had been almost pathetically grateful that someone else was making decisions at a time when she felt barely capable of remembering her own name. Kate snipped another dead blossom and dropped it in the sack, then let her hand fall to her side while she stared unseeingly at a pollen-laden bee that was waddling along the edge of a half open rose.

Sometimes it bothered her that everything seemed to be working out so well. Her marriage was... Well, it wasn't exactly a marriage at this point. It had been her idea that they should have separate rooms. She smoothed one hand absently over the slight swell of her stomach. Looking back, it seemed like a case of shutting the barn door after the horse was out, but at the time, it had made sense—at least to her. And Nick hadn't argued. He hadn't offered even a mild protest.

Kate's teeth worried the inside of her lower lip as she considered their unique sleeping arrangements. Maybe Nick hadn't argued because he hadn't wanted her to change her mind about marrying him. Did he still *want* her? Did she *want* him to want her? They hadn't really discussed anything beyond the bare fact that they were going to be married. They hadn't asked any of the questions that had occurred to her since then. How long was this marriage going to last? Would it eventually be a real marriage?

Questions she was half afraid to ask, she admitted.

She wasn't ready to risk upsetting the status quo. Living at Spider's Walk with Nick and Harry, she'd found an odd sort of contentment—odd because it was so unexpected. By rights, she should have been miserable, if for no other reason than that she deserved to be miserable after hurting Gareth the way she had. But whether she deserved it or not, she'd been almost...happy.

"If you keep scowling at that bee, he's likely to take offense," Nick said from a few feet away.

"Oh!" Kate jumped, her head jerking toward the sound of his voice. He was standing in the middle of the main pathway, a coffee cup in each hand. Leroy stood next to him, looking bored. "I didn't hear you."

"Sorry. I guess I had my sneakers in creep mode."

Her eyes dropped to his feet. "You're barefoot."

"No, I'm not. I'm wearing purple Nikes with silver glitter on the toes. But not only are they in creep mode, they're also set for invisibility." He closed the gap between them as he spoke, and Kate could see the laughter in his eyes, though his expression remained serious. The way he could smile with just his eyes was one of his most endearing characteristics, she thought, feeling her heart clench a little.

"Silver glitter?" She raised her brows. "Sounds a little flashy."

"Too gaudy, do you think?" he asked anxiously.

"For you?" She pretended to consider the question. This sort of nonsensical conversation was typical of Nick. She'd smiled and laughed more in the past two months than she could ever remember doing in her life. "I think it's just right."

Nick frowned. "I'm not sure, but I think I've just been insulted. And after I came all the way out here to offer you sustenance." He offered her one of the cups. "Decaf." Leroy sat beside him with an almost human sigh.

"Thanks." Kate bent her head over the cup, feeling her cheeks warm at the oblique reference to the baby. Despite the fact that her pregnancy was the whole reason for getting married, they hadn't talked about it much. She was stupidly self-conscious whenever the subject did come up. It was ridiculous to feel embarrassed. He certainly knew she was pregnant and how she'd gotten that way. Even if he did seem to have forgotten that part of it lately.

Despite herself, her eyes slid in his direction. He was standing with his feet braced slightly apart, one hand wrapped around his coffee cup, the thumb of the other hooked in the pocket of a pair of faded jeans that rode low on his hips. An ancient gray T-shirt molded the solid muscles of his chest. His dark hair was slightly rumpled and his eyes had a sleepy look, as if he hadn't been awake for very long, which he probably hadn't been. She knew he'd worked until at least two in the morning because she'd heard him downstairs when she got up to make one of her increasingly frequent trips to the bathroom. He hadn't shaved yet and a dark growth of beard shadowed his jaw, giving him a vaguely dangerous look that made her heart beat a little faster.

"You know, most people prefer live flowers," he commented, glancing into the bag of faded blossoms. "And I'd think those short, stubby little stems would make it real tough to get a good arrangement going."

"I thought I'd just float them in a bowl of water."

"Aren't they a little...faded?"

"Don't you think it's a little shallow of you to only admire blossoms that are in the full flush of youth?" she asked crisply.

"I never thought of it that way." Nick glanced into the bag again. "So what you're saying is that, if I were a deeper person, I'd actually think all those bald sticks and rotten petals in there were beautiful."

"Exactly."

"Hmm." He frowned and shook his head. "Nope. I guess I'm just destined to remain a shallow hedonist," he admitted without visible regret. "I like flowers that actually look like flowers."

His grin was irresistible. The corners of Kate's mouth curved in a smile despite her best efforts to look stern. "Peasant."

"To the core." He gave her a conspiratorial look and leaned closer. "Not only that but I actually like Norman Rockwell more than Picasso. All those women with only half a face and funny skin tones and breasts in the wrong place." He shuddered. "They always make me feel like I ate the wrong kind of mushrooms for lunch."

"I'm not sure but I think that could get you permanently kicked out of the in-crowd."

"I know." He sighed and shook his head sadly. "Once a geek, always a geek."

Kate nearly choked on a mouthful of coffee. She'd never seen a more unlikely candidate for geekhood in her life. "You hide it well," she said dryly.

"A mere mask, hiding a deep-seated anguish. Makeup concealing the tears of a clown. A facade to—" Leroy's loud yawn interrupted the dramatic recital. Nick scowled at the huge dog. "Everybody's a critic," he complained.

Kate's laughter spilled over. Pleased with himself, Nick grinned. He had the feeling that she hadn't laughed nearly enough in her life. She always seemed faintly surprised by the sound of her own laughter. In the first couple of weeks after the wedding, even her smiles had been fleeting and guilty. He understood. Guilt had become an all too familiar companion lately. When he let himself think of the pain he'd caused his brother, it threatened to choke him. But he was a realist. He couldn't change what had happened, and if he was honest, he didn't want to. Kate was his, the child she carried was his and not even to heal Gareth's pain could he wish it any other way.

As she took a sip of coffee, Nick let his eyes drop

to her waist. She wore jeans and a faded olive green shirt, the tails worn out. The layers of clothing concealed the changes that pregnancy had made to her body but did nothing to stifle his curiosity. Was her waist thicker now? Were her breasts more sensitive?

Damn. Aware that he was becoming aroused, he looked away. Focusing his attention rather ferociously on an overblown rose in an eye-searing shade of red, he took a large swallow of hot coffee. Questions like that had contributed to quite a few sleepless nights lately. And seeing her like this, with the sunlight turning her hair to pure gold and her blue eyes smiling at him, he had to fight down the urge to sweep her up and carry her into the house where he could strip off the annoying layers of clothing and see exactly what changes his baby had caused.

Not part of the bargain, he reminded himself. When she'd agreed to marry him, it had been on the condition that they have separate bedrooms. He hadn't argued. He'd figured they could work out the details later. At the time, his main concern had been getting a wedding ring on her finger.

Looking back, he was sure he'd made the right decision, but that wasn't much consolation when he was lying awake, knowing that she was just down the hall, wearing his wedding ring, carrying his child. His memory was a little too sharp at times like that and all too eager to present him with crystal-clear images of the taste of her mouth, the scented softness of her skin and the hot, damp welcome of her body.

Swallowing a groan of frustration, Nick forced his thoughts in another direction. There was no point in torturing himself, especially since he wasn't willing to do anything to upset the fragile peace they'd achieved. If she'd shown the least sign of wanting to alter their arrangement—but she hadn't.

"I thought this was your day off," he said, nodding to the clippers in her hand. "Isn't this what they call a busman's holiday?"

"I suppose it is." Her smile was self-deprecating. "But it's such a beautiful day and—"

"You figured you'd spend it beheading roses," he finished for her.

"That's one way of putting it, I guess." Kate sighed and looked around the rose garden with an expression of pure joy. "This place is just so beautiful. Working here doesn't even feel like work."

"Harry thinks you're doing a great job with the place," Nick said, even as he wondered if it was possible to be jealous of a garden. He would have given a great deal to hear her express such open delight in his company.

"Harry doesn't care what I do as long as I don't ask him to make any decisions," Kate said dryly. She'd gotten to know Harry fairly well over the last couple of months. Though he was staying in the guest house, he usually joined them for dinner, and she'd found that her initial impression of him had been accurate. He was charming and a great deal shrewder than his perpetually wrinkled appearance would lead you to believe.

"I think he might register an objection if you decided to put in an amusement park," Nick said judiciously. "He also likes your cooking."

"Harry likes *anything* he doesn't have to cook himself," Kate pointed out.

"There's a certain truth in that," Nick admitted, grinning. "But he's still talking about that pot roast you made last week—the one you said was your mother's recipe. You got any more of her recipes stashed away?"

"A few." Kate reached out to snip a faded rose.

Nick saw the sudden tension in her face. He saw the same reaction whenever the subject of her family came up, which wasn't very often. Ordinarily, he was willing to follow her lead but today he felt like pushing a little. They were married, not roommates, no matter how comfortable she seemed with that pretense.

"How old were you when your mother died?"

She let a few seconds pass before responding and then her answer seemed pulled from her. "I was twelve."

Nick winced. "That's a rough age to lose a parent."

"Is there a good age?"

"No, but there are better ages than that."

She shrugged and said nothing. Nick almost dropped the subject but something pushed him to probe a little further.

"Were you very close to her?"

"Not particularly." Kate reached out and cut a perfectly healthy rose off the shrub, dropping it blindly into the bag at her feet. "She pretty much lived and breathed for my father. I don't think she had much left over for her...for me."

Nick groped for something to say, but her tone made it impossible to offer sympathy. He was starting to wish he hadn't given in to the impulse to probe for information about her family. But he wasn't quite ready to let the subject go.

"Is your father still alive?"

"I had a card from him at Christmas." Her knuckles had turned white with the force of her grip on the pruning shears. "It's a little difficult to keep track of him. He moves around a lot."

More than ever, Nick wished he hadn't given in to the impulse to ask about her family. He'd been left with more questions than answers and accomplished little beyond upsetting Kate. He opened his mouth to apologize but before he could say anything, she gasped and put her hand against her stomach.

"What is it?" His coffee mug hit the ground with a soft thud as he moved to her side.

"It's nothing." She shook her head. "Nothing

wrong, I mean. The baby moved and it startled me. That's all.''

"Does he move often?'' Nick asked, staring at her stomach with open fascination.

"Quite a bit.''

The compulsion to feel his child moving within her was too strong to resist. As if drawn by a magnet, Nick's hand came out and settled against the gentle swell of her belly.

Surprise held Kate still. It was the first time he'd touched her—really touched her—since the chaste kiss they'd exchanged at their wedding. She could feel the heat of his palm through the layers of her clothing. As if in response to his father's touch, the baby kicked again. Nick sucked in a sharp breath and lifted his eyes to her face. Pure happiness blazed in them, sharp and almost fierce in its intensity.

"He feels strong and healthy.''

"It could be a girl,'' she said, smiling at his excitement.

"Either way is fine with me. Do you have a preference?''

"No.'' She shook her head. "Just as long as he or she is healthy.''

"I guess we're going to have to pick out names.'' Nick's fingers shifted slightly against her belly, his touch becoming subtly caressing.

"I haven't really thought about that yet.'' She felt mesmerized by the intensity of his gaze. The sun-soaked garden wrapped them in a gentle cocoon, creating a sense of isolation, as if the rest of the world no longer existed.

"We've got time." He brought his other hand up and set one fingertip against the pulse that fluttered at the base of her throat. "We've been married for two months, Kate."

"I know." It was hard to force words out past the constriction in her throat.

"Two months, and I haven't really kissed you."

"No." She couldn't have said whether she was agreeing with him or protesting his obvious intention to make up for lost time.

Her thoughts were careening inside her head, a frightened need to retain the status quo bouncing off the purely feminine satisfaction of knowing that he wanted her. She wanted to lean toward him, feel his arms come around her. And she wanted to pull away, protect herself from the danger he represented. Caught between the conflicting urges, she did nothing.

Nick took her silence for acceptance and slid his hand around the back of her neck. She swayed toward him, her eyes closing, and he lowered his head.

"Hullo."

A siren couldn't have had a more powerful effect than that single word, offered in a piping little voice. Kate's eyes flew open and she stepped back so quickly that she nearly fell over her own feet. Nick's head jerked up and his entire body flinched as if from a physical blow. He sucked in a sharp breath and barely controlled the urge to release it on an even sharper epithet. With an effort, he gathered his self-control and turned to look at their visitor. Laura was standing next to Leroy, her big blue eyes wide with curiosity.

"Were you two kissing?"

"No."

"Yes." Nick's flat confirmation overrode Kate's breathless denial. "We were *about* to kiss," he told the little girl, hoping she'd take the hint—and her small person—elsewhere.

"Mommy and Daddy kiss sometimes," she informed them.

"Lucky Mommy and Daddy," Nick muttered and heard Kate's stifled snort of laughter behind him.

"Once, when they didn't know I could see, Daddy put his hand in Mommy's blouse." She reached out to scratch Leroy behind the ear, oblivious to the effect her words were having on her listeners. "Mommy seemed to like it but I thought it looked silly."

At a loss for words, Nick threw a pleading look over his shoulder at Kate, who was doing her best not to laugh out loud. Laura's matter-of-fact recital of her parents' behavior was bad enough, but the utter panic in Nick's eyes was almost too much for her self-control.

"I know where babies come from," Laura announced. She threw one arm around Leroy's thick neck and fixed them with a superior look as she prepared to educate. "The daddy puts his—"

"I have to go," Nick said loudly. "I have to, uh, take a shower." He bent and scooped his cup from where it had fallen in the grass and fled the scene as if the Hound of the Baskervilles was nipping at his heels.

Kate dissuaded Laura from her intended lecture and also managed to contain her laughter. She felt a modest amount of pride in both accomplishments. She detached herself from the little girl—not a difficult feat since Laura made no secret of the fact that she preferred Nick's company—and made her way to the house. Deadheading the roses had lost its appeal. It was getting close to lunchtime and her stomach was starting to send up polite inquiries.

When she entered the kitchen, she could hear the shower running upstairs. She went to the refrigerator and got out the ingredients for a salad but her thoughts were elsewhere. Her mind was filled with the unwanted and irresistible image of Nick standing in the shower, water beading in the hair on his chest, sluicing down his body. Her fingers clenched around the bottle of salad dressing and she drew a shaky breath.

Good grief, it wasn't like this was the first time

she'd heard him take a shower. But it was the first time since he'd touched her, almost kissed her. Her body was tingling with renewed awareness of him, all her senses alert and hungry.

The very intensity of her reaction made her uneasy. It was dangerous to want anything too much. Dangerous to let herself become too involved.

Like being married to the guy and pregnant with his child isn't already pretty damned involved?

Kate shook her head as she carried the salad ingredients to the counter. There was involved and then there was *involved.* Nick cut through her defenses too easily, made her trust him, made her want him. He posed a threat to her that Gareth hadn't. She couldn't articulate it clearly, even to herself, but she knew it was the truth. If she wanted to protect herself, she needed to keep Nick at a distance.

The question was, which did she want more, safety or Nick?

The gentle chime of the doorbell was a welcome interruption and Kate went to answer it. She'd rather deal with a small child selling astoundingly overpriced and completely inedible chocolates than face the turmoil of her thoughts.

But it wasn't a neighborhood child raising funds standing on the other side of the door. Kate felt as if the air had been knocked from her when she saw who it was.

"Gareth."

"Hello, Kate." His smile was nothing more than a token curve of his mouth, leaving his dark eyes cool and wary. "Have I caught you at a bad time?"

"No. No, not at all." She forced strength into her knees and moved back from the door. "Come in."

"Thanks." He stepped into the entryway and she closed the door behind him. "I wanted to talk to you, if you've got a few minutes."

"Of course." She hadn't seen him since that horrible scene at his parents' home. It didn't seem likely that he'd waited two months to continue castigating her, but she couldn't imagine what else he might have to say to her. "I...was about to make a salad," she said, breaking the awkward silence. "We could talk in the kitchen, if that's okay."

"It's fine."

She led the way into the kitchen, acutely aware of him behind her. "Can I get you something to drink? A cup of coffee or a soda maybe?"

"No, thanks. I can't stay long."

She reached for a head of leaf lettuce, broke a leaf from the base and began tearing it into bite-size pieces and dropping them into the big wooden bowl she had ready. Gareth watched her, his expression unreadable. Kate heard the shower go off upstairs and was suddenly acutely aware that Nick would be coming downstairs soon. How would the brothers react to seeing each other for the first time since Nick had returned her engagement ring?

"You said you wanted to talk," she prompted when Gareth made no attempt to break the silence.

"Actually, I came with an invitation. Mom and Dad are hoping that you and Nick will come over for dinner Saturday night—nothing special. Just the family."

"I...I don't know. I guess it would be okay. If Nick agrees." Kate knew it was much more than a simple dinner invitation. It was an attempt to heal the breach in the family. "Philip and Sara came to see us a few days after we...after the—"

"After you and Nick went to Vegas and got married?" Gareth filled in the words she couldn't seem to find.

"Yes." Kate looked at the lettuce leaf she was tearing up. "They were very...kind." It was the truth as far as it went. They had been kind. They'd also been hurt and confused and upset, but they'd welcomed her into the family and wished her and Nick well.

"They want to patch the family back together again," Gareth said.

Kate gathered her courage and looked at him. "Do you want to put it back together again?"

Gareth shifted restlessly, shoving his hands in the pockets of his jeans and hunching his shoulders. He looked away from her for a moment and when his eyes met hers again, some of the wariness was gone.

"Yes, I want the same thing. I've lost enough family for one lifetime. I don't want to lose any more."

Kate's heart twisted with regret. "We— I never meant to hurt you. It was the last thing in the world I wanted to do."

"I know." He pulled his hands out of his pockets and looked at them for a moment before shoving them back into hiding. He glanced at her and then away. "You look well."

"I'm fine."

"Good." He pulled one hand free and used it to arrange two carrots at perfect right angles to each other.

Watching him, Kate was aware of a deep sense of loss. In the past few weeks, she'd realized that she loved the *idea* of Gareth more than she'd ever loved the man. He'd seemed to be everything she'd wanted in a husband, and she'd convinced herself that that was the same as love. But she'd cared for him. She'd *liked* him, and it hurt to know that she'd lost a valued friend.

Tears burned her eyes. Before she could blink them back, a movement in the doorway caught her attention. She looked up and saw Nick standing there. His gaze went from her to Gareth and then back again. His expression unreadable, he looked at her for several long seconds. Kate had the feeling he could see straight through to her soul.

And then he looked away, leaving her to wonder what he had seen there.

Chapter Sixteen

Nick spent the afternoon replacing a section of the front porch railing. It was a straightforward job, leaving him more time than he wanted for thinking. And what he thought about was Kate. And Gareth. That moment when he'd walked into the kitchen and seen the two of them together, Kate looking at his brother with tears in her eyes.

It was the first time he'd seen Gareth since the day he'd returned Kate's engagement ring. They had exchanged stiff greetings. Even with jealousy clawing at his gut, Nick had regretted the stiffness between them. Not that he'd expected anything else. The wounds were too deep to heal quickly or easily. He hoped, given time...

At least the dinner invitation from his parents was a start. The fact that Gareth had been the one to deliver it said that he was ready to try to move forward. Grateful as he was for that, it didn't stop Nick from wondering about the scene he'd interrupted.

He tugged on a rotten section of railing, but it held firm. When he'd rushed Kate into marriage, he'd been betting heavily on the conviction that she had never really been in love with Gareth. He might have had doubts about everything else, but he'd been sure of that. He'd used that conviction to stomp the guilt down to a manageable level.

So, if he was right, why had Kate been looking at Gareth as if her heart was broken? Was it because seeing Gareth reminded her so painfully of her loss?

The muscles in his shoulders bulged as he used brute force to jerk the railing loose. The harsh groan of splitting wood cut across the afternoon quiet like a scream. She wasn't in love with Gareth.

Was she?

He'd never seen any sign of it when they were together. They'd always seemed more like good friends than lovers. Or had he been seeing what he wanted to see?

He scowled at the discarded section of railing. He kept seeing the tears in Kate's eyes, the pain in her expression. What if he was wrong? What if she did love Gareth? He rubbed his hand against his breastbone, aware of a sudden tightness in his chest. What if she was married to him, carrying his child but still in love with his brother? Jesus, a talk show host could have a field day with that one! The moment of black humor faded too quickly, leaving him bleak and empty.

What the hell was he supposed to do now?

Kate rolled onto her back and stared at the ceiling. She'd been lying in bed for over an hour but, so far, sleep had proved elusive. She closed her eyes. If she could just stop thinking for a little while. But her brain refused to cooperate. With a hiss of frustration, she threw the covers back and sat on the edge of the bed.

Gareth's visit had effectively cracked the tidy little shell she'd built up between her and the real world these past few weeks. She'd been drifting along without thinking too much about anything. It had been remarkably pleasant, but she couldn't continue that way forever, she thought with a twinge of real regret. Seeing Gareth—now part of her past—had made her wonder about the future. Or maybe it was the fact that Nick had almost kissed her in the garden that was making her feel so restless.

Kate pushed her feet into a pair of pink backless slippers and pulled a soft robe over her plain white cotton nightgown. She snugged her belt around her thickened waistline as she pulled the door open and went into the hallway. Hesitating at the top of the stairs, she listened to see if she could hear any indication that Nick was still up. It was after midnight but he often worked much later than this. The big old house was quiet around her and the only light she could see was the one always left burning in the entryway.

She hadn't heard him come up to bed, but he moved quietly for a man his size, so that didn't mean much. She glanced down the hall toward Nick's bedroom, which was on the opposite side of the staircase from hers. From here, it was impossible to tell whether the door was shut or just pulled against the frame. There was nothing to stop her from tiptoeing over to get a closer look. Nothing except the fear that Nick would hear her and open the door to find her creeping around in the hall like a junior-grade spy.

What difference did it make, anyway? She wasn't going to turn into a pumpkin if she saw him after midnight. Irritated with herself, Kate started down the stairs, automatically avoiding the center of the third step from the top, which had a tendency to creak loudly if asked to bear any weight. She glanced at the archway into the living room as she crossed the entry hall. Nick had been working in there earlier this afternoon but it looked dark now. And that was the last thought she was going to give to his whereabouts, she told herself as she went into the kitchen.

Maybe some warm milk would help her relax. She could take it to her room and sip it in bed. There was a new catalog from White Flower Farms on the nightstand that she hadn't had a chance to read yet. She reached for the refrigerator door.

"Everything okay?" Nick asked from behind her.

With a stifled shriek, Kate spun to face him, one hand pressed to her chest, as if to still the sudden pounding of her heart. "I thought you were in bed," she said, fright making her tone accusing.

"Sorry." Nick's brows rose. "I didn't mean to startle you."

"That's okay." She waved one hand dismissively. "I didn't mean to snap."

"No problem. You feeling okay?" His dark eyes skimmed down her body in a searching look that made her skin tingle and made her aware of the bareness of her body beneath the thin cotton layers of robe and nightgown.

"I'm fine. I couldn't sleep and thought some warm milk might help."

He grimaced. "I always figured that, if the only way I could get to sleep was by drinking warm milk, I'd rather stay awake."

"It's not so bad." She pulled open the refrigerator door, grateful for the excuse it gave her to turn away from him for a moment and get herself together.

"I've heard people say a root canal isn't so bad but that doesn't make me want to have one," he said as she set the milk on the counter and got a small pan out of a cupboard near the stove.

"I'm not sure you can put warm milk and root canals in the same category."

"I can."

Kate glanced at him out of the corner of her eyes, trying to judge his mood. He'd been quiet at dinner. Even Harry had commented on it. Nick had shrugged off the old man's concern, smiling and saying he was tired from working so hard trying to get the house ready so Harry could put it on the market. The comment had made Harry grumble that there was no rush and it had also kept him from pursuing the subject, which was, she suspected, exactly what Nick had intended.

She hadn't bothered to turn on the overhead light, only the small task light over the stove, which left most of the room in shadow. She could make out Nick's form, the familiar length of denim-clad legs, a soft gray T-shirt that clung to the flat plane of his stomach and outlined the solid width of his chest and shoulders. His face remained in shadow, his expression unreadable.

She sought for a casual topic of conversation but found her mind uncooperatively blank. She wondered what he was thinking.

Nick watched Kate pour milk into a pan and set it on the stove. She turned the burner on and he caught the faint, sharp scent of heat as the flame came on. He'd been sitting in the living room, staring at the empty fireplace and contemplating the mistakes he'd made in the past few months, starting with coming home in the first place. He wondered if he should add marrying Kate to the list, but something inside him insisted that he hadn't been wrong there. He'd been trying to decide whether it was instinct or stupidity that made him feel that way when he'd heard her go into the kitchen.

Looking at her, he felt a sharp wave of possessiveness rise in him. She was *his*. And the child she carried was his. Both of them. His and his alone. It wasn't an enlightened attitude. It sure as hell wasn't politically correct, but it was how he felt. It occurred to him that he'd never felt this way about Lisa, but he shied away from the thought. He didn't want to think about the past, not tonight.

What was it about her, he wondered, almost despairingly. She stood there, wearing a virginally simple robe, her hair tumbling over her shoulders, doing absolutely nothing that could be construed as seductive, and he wanted her so badly, he ached with it. Swallowing a sound that might have been either a laugh or a groan, he lifted the glass of Scotch he'd carried in with him.

Kate had been trying very hard to pretend that she'd nearly forgotten his silent presence but it was difficult to convince herself when her entire being seemed focused on his every move. She glanced at him in time to see him take a swallow from the old-fashioned glass she hadn't even been aware he was holding. It was only the second time she'd seen him drink anything stronger than beer. The first time had been the night their child was conceived, and that was a memory that brought mixed feelings.

Nick saw her stiffen and caught the look of dislike she shot the glass as he lowered it. He raised his brows in question. "You don't like Scotch?"

Kate shrugged and looked away, pretending an interest in the milk she was warming on the stove. "I'm not particularly fond of alcohol in general. I've seen what it can do to people."

Nick's brows climbed higher. "Do you think I have a drinking problem?"

"No." She shrugged again. "At least, I don't know that you do. It's just— I know how easy it is to start using it as a crutch." She glanced in his direction but her eyes veered away as if she didn't want to look at him directly. "My father drank," she said, and the words startled her. She'd never said it out loud, had hardly even let herself think it. But now that it was out, she felt compelled to add to the flat statement. "He always drank—a glass or two in the evenings after work, maybe a little more on the weekends, but after my mother died, he started drinking more and more until he was drunk most of the time. I guess it was his way of dealing with the pain."

"Not exactly the best way to handle things, especially when you've got a child dependent on you."

A ring of tiny bubbles had begun to form around

the edge of the milk and she shut the burner off. She didn't reach for the mug immediately but stared into the opaque liquid as if viewing the past on its surface. "It was a...difficult time." She seemed to shake herself and shrugged again. "I guess it just left me with a permanent distaste for alcohol, but I shouldn't have said anything to you. It's none of my business whether you do or don't drink."

"I think a marriage license gives you some say," he said mildly. He glanced at the glass in his hand, shrugged and set it on the counter. "If you don't like it, I won't drink."

The pan Kate had just picked up hit the stove with a thud, sloshing milk dangerously close to its rim. Ignoring it, she turned her head to look at him, her eyes wide and startled.

"You don't have to do that."

"If my drinking worries you, I'll quit."

"You'd do that for me?" She obviously found the idea astonishing and Nick's smile took on a rueful edge as he moved toward her.

"Much as I'd like to let you believe that I'm making a terribly noble sacrifice on your behalf, Kate, I don't really drink all that much anyway. I've been nursing that glass for a couple of hours. Giving it up won't cause me more than a mild pang of regret. I reserve the right to an occasional beer for ceremonial purposes, however."

"Ceremonial purposes?"

"Watching football, eating ribs—profound moments like that. As long as you don't mind."

"I...I don't mind." She stared at him uneasily. The idea that he was willing to change his life for her, even in this small way, bothered her, though she couldn't put her finger on the exact reason. And when had he gotten so close? She tried to shift casually away but found herself trapped by the counter at her back. "I don't want you to give up something you enjoy for me," she muttered.

"You're my wife, Kate. I'd give up a hell of a lot more than an occasional glass of Scotch for you."

That was it. That was what bothered her about this. It made their marriage seem real. Permanent. Permanence wasn't something they'd talked about.

"I...I just—" She broke off, shivering as his hand slid under her hair, cupping her nape and pulling her subtly forward.

"The problem is, I think we've both forgotten," he murmured.

"Forgotten what?" She stared, mesmerized, as his mouth dipped toward hers.

"That you're my wife. Mine," he whispered as his mouth covered hers.

For an instant, less than a heartbeat, she held herself stiff, half frightened of the way he'd simply walked through her defenses as if they didn't even exist. His tongue slid along her lower lip, and Kate felt her knees weaken. It had been so long since he'd held her. Kissed her. What harm could it do to give in to the desire rising inside her? They were married. No one would be hurt by it. No one but herself, and she'd take care not to let that happen.

Even as the justifications argued themselves out in her mind, her hands were coming up to rest against his chest, her fingers curling into the thin fabric of his T-shirt, feeling the heat of his skin beneath. She'd been aching for this. Aching for him. Her mouth opened to him and she let her body sway against his, giving in to the hunger rising in her, a hunger only he had ever ignited in her.

The feel of her surrender exploded through Nick, burning away his already tenuous self-control. Arousal was instantaneous and powerful. His tongue plunged into her mouth as his hands slid down her slender back, pulling her so close that not even a shadow could have come between them. His fingers curved around the yielding softness of her bottom, lifting her against the hard length of his erection. He heard her whimper and then her legs parted to cradle him against the feminine heart of her.

It was just like it had been before, he thought. The hunger raging through him, burning away everything but the need to have her, the need to sheath himself in the damp heat of her. She rocked forward and a groan tore from his throat. He was hard as steel, aching with need. He had to have her. Now.

Kate felt the edge of the counter dig into her back

and for one delicious, half-terrified moment, she thought he was going to take her right there in the kitchen. With her pulse beating in her ears, her whole body thrumming with hunger, she wouldn't have offered so much as a word of protest.

But Nick gathered the last shreds of self-control and lifted her. Kate's legs parted automatically, twining around his hips, her arms circling his shoulders as he carried her from the kitchen. The full skirt of her nightgown caught between her legs, offering her tender flesh protection from the rough denim of his jeans, none at all from the rigid bulge beneath. Every step rubbed his swollen length against the aching softness of her, intensifying her arousal so that, by the time he'd reached the top of the stairs, she was nearly frantic with it.

Nick was in no better shape. It had taken a considerable effort of will to keep from having her on the damned stairs or pushing her against a wall and taking her standing up. He wanted her anyway, anywhere, as long as he could be inside her. Kicking open his bedroom door, he carried her inside and set her on the floor next to the bed, keeping one arm around her waist when her knees threatened to buckle.

He stripped the robe away from her shoulders, letting it drop to the floor. His T-shirt ripped as he jerked it over his head. An instant later he shoved his jeans and shorts down and kicked them aside. He reached for her nightgown again, only to stop, his breath leaving him on a strangled groan as her hand closed over his naked shaft. He froze, his entire body going rigid as her cool fingers explored his burning flesh. It was the sweetest torture imaginable.

Too sweet.

Groaning, his control in shreds, he grabbed her hand and drew it away and then stripped her nightgown off before lowering her to the bed. Moonlight spilled in through the open curtains, gilding the room with soft, silvery light. Nick wanted to linger over her, wanted to trace the changes his child had made in her body, wanted to explore every inch of her, taste the heat of her arousal. But his heart beat like a drum and his entire body ached with the need to have her *now*. Kate reached for him, her face taut with need, and he was lost.

Kate's legs parted for him, her hand reaching to guide him to her. Nick fisted one hand in her hair, tilting her head and lowering his mouth to hers, even as his body surged into her welcoming heat. He tasted her pleasure, felt it in the way her body arched to take him deeper, not just accepting his possession but demanding it.

In the months since he'd last held her like this, he'd tried to convince himself that it hadn't been as extraordinary as he remembered. It was just sex, after all. He'd lied. Sweet Jesus, how he'd lied. Nothing had ever been like this.

It was too intense to last long. They strained together, their bodies moving toward a shared goal.
The room was full of the harsh sound of their
breathing, the rhythmic thud of the headboard against
the wall and the earthy scent of sweat and sex.

When it came, the peak was hard and fast as the
climb toward it had been. Kate sobbed with the force
of it, her fingers clinging to Nick's shoulders as the
only solid thing in a world that spun madly around
her. The feel of her completion called up his, and
Nick thrust deep into her welcoming heat, a ragged
groan tearing from his chest as pleasure washed over
him.

It was a long time before either of them moved,
and then it took every bit of Nick's strength to ease
himself onto the bed next to Kate. She made a soft
sound of protest but it ended on a sigh of pleasure
when he slid his arm under her shoulders and pulled
her against him. She cuddled into the hard warmth
of his body, her head on his shoulder, one hand nestled in the soft mat of hair on his chest.

Nick thought vaguely that there were probably all
kinds of profound things that needed to be said right
about now but he couldn't think of what they might
be. He ran his hand up her back and felt a shiver of
awareness run through her. As if it was a signal, he
felt hunger stir in his gut. A moment before, he'd felt
drained, sated. But the need was still there, a warm
pulsing in his veins. He shifted his hand, sliding it

up her side until his palm rested against the soft globe of her breast. He felt her nipple harden against his side, heard her breath catch and knew it hadn't been enough for her, either.

With a muttered curse, he came up on his elbow, pressing her flat on her back as he leaned over her, staring into her eyes.

"Two things," he said as his hand closed over her breast.

"Two?" she repeated unsteadily.

"No more separate beds." He bent to trail soft kisses along the line of her collarbone while his thumb stroked the sensitive peak of her breast.

"O—okay." Kate gasped as his tongue flicked across her other nipple, rousing it to instant attention. "What's the other thing?"

"This time, we make it last all night," he said and closed his mouth over her breast.

She moaned, her fingers curling into the silky dark thickness of his hair, pressing him closer. Against her thigh, she could feel him growing hard again. Her last coherent thought was that he was probably going to have to settle for one out of two.

Sharing a room was only the most tangible change in Kate's life after that night. The other changes were more subtle, yet in an odd way even more profound. Suddenly her marriage was real, no longer words on a piece of paper she could barely remember signing.

It wasn't possible anymore to think of Nick as her roommate. He was her husband, in every sense of the word.

She'd always considered herself one of the least impulsive people she knew, especially when it came to making major life changes. Yet, in the past few months, her life seemed to have been ruled by impulse—sleeping with Nick, marrying him and now making their marriage real. There were moments when she thought that perhaps she should be very worried about her uncharacteristic behavior but she couldn't seem to whip up any real concern.

Nick was not only a passionate lover, he was fun. She laughed more with him than she ever had in her life. He had a deep appreciation for the absurd, wherever he happened to find it.

She came home from work one afternoon and found him sprawled on the sofa, his attention riveted on the soap opera playing on the television. Kate stared in disbelief, but when he looked up, he showed no trace of embarrassment.

"You wouldn't believe what these people are up to," he said, as if continuing a conversation they'd been having.

"You watch soap operas?"

"How else does anyone learn about life?" He gave her a surprised look. "Where else can you find out how to behave when you find out that your fiancé is possessed by the devil and has been stalking your sister, who's also his sister because his father was once married to your mother only they're divorced now and your father is married to your other sister who's not related to him by blood because she's a product of your mother's *first* marriage? Only the truth is that she's really your mother's sister, which no one knows yet.''

"Your mother thinks her sister is her daughter?'' Kate asked, coming farther into the room and staring, fascinated, at the screen.

"Not *my* mother but Caitlin's mother.''

"Isn't that a little far-fetched?''

"Not at all.'' He moved over to make room for her on the sofa and she sat down absently. "It makes perfect sense. You see, Caitlin's mother, whose name is Susan, was drugged by her father—''

"Caitlin's father?''

"No, *Susan's* father drugged her and hired a hypnotist to implant false memories of pregnancy and childbirth so when she came out of hypnosis she *thought* she'd had a baby.''

"Did he have a reason for doing this or was it just a slow day?''

"The baby was actually his illegitimate child, fathered on a Gypsy fortune-teller who died in childbirth.''

Kate dragged her eyes from the screen and stared at him. "You're making this up, aren't you?''

"Are you kidding? If I had enough imagination to

make something like that up, I'd be writing screen-plays and getting rich.''

"How long have you been watching this show?''

"A couple of weeks. I leave it on in the background while I'm working.''

"You found out all of that stuff about these characters in two weeks?'' she asked, incredulous.

"No. Turns out that Laura's mother has been watching it for years. She came over to borrow something and recognized the theme music so she filled me in on the juicy details.'' He suddenly pointed to the screen where an actor with improbably perfect features and thick white hair was sitting at a desk looking thoughtful. "See that guy?''

"Don't tell me—he's married to his own mother but thinks she's actually his long-lost love who ran off to join the circus when she was a child.''

Nick turned his head slowly and gave her a surprised look. "How did you know?''

Nick hadn't realized just how much he needed to have Kate sharing his bed until it happened. It wasn't just the sex, though that was certainly incredible. But even more than that, he'd needed to be able to touch her, hold her, feel the changes his child had made to her body.

He'd never felt this primal need to hold, to possess a woman before, and the strength of it made him uneasy. With Lisa, he'd wanted to care for her, to protect her. He wanted to protect Kate but he also wanted to know that she was his.

Not that sex had magically vanquished all the barriers between them, but it was a step in the right direction. Maybe she'd been as frustrated by their marriage in name only as he had, because she seemed to relax with him, let him inside at least some of the walls she'd thrown up for her own protection. She smiled more easily, laughed more often.

"What are these doing in here?"

Nick had been shaving. At Kate's question, he glanced over to see her holding up a box of Band-Aids. He arched one brow in surprise.

"Did you catch them doing something illicit?"

"No. But I don't understand what they're doing here." She sounded genuinely puzzled.

Nick frowned at her. "Why shouldn't they be there?"

"It just seems kind of odd, that's all." She glanced at him and he thought he saw laughter in her eyes but she looked away too quickly for him to be sure.

"What's odd about it?" he asked, confused. He picked up a washcloth and wiped the last of the shaving cream from his jaw. "It seems fairly normal to keep first-aid supplies in the bathroom."

"Yes, but for you?" She lifted one shoulder. "I figured that, if you cut yourself, you'd—you know—wave a magic wand and the cut would just go away."

She looked at him again, and there was no mistaking the mischief in her eyes.

Nick stared at her, his mind blank with shock. My God, she was teasing him about his ability to heal! Since the day he'd discovered his gift, he couldn't remember anyone ever referring to it in normal conversation, let alone joking about it. His family had always treated it as a secret—not something to be ashamed of but certainly not something to joke about.

When he didn't say anything, Kate's smile faded and her fingers tightened over the metal box. What an idiot! She couldn't believe she'd mentioned his gift, especially when she knew it was a source of conflict for him. It had been an impulse—a bad one, obviously.

"Nick, I didn't...I wasn't think—"

His shout of laughter cut her apology off in midword. It was probably more laughter than the fairly mild joke deserved, but it was the first time he'd ever laughed about his ability to heal. It felt wonderful. If he'd known how good it would feel, he'd have laughed about it years ago.

"Thank you." He hooked his hand around the back of her neck and dragged her close so that he could kiss her thoroughly.

"You're welcome," Kate said when he released her. "What did I do?"

"You made me laugh."

Kate started to say something but the chime of the

doorbell interrupted them. "Oh, no! That must be Brenda." She hurried into the bedroom, grabbed a hairbrush off the dresser and began dragging it through her hair. "I told her I was taking the truck in for a tune-up and she said she'd pick me up today."

"You two doing okay?" Nick asked, following at a more leisurely pace.

Kate's hand faltered for a moment. When her engagement to Gareth had come to such an untidy ending, her friendship with Brenda had been an unexpected casualty. Brenda had had a hard time understanding how Kate could so completely betray Gareth. There was still a slight distance between them but she thought they were getting past it. Nick knew about the rift and knew how much it bothered her.

"I think we're going to be okay," she told him and hoped she wasn't wrong. She picked up one shoe and looked around for the other one. "Could you get the door and tell her I'll be there in a minute?"

"Sure." Nick left the room and she heard him running down the stairs.

The missing shoe was halfway under the bed. She put it on, grabbed a scarf to tie her hair and hurried from the bedroom. A glance at her watch confirmed that Brenda was early—a practically unheard of event.

She'd expected Brenda to be in the entryway, or

in the kitchen watching Nick make coffee. But the entryway was empty. As she reached the bottom of the stairs, Nick came out of the living room.

"It isn't Brenda," he said. Something in his expression made her uneasy, and she hesitated on the last stair.

"Who is it?"

"He says he's your father."

Kate felt the bottom drop out of her stomach and her fingers clenched over the wooden banister. She looked past Nick to the man who'd come to stand behind him. He was nearly as tall as Nick, though his shoulders weren't as broad. His hair was dark, his features even, his eyes a dark gray-blue. He looked familiar and yet totally alien standing here in this house that she'd come to think of as her home.

"Hello, Katie." He smiled, delighted to see her.

"Dad." The acting skills she'd developed in a lifetime of pretending weren't enough to put any warmth in her voice. She saw Nick's eyes sharpen with question as she left the illusory safety of the stairs and went to greet the father she'd hoped never to see again.

Chapter Seventeen

His curiosity aroused, Nick turned to watch Kate greet her father. She accepted the older man's hug but did not return it, stepping back the moment his arms loosened.

"What a surprise," she said. "I thought you were in Seattle."

"I was, but the work there was running out and I figured it was time to move on." He chuckled, his blue eyes sparkling with humor as he looked at her. "You know how I am."

"Yes. I do." Kate turned to Nick, her expression revealing none of her father's amusement. "I assume you two have already met," she said.

"More or less." Nick came forward to take the hand she'd held out. The gesture surprised him. Despite the new closeness that had grown between them, outside the bedroom she rarely reached out to him. He suspected it was a measure of how much her father's unexpected visit disturbed her that she'd done so now.

"I introduced myself," David Moran said, smiling at Nick. "You wrote and told me you were engaged but I didn't think the wedding was coming up this soon."

Nick felt Kate stiffen. Obviously, her father knew nothing about her broken engagement and abrupt change of groom. "I rushed Kate into marriage," he said easily, glancing at her. "We ran off to Vegas."

"Vegas, huh?" David's smile widened. "That's where her mother and I were married. I guess that makes it something of a family tradition, doesn't it, Katie?"

"It would seem so." Her smile was perfunctory.

There was an awkward little silence. Nick wondered if he should suggest that they go sit down, rather than stand around awkwardly, but he hesitated in the face of Kate's cool response to her father. She didn't look as if she wanted to do anything that might prolong the visit. Still, they could hardly stand here like a bunch of statuary. He put his arm around Kate's shoulders and drew her against his side, ignoring her stiffness.

"I was about to make some coffee," he said. "Would you like some?"

"I wouldn't say no to a cup," David said. Then

he looked at Kate, his expression oddly hesitant. "As long as it won't be too much trouble."

"It's no trouble at all," she said. She smiled and Nick thought he could feel the effort it cost her. He felt her hook her fingers through the belt loop on his jeans as if she needed something to hold onto. "But I should warn you, Nick uses any leftover coffee as paint stripper."

"Sounds good to me," David said. His tone was a bit too hearty, and Nick's curiosity sharpened. Just what was going on?

A change of setting didn't do anything to dispel the tension between Kate and her father. While he made coffee, he tried to keep the conversational ball rolling because it was clear that, if he didn't do it, no one would. As it was, Kate's contribution to the conversation consisted of a few strained smiles and an occasional comment. David Moran was more forthcoming, though he didn't seem any more at ease than his daughter.

He seemed to have left Seattle on a whim, without a particular destination in mind. He was thinking about going to Texas or maybe Michigan and hadn't decided yet. "I've saved up a few dollars so I don't have to make any quick decisions. A friend of mine has a job lined up for me in Saginaw, but I hear they're building in Texas again so I might go there first. 'Course, summer isn't exactly the best time of year to be visiting Houston." He glanced at Kate, smiling. "Remember the summer we spent in Galveston? You were about eight, I think. You and your mother spent quite a bit of time on the beach."

"I remember." The memory didn't seem to bring her any pleasure. "It was after Miami and before Tucson. Mama liked Galveston."

"So she did." David's smile faded and he looked at his hands. They were strong hands, long-fingered and supple—an artist's hands, Nick thought. When he looked up, his smile was back in place. "She liked Tucson just fine, though. Said it was a good place to spend the winter."

"She never complained," Kate said expressionlessly, leaving the flat statement open to interpretation.

Nick saw her glance at the clock and guessed she was counting the minutes until Brenda arrived and put an end to this meeting. He couldn't blame her. The undercurrents in the room were strong enough to pull under an Olympic-class swimmer.

"Kate said you're a carpenter," he said, hoping to move the conversation onto neutral territory, not an easy task when he didn't know what war was being fought.

"That's right. I do finish work, some custom cabinetry, things like that. The pay's good and I can usually find work without too much trouble."

"While you're here, maybe you could give me some suggestions about some of the work around here. I'm more of a handyman than anything else and I'd—"

"Actually, Nick is an architect—a very good one," Kate interrupted. From her tone, it was difficult to tell whether she was praising him or throwing his degree out as a challenge. Nick couldn't begin to guess which it might be.

"Is that so?" David said, looking interested.

"More or less. I haven't done any designing recently, though." Nick turned to get cups out, grateful for something to do. He felt like he was walking through a minefield—one wrong step and the situation would blow up in his face. He set the cups down and looked at Kate. "Do you want me to put water on so you can boil some weeds for tea?"

"Weeds?" David raised a questioning brow.

"Herb tea," Nick said, grinning at Kate. It was an ongoing joke between them.

"I gave up caffeine a couple of years ago," Kate lied calmly. "It was making me uptight. Nick doesn't approve."

"I just think the stuff tastes like wash water." He picked up her lead immediately and saw her eyes flicker with relief and something that might have been gratitude. He added another question to the growing mental list he was keeping. Why didn't she want her father to know she was pregnant?

Kate looked at the clock again. This time, as if in answer to a prayer, the doorbell rang.

"That will be Brenda," she said immediately and even managed not to sound openly relieved. She looked at her father. "My truck is in the shop so my boss is picking me up this morning."

"Nice boss," he said.

"Yes, she is. I'm sorry to cut this short."

"That's okay." David straightened away from the counter he'd been leaning against. "I should have called before I came over. I knew it was a bit early to be dropping in but I was anxious to see you."

"Will you be staying in town long?" Kate asked, avoiding any direct response to his comment.

"I haven't made any plans." He smiled. "You know me—always going where the wind blows me."

"Yes. I remember." For just a moment, her expression was chill and then she gave him another of those quick, meaningless smiles. "We'll have to get together for dinner while you're here," she said as if she was talking to a casual acquaintance.

"I'd like that," David said eagerly.

The doorbell rang again.

"I have to go," she said.

"Not without a kiss," Nick said lightly, catching her hand and pulling her. Their eyes met, his searching, hers shuttered. He had a thousand questions but this was not the time to ask them. Resigning himself to frustration, he dropped a kiss on her mouth.

She was gone the moment he released her, and Nick looked after her thoughtfully. Considering the tension between them, he was a little surprised she'd been willing to leave him alone with her father. He wondered if he should be flattered that she trusted him that much or if it was just a measure of her desperate need to escape.

His gaze shifted to his father-in-law. The older man was looking after his daughter with such an expression of pain that Nick looked away, feeling as if he'd intruded on something private. He felt as if he'd been dropped into the middle of a play without the least idea of what the plot might be.

Just what was going on between Kate and her father?

Nick didn't get a chance to talk to Kate alone until after dinner. Harry joined them for the meal, as he almost always did. Nick thought it was interesting that Kate didn't mention her father's unexpected visit to Harry. Was she hoping David Moran would leave as abruptly as he'd appeared, without her having to acknowledge his presence to anyone? If he hadn't happened to be home this morning, would she even have told *him* about her father's visit?

He waited until Harry had gone to the guest house, leaving them alone, before he broached the subject.

"You want to tell me what was going on this morning?" he asked as he snagged a flour-sack towel from the rack and picked up a dish to dry.

"I don't know what you mean." Kate didn't look

at him as she rinsed another plate under running water and set it in the drainer. "You don't have to do that. They'll air dry just fine."

"It gives me something to do while we talk."

"I don't want to talk about my father," she said flatly. She dropped a fistful of silverware into the sink, letting it clatter against the porcelain as if punctuating her statement.

"There's obviously a problem—" he began, but she cut him off ruthlessly.

"If there is, then it's *my* problem."

Nick finished drying a plate and set it on the counter before reaching for a glass. He let the silence stretch while he debated whether or not to push. She'd said she didn't want to talk about her father and that should be an end of it. And yet... And yet, he couldn't shake the feeling that, whatever it was, it should be brought out in the open.

"Did he stay long?" she asked abruptly, almost as if against her will.

"Half an hour or so."

"Did you— What did you talk about?" Every word seemed pulled from her. She didn't look at him but kept her eyes on the fork she was washing as if the fate of the world depended on it being perfectly clean.

She was obviously upset, and Nick would have given a great deal to be able to comfort her, but there

wasn't much he could do when he didn't know what
was wrong.

"We talked about the work on the house," he told
her. "He obviously knows his stuff. I didn't tell him
about the baby, if that's what you're worried about."

She shrugged. "It doesn't matter, I guess."

"It seemed to matter this morning."

"I was...surprised to see him and I guess I overreacted."

"Actually, I think the word should be under-
reacted. I've seen people greet IRS agents with more
enthusiasm." Nick was careful to keep any hint of
criticism from his tone, but Kate's head came up, her
eyes bright with anger when she looked at him.

"I don't owe him *anything*," she said fiercely.

"I didn't say you did."

"Not everyone has a close family like yours." She
was very much on the defensive.

"I know that." He tossed the towel over the edge
of the drainer and leaned one hip against the counter,
watching her. "You want to tell me about it?"

"No." But there was no force behind the word.
Kate stared at the water in the sink. She trailed her
fingers through the slowly dissipating suds, vividly
aware of Nick watching her. Waiting.

Seeing her father had stirred up emotions she'd
thought were long dead and buried. Things she'd told
herself were all but forgotten, anger she'd convinced
herself she no longer felt. She'd spent the day feeling

restless and with a knot in her stomach the size of a fist. The emotional turmoil had exhausted her, and yet she was too wired to think about resting. She felt as if her skin hummed with nervous tension.

She didn't want to talk about her father, didn't want to *think* about him.

"Did he say anything more about how long he's going to be around?" The question had been haunting her all day.

"No. Just that he didn't have any firm plans."

"That figures." She pulled the plug from the sink and stood watching the water drain. "He never liked to plan more than a few days in advance, if he could avoid it."

"A spontaneous kind of guy?" he questioned cautiously.

"A selfish, self-centered, self-indulgent kind of guy," she said and immediately wished she could call the words back. "I don't want to talk about him."

"Maybe you don't want to, but I get the feeling you need to." Nick offered her a towel to dry her hands.

"Don't tell me what I need!" she snapped, jerking the towel from him. His brows rose at her tone and she felt herself flush. "I'm sorry. I... It's not your fault. I just... I wasn't expecting to see him."

"I know his job required a lot of moves when you were a child," he said cautiously.

"It didn't require moves," she corrected him. She began pleating the towel, starting at one end and making neat little back and forth folds, keeping her eyes on the process. "He *chose* to move. I never went to school in the same place twice. We moved every year. Every year, I was the new kid. I'd eventually make friends but then we'd be gone again. I finally stopped trying to make friends."

"Didn't he see how hard it was on you?"

"I don't think he wanted to see." Kate threw the towel on the counter and shoved her hands in the pockets of her slacks. She didn't look at him but focused her gaze on the clock on the wall, watching the second hand tick its way around the dial. "He just had to keep moving, always looking for... something. I never did know what. The perfect job. The perfect town. I doubt if he even knew what he was looking for."

"What about your mother? How did she feel about moving so often?"

"His happiness was always her primary concern. Everything else came second to that." A tired kind of bitterness colored the words. "She did insist that we didn't move in the middle of the school year, but that was as far as it went."

"Maybe she liked moving?" Nick hazarded. Once again, he had the sensation of picking his way through an emotional minefield.

"I don't think she cared one way or another,"

Kate said, shaking her head. ''As long as she was with him, she was happy. He felt the same way about her. They were...complete. Children were nice, but we weren't necessary.''

''We?'' Nick pounced on the word, his expression startled. ''You have brothers and sisters?''

''Had,'' Kate said softly, almost as if speaking to herself. ''I had a brother and a sister.''

Nick stared at her, feeling as if he'd just been kicked in the chest. ''What happened?''

''My mother died when I was twelve. We were in Denver then. Joshua was three and Mary was just over a year old—just babies, both of them. Mother got pneumonia and it just didn't respond to treatment. Before she died, she asked me to take care of them and of Daddy. I told her I would. I promised her.''

As she spoke, her voice became subtly higher and lighter until Nick had the eerie sense that he was listening to a twelve-year-old Kate. Her eyes were distant, almost unseeing, as if she was looking into the past.

''After she died, I kept my promise. I took care of the children and looked after Daddy. I had to go to school but I always came straight home so I could spend time with Joshua and Mary and take care of the house, cook supper. I never minded. They were such good babies.''

Nick's heart ached at the picture she was painting. She'd been just a child herself, too young to be trying to be mother to her brother and sister. "What happened?" he prompted when she didn't continue.

She blinked and shook her head, as if physically shaking off the memories. When she looked at him, there was a fierce, burning anger in her eyes. "He gave them away," she said. "He gave them away like they were unwanted packages that he was returning for credit."

"Gave them away?"

"It was a private adoption." Kate picked up the towel again, wrapping either end of it around her hands and jerking it back and forth with tightly controlled violence. "After Mama died, he started drinking heavily. I used to wonder if he'd sold my brother and sister for money to buy booze."

"Did he?"

"I don't think so." She scowled at the towel stretched tautly between her hands. "I...could never really believe *that* of him. I think he just gave them up. I came home from school one day and they were gone. He said he did it for me, that I was too young to be trying to take care of my brother and sister."

"You *were* only twelve," he began but Kate's head came up and her expression cut his words off short.

"I was taking care of them. They knew me. They loved me. We were fine!" she said fiercely. "But he didn't care about that."

"Maybe he really was worried about you," Nick

said carefully. He'd seen David Moran's face this morning, had seen the longing in his eyes when he looked at his daughter. He didn't doubt that, whatever his faults, the man loved her.

"He was drunk and crying when he told me they were gone," she said, as if he hadn't spoken. Her voice caught suddenly. "I didn't even get to tell them goodbye."

Nick stared at her helplessly. He knew what it was to lose people you loved and he knew that there were no words that could take away the hurt. It was all too easy to picture her as a child, losing her entire family in a matter of months. First her mother, then her brother and sister and then, just as surely, her father. He wondered if, in some ways, the loss of her father hadn't been hardest of all because it had seemed like a deliberate betrayal.

"He may have meant well," he said finally, knowing the words were hopelessly inadequate. "You can't know what someone else is thinking."

"I know," she said coldly, her expression implacable. "I know him and I'll never forgive him for what he did."

"Kate." He reached out to take her hand but she stepped back and he let his hand drop to his side. "It's not good to hang onto anger."

"Are you telling me I should forgive him?" she asked incredulously. In a heartbeat, her mood shifted from icy rage to white-hot anger. "What he did was unforgivable, and he didn't do it for me or for Joshua or Mary. He did it for himself because he was weak and selfish and he didn't want the responsibility. Don't you dare tell me to forgive him!''

"I'm not saying that." He'd never seen her like this—so angry that she was trembling with the force of it. "I'm just saying that you have to let go of the anger.''

"I don't have to do anything. You don't know what it's like to lose—'' She caught her breath and stared at him in shocked realization.

"I don't know what it's like to lose people you love?'' he asked mildly.

"I'm sorry,'' she muttered, looking away. "I know you've lost—more than I have. At least I can assume that Joshua and Mary are still alive.''

"They're still lost to you,'' Nick said gently. This time, when he reached out to take her hand, he ignored her attempt to pull away. He tugged her toward him, drawing her into his arms and holding her. She didn't try to pull away, but neither did she relax in his hold.

"You can't hold onto the anger forever, Kate. Sooner or later, it turns on you and starts eating you alive. You have to find a way to let it go.''

She didn't say anything, but the stiffness slowly eased from her body and she allowed herself to lean against his chest. Nick rested his cheek on top of her head and tightened his arms around her. He hoped

he'd gotten through to her. He knew from experience
what that kind of anger could do to your soul.

The Red Lake Motel was on the south end of town,
conveniently located near the highway. The name
came from the swimming pool built by the original
owners, the bottom of which had been surfaced in an
imaginative, but not particularly attractive, terra-cotta
colored plaster. The intention had been for the pool
to be striking and memorable—and it had succeeded
on both those counts. Unfortunately, a red pool
wasn't exactly a *positive* memory for most guests,
making them think of horror movies and great white
sharks rather than basking in the California sunshine.
The pool had eventually been resurfaced, but the
name had remained, providing a minor mystery for
the guests.

Nick turned the Harley into the narrow parking lot
that fronted the low pink stucco building. If Eden had
a tourist season, it obviously wasn't the middle of
summer, if he could judge by the number of open
parking spaces. He pulled into a spot that boasted a
pencil-thin strip of shade, courtesy of one of the ubiq-
uitous Mexican fan palms that had been planted with
military precision along both sides of the street in
classic California style.

He swung off the bike, tugged off his helmet and
stood for a moment, debating the wisdom of what he
was about to do. Kate would be furious if she knew

he'd sought out her father. Actually, seeing her furious would almost be a relief, he thought, frowning.

Since David Moran's arrival two weeks ago, she'd been so tightly controlled that it seemed as if she didn't feel anything at all. She smiled, she even laughed occasionally, but there was always the sense that she was just going through the motions, that the real Kate, the one who let herself feel things, was locked away somewhere with her eyes closed and her hands over her ears.

He'd tried to get her to talk to him but she just smiled politely and said there was nothing wrong. It was that politeness that bothered him more than anything else. If she'd told him to mind his own business, shouted at him to leave her alone, it wouldn't have been as frightening as that cool little smile and those empty eyes. He was obviously on the other side of whatever wall she'd retreated behind. She wasn't going to come out, and she had no intention of letting him—of letting anyone—inside. He couldn't shake the feeling that, if he didn't do something to break down that wall, she was going to close herself off so completely that he'd never be able to reach her again.

Nick bounced the helmet lightly between his hands for a moment before coming to a decision. He wasn't sure what a visit to her father might accomplish. But he had to do *something*.

Leaving the helmet with the bike, he turned toward the motel. David Moran's room was at the far end of the building, through the courtyard and past the pool. There was a couple lounging next to the pool, pale faces turned up to catch the blazing heat of the sun. From the look of them, they were attempting to go from winter white to California tan in one afternoon. He hoped they'd brought a good supply of sunburn cream.

Nick hesitated outside David's door. Did he know what he was doing here? The answer came promptly. *Not really.* With a rueful smile, he lifted his hand and knocked. He'd already seen David's camper in the parking lot so he didn't waste any time hoping to be saved from the consequences of his own folly by the other man's absence.

"Nick!" David looked surprised but welcoming when he answered the door. "Come on in."

"Thanks." Nick stepped inside. The contrast between the heat outside and the air-conditioned room chilled his skin. It was like stepping out of an oven directly into a refrigerator.

"I'd forgotten how hot summers in this part of the country could be," David said. "Last few years, I've been spending most of my time farther north. It's got to be close to a hundred out there today."

"Hundred and one, according to the thermometer on the bank. But the heat wave's supposed to break tomorrow. Should be down to around eighty-five or so."

"Break out the heavy coats," David said, giving an exaggerated shiver.

Nick grinned and shrugged. "It's all relative. Compared to a hundred and one, eighty-five is practically a cold snap."

"I guess so." He bent to turn down the sound on the television set, muting Rosie O'Donnell's monologue. "Keeps me company," he said, nodding to the television set. "Silence gets overwhelming sometimes when you live alone."

"It can." Nick thought of the years he'd lived in New York, all the long, empty nights spent watching Leno and Letterman."

"You want something to drink?" David asked. "This place has a kitchen—more or less. It's not much more than a closet but it saves me from having to eat out every night. Or cadge meals from my in-laws," he added, smiling over his shoulder. He'd had dinner with them twice, both times at Kate's invitation, though she'd barely spoken a word during either meal. He pulled open a pair of louvered doors to reveal a small kitchen area. "I've got Four Roses, Chivas and some single-malt whiskey. Name your poison."

"It's a little early in the day for me," Nick said easily. "You have anything cold and wet?"

"Beer and I think there's a couple of Cokes."

"A Coke would be great." Nick took the ice-cold can from him and opened it, watching while David threw some ice cubes in a tumbler and splashed whiskey over them.

"Place didn't come with much by way of bar glasses," he said, lifting the tumbler as illustration. He smiled and shrugged. "When you travel as much as I do, you get used to making do."

"Sounds like you've seen most of the country," Nick said.

"Pretty much. Have a seat." David gestured toward the room's one overstuffed chair. "I've traveled through every state except Hawaii." He sat on one of the straight-backed chairs that flanked the tiny table. "Only reason I've missed Hawaii is because you gotta leave the ground to get there. I don't do planes or boats," he added with a self-deprecating smile.

"That puts Hawaii pretty much out of reach unless you're one hell of a swimmer."

"Not that good." David's chuckle ended on a wistful sigh. "It's a pity, though. It would be nice to make it a grand slam. Every state in the union."

"Trying for a spot in Guinness?"

"No. Just like to see what's over the next hill. I never could settle in one place for very long. Always had the feeling I was missing out on something."

"More hills, usually."

"More often than not," David agreed. "But now and again, there's something new. It makes it worthwhile." He took a swallow of his drink and shot Nick a shrewd look. "I imagine Katie told you we moved a lot when she was a little girl."

"She told me." Nick kept his tone neutral.

"She hated it." David shifted his eyes to his glass, swirling it lightly so that the whiskey slid in thin, amber curtains over the silvery ice cubes. "I always told myself she'd learn to love it, given time. But she never did." He shook his head. "I used to think that children sort of grew up in the direction you aimed them, but it doesn't always work that way. Katie hated every move."

"Then why did you keep moving?" Despite himself, there was an edge to the question.

David's fingers tightened around the glass and then relaxed slowly. "I thought about settling down. Even tried it a time or two. But I couldn't do it. After a few months, I'd get the itch and I just had to move along."

No matter what it did to your family? But Nick didn't ask the question.

"Sally—Katie's mother—she never minded," David said. The words held a faintly defensive edge. "She didn't care where we lived. Long as we were together, she was happy."

Nick remembered Kate saying the same thing, remembered also the old hurt in her eyes. He felt the sides of the Coke can start to bend under the pressure of his grip and made a conscious effort to loosen it.

"You were lucky."

"And I always knew it." David looked at him again. "Did Katie ask you to come here?"

"No." Nick raised his brows in surprise. "Why would she?"

"I don't know." David frowned at his glass. "She...I never did understand her. I never knew how to talk to her. She always seemed to see too much."

"What do you mean?"

"I always felt like she could see right through me, see who I really was." His eyes, the same smoky blue as his daughter's, focused on a point past Nick's shoulder, looking into the past. "She'd look at me with those pretty blue eyes and she'd see right through all my lies to the truth."

Nick said nothing. He hadn't known what to expect from this visit, but he certainly hadn't expected the other man to open up to him like this. He glanced at the whiskey and wondered if it was David's first of the day and if that was what had loosened his tongue.

David's eyes met Nick's for an instant before flickering away. "I suppose she told you about Joshua and little Mary?"

"She told me," Nick said, making an effort to keep his tone neutral. He didn't want to do anything to discourage this flow of information, and he was curious to see what Kate's father had to say about his two younger children.

"I shouldn't have let them go, I suppose." David

rattled the ice nervously in his glass and then got up abruptly to splash more whiskey over the half-melted cubes. He sat down again and took a deep swallow, as if fortifying himself to continue. "I told myself—told everyone—that I did it because it was what was best for them, what was best for Katie. I said she was too young to be taking care of her brother and sister."

"She was just a child herself."

"Yes, but she was so much older than her years. And she knew." He sighed and let his head fall forward until his chin nearly touched his chest. His voice dropped to a whisper. "I could never fool her. She always knew why I did it."

"Why did you?" Remembering Kate's anguish, Nick had to struggle to keep his voice level.

David didn't speak right away, and Nick wondered if he was going to ignore the question. But then he lifted his head and met Nick's eyes for a moment, his expression an odd mixture of defiance and pleading. "I did it because I was weak." He looked away. "I did it because I wanted to bury myself in the bottle, and I couldn't do it with two little ones depending on me."

"What about Kate? She was depending on you, too." Despite himself, Nick's voice vibrated with anger. David heard it and shook his head.

"Katie never let herself depend on anyone, least of all me," David said. His mouth twisted. "I used to wonder, if she'd been different—if she'd been the kind of child who clung to you and always needed someone to take care of her—if maybe things would have been different between us. But even as a child, she stood on her own two feet.''

"Maybe she felt she didn't have a choice," Nick said coldly. He could no longer conceal his anger but the other man either didn't notice or didn't care.

"Maybe." David lifted the glass again. "It's funny how you spend your whole life looking for something—chasing a dream, always looking ahead. And then, all of a sudden, you look up and you realize you're not a kid anymore and you don't have a damned thing to show for all those years of dreaming.''

Nick didn't leap to fill the silence that followed. The other man's loneliness was palpable, but he'd created his own hell, and there was nothing anyone else could do to change it.

"I guess it was a mistake to come here," David said when Nick didn't speak. "I didn't mean to upset Katie. I just wanted to see her again. I hoped we could—I don't know. Maybe we could be friends.''

Despite himself, Nick felt a twinge of pity for him. But his primary concern was for Kate.

"I don't think that's likely," he said quietly.

David winced a little but he didn't argue. The ice clinked against the sides of the glass as if his hand trembled slightly. "She's pregnant, isn't she?''

Nick hesitated a moment before nodding. It wasn't the kind of thing that could be kept a secret. Kate's condition was already obvious to anyone who cared to look, which, obviously, her father had.

"A grandchild." David seemed to roll the word over in his mind and then shook his head. "Hard to imagine it."

There was nothing in his tone to indicate whether the idea pleased him or not. He lifted the glass and drank down the last of the whiskey. When he lowered it, he looked at Nick, his eyes clear and direct.

"You love her very much, don't you?"

"Heart and soul." Nick's answer came without hesitation and he felt a tremendous sense of relief at finally having said it out loud. The knowledge had been hovering for weeks—maybe months but he'd avoided recognizing it, more than a little uneasy about allowing himself to love someone again. It felt good to face the truth. "Heart and soul," he said again, savoring the truth of the words.

David nodded, as if the answer pleased him. He seemed to hesitate and then exhaled slowly. "I guess it's time for me to be moving on." It was a statement.

Nick nodded. He hadn't come here intending to ask him to leave but now, it seemed obvious that that was exactly what had to happen. As long as he was near, Kate was going to keep building those internal walls higher and higher until she forgot how to live without them.

For just a moment, he saw a flash of real pain in the older man's face but it was gone in an instant, replaced by a smile that didn't quite reach his eyes. "I'd just about made up my mind to head for Saginaw anyway. Weather's got to be cooler there."

Chapter Eighteen

Kate was halfway down the stairs when the front door opened and Nick came in. He didn't see her immediately, and she was seized by an almost over-powering urge to turn and run upstairs before he saw her. It was ridiculous, of course. There was no reason to run from Nick. Besides, she'd never make it, she thought with a flash of bleak humor. As if in answer to her thought, Nick looked up and saw her.

"Kate!" His smile sent a shiver of awareness down her spine. She ignored it and continued down the stairs. "I didn't expect you home," he said, coming forward to greet her.

"We had a problem with a water pipe at the nursery. No permanent damage but it created a small swamp so we decided to close a couple hours early."

"Your customers' loss is my gain." He caught her hands and pulled her forward.

Kate responded to his kiss but drew back quickly. Being close to him made her want to lean on him. And she didn't want to lean on anyone—didn't *need* to lean on anyone. It was always a danger to depend on other people.

"I'm going to spend some time in the garden," she said, pulling away from him. "In this kind of heat, everything needs extra water. By the way, Harry said he was going to pick up Chinese for dinner tonight—his treat. I reminded him that not everyone has a cast-iron tongue. Hopefully, at least one or two dishes will come without hot peppers."

She was walking across the hallway as she spoke, headed for the kitchen and the back door. The gardens were the one uncomplicated thing in her life right now and she was anxious to escape into them.

"I went to see your father. He's leaving for Michigan tomorrow." Nick's tone was so casual that it took Kate a moment to realize what he'd said.

"You did what?" She'd almost reached the door but she stopped and turned to look at him, the peace of the gardens forgotten. "Why?"

"Because I could see what having him around— seeing him—was doing to you."

"I was handling it."

"No, you weren't. You were hiding from it."

Kate opened her mouth to snap out a denial and

then closed it without speaking. Maybe he was right. And what difference did it make, anyway? What mattered was that her father was leaving. She took a moment to let the relief of that sweep over her.

"Did you...did you tell him to leave?" Kate wrapped her fingers around the edge of the door frame, needing a little extra support.

"No, I didn't." He met her eyes directly. "But I would have if I'd been sure it was what you needed."

She stiffened. "I don't know what you mean. I don't *need* anything from him."

"Or from me?" Nick asked, arching his brows questioningly.

Kate flushed because that was exactly what had gone through her mind. "I didn't say that."

"No, but that's what you meant."

She shrugged and looked away. There was something in his eyes that made her uneasy, something about his mood that disturbed her.

"Why is he leaving?" she asked, leery of letting silence build between them.

"I think he realized that there really isn't much here for him." Nick hesitated before continuing. "You know, for what it's worth, I think he loves you."

"As much as he's capable of loving anyone," she agreed without hesitation. She pushed her hands into her pockets and walked away from the doorway, her movements restless. "But he doesn't love me as much as he loves the road—or the bottle."

"People can't always help what they are," Nick said quietly.

"He never really tried to." Kate looked down, tracing the line between two boards with the toe of her battered tennis shoe. "I thought about what you said, about letting go of my anger." She shot him a quick sideways glance before returning her attention to the floor. "If it was just the constant moving, I could accept that. Lots of kids grow up on the move and they do okay. Even the drinking—I know it's an illness and that maybe he can't stop that without help. But I can't forgive him for—" Her throat tightened abruptly, cutting off the words.

"For giving away your brother and sister," Nick finished for her.

"Not for that," she agreed, her voice husky. "I can't just set that aside. Not just because it hurt me. I can't ever forget how frightened and confused they must have been. Especially Joshua. He'd just lost his mother and I was...I was all he had. And then suddenly I was gone, too, and he wouldn't have understood why or even have known that I cared." She stopped, struggling to get her voice under control. "I can't forgive him for that. Not ever."

"That's your choice," Nick said, surprising her. She'd expected him to argue, to urge her to forgive. Instead, he changed the subject abruptly. "What would you say if I told you I was thinking about moving back to New York? I could get a job with my old firm. The money's good and there's always something to do—plays, museums, the kind of thing we don't get much of around here. What would you think?''

It took every bit of Kate's self-control to keep her expression calm. Inside, she felt a chill that started in her chest and slowly crept outward until even her fingertips felt icy. She should have known this was coming. He'd never said he was staying in Eden, never made any promises.

''No comment?'' he asked when she simply stared at him as if struck dumb.

''I...I wish you luck,'' she got out. She turned blindly toward the door but Nick reached out to catch her arm and stop her. She jerked away as if stung. It hurt to have him touch her. It hurt to think of what a fool she'd been—believing in promises he hadn't even made. She should have known.

''That's it?'' he asked. ''Goodbye, good luck, don't call me, I'll call you?''

''I don't know what you want,'' she said stiffly. ''If you want me to go with you, the answer is no. I'm not leaving here.'' She set her hand against the slight swell of her stomach, as if to comfort the child she carried. Or maybe she was the one seeking comfort. ''I'm not leaving,'' she repeated.

''I didn't say I was, either,'' Nick said softly. He

waited until her head came up and her eyes met his. "All I did was ask what you'd say if I told you I was thinking about it, and you had me out the door in nothing flat. Not all men leave, Kate. Some of us stay put."

Too late, Kate saw the trap he'd set. And she'd walked right into it, she thought bitterly. To her, when he'd mentioned leaving, he'd been as good as gone. He'd known exactly how she would react, damn him.

"I don't really feel like playing Psych 101 with me as the patient and you as the analyst," she said coldly. "I've got better things to do with my time."

"Tough," Nick said flatly. He took hold of her arm again and led her into the living room. He nudged her gently in the direction of the sofa, but Kate ignored the hint. "You're not going anywhere until I've finished saying what I have to say."

"I don't want to hear it," she snapped, feeling her self-control start to shred.

"Tough, because you're going to listen anyway, even if I have to sit on you to keep you here."

"How mature," she sneered, concealing her shock. "Using superior physical strength to get your way."

"Whatever works," he said and didn't even have the grace to look guilty. "Are you going to listen?"

"I don't seem to have much choice." She crossed her arms over her chest and waited impatiently.

"I talked to Jack this morning," Nick said, as calmly as if they were having a pleasant chat. "He's been after me to pick up our partnership again and I've been putting him off because I wasn't sure what I wanted to do, but I finally came to a decision."

"Bully for you," she muttered and then flushed with embarrassment. Good grief, she sounded like a bratty ten-year-old. Pretty soon, she'd be sticking out her tongue and saying nanny, nanny. What was wrong with her? She grabbed hold of the tattered shreds of her maturity and tried not to resent the fact that Nick was simply ignoring her less than gracious response.

"I told Jack I'd do it," he said. He slid his hands in his pockets and rocked back on his heels. "We still have to draw up all the legal documents, but as of this morning, the firm of Sinclair and Blackthorne is back in business."

"That's...great." *This* was what he'd dragged her in here to tell her?

"I'm staying, Kate." His mouth twisted with a touch of self-mockery. "I want to buy a house—for us." He looked around at the drop cloths, paint cans and partially stripped woodwork and his smile widened. "Hell, if Harry ever makes up his mind to sell this place, we could buy it. You like the gardens, and give me another ten or fifteen years and I might have the house in livable condition." He looked at her again and his smile faded, replaced by something so intense that Kate had to look away. "I'll put down roots so deep, it will take a major explosion to blast them loose. We don't even have to go on long vacations, if you don't want to."

Kate's heart was thudding against her breastbone as she realized what he was saying. She didn't want anyone making sacrifices on her behalf. She didn't want to feel that kind of obligation.

"I haven't asked you to make sacrifices for me," she said defensively.

"Who said anything about sacrifice?" Nick asked tartly. This wasn't exactly the reaction he'd been hoping for. "I'm talking about us building a home together, not immolating myself on the altar of duty. We're married, Kate. What did you think was going to happen with that? Did you think it was just going to go away?"

Kate shrugged weakly and looked away. "I haven't really thought about it," she muttered.

"Well, think about it now," he snapped. "And while you're thinking about it, think about this—I love you."

The moment the words were out, Nick wished them unsaid. This sure as hell wasn't the way he'd envisioned telling her how he felt. He'd been picturing candlelight and wine and soft music, not paint cans and sawdust. "Dammit all to hell." He thrust his fingers through his hair and laughed roughly. "I didn't mean to say that. Not that way. I... Dammit,

Kate, I've never known anyone who could throw me off stride the way you do.''

Kate heard him speaking but the words barely registered. He *loved* her? She didn't know how to react to that. She hadn't thought about love—hadn't allowed herself to think about it. She didn't want to think about it now. Loving Nick wouldn't be like loving Gareth. That had been sweet and warm and...comfortable. Loving Nick wouldn't be any of those things.

''You can't love me.''

''Is there a law against it?'' She was too caught up in the turmoil of her emotions to recognize the vulnerability behind the half joking question.

''I don't want to love you.'' Too upset to be tactful, she blurted out the truth.

Nick jerked as if she'd slapped him. He'd told himself not to expect too much. After talking to her father, he thought he knew how she might react, but he hadn't been prepared for how much it would hurt.

''Should I take it that you *do* love me, like it or not?'' he asked, struggling to keep his voice even.

''No.'' She shook her head, in answer to his question or denial of her own feelings. She started to turn away but he caught her arm and pulled her around to face him.

''This isn't something that's just going to go away, Kate. You know, it's usually considered a good thing to love the person you're married to.''

"You don't understand." How could he, when she didn't understand it herself? "I can't love you. What about Gareth?"

Nick's fingers tightened around her arm for an instant, and he released her abruptly. "What about him?"

"I...I was going to marry him. I loved him."

Thin lines bracketed his mouth as he struggled for control. His voice was tight with suppressed emotion. "You weren't in love with Gareth. You were in love with the idea of him. There were no deep waters with him. You could marry him and build a life without ever having to risk yourself. You didn't have to worry about loving him so much it would tear you apart inside to lose him. He was safe."

He hadn't said anything she hadn't already known. She'd thought about her feelings for Gareth, worried over how she could have betrayed him so easily. She might not have put it in exactly the same words, but what Nick was saying was true—she hadn't loved Gareth, not the way you should love the man you're going to marry. What frightened her was that Nick had made her realize how different her feelings for *him* were. There was nothing safe about what she felt for him. Living with him—loving him—she'd be risking everything.

Kate thought of the way her mother had been willing to set aside everything—her own desires, her children's best interests—to keep her father happy.

From the time she was old enough to see what was happening, she'd told herself that she would never be like that, never let someone become so important to her that everything was sublimated to the need to please them.

Nick saw the fear in her eyes and felt his anger dissolve. This wasn't the way it should be, dammit. They shouldn't be fighting about this, of all things. He'd handled this all wrong, and now she was looking at him as if he'd just shattered her world.

"I'm sorry, Kate. I didn't mean to snarl at you." He drew a deep breath and forced a half smile. "This isn't exactly the way I envisioned this conversation going," he admitted ruefully. He reached out to take her hand, but she pulled away.

"I need to think," she said. She brushed her hair from her face and looked around a little dazedly. "I have to think."

"I won't push." The promise didn't come easily, because he wanted to push. He wanted—needed—to hear her say that she loved him the way he loved her—heart and soul, without reservations. "You know, when you think about it, this isn't exactly sudden. Five years ago, the first time we met, if things had been different then—we might have had this conversation a long time ago. Maybe it was fate or Kismet or whatever that brought us together again."

Kate shook her head, not in denial but in an attempt to clear it. It was too much, too fast. First her father showing up, bringing back old memories, old pain, then this. She wasn't ready for this. She felt as if she'd been thrown into an emotional whirlpool without so much as a life vest to keep her afloat.

"Nick, I—"

The phone rang, the sharp, electronic buzz cutting through her words like a knife. Just as well, she thought. She didn't know what she would have said anyway.

"Let it ring," Nick said. "The answering machine will get it."

"No, answer it. Please." She dragged up something that was almost a smile. "I need a minute."

He hesitated. He didn't give a damn who was calling.

"Please," she said when the phone rang again. With a muttered curse, he turned and went to answer it.

"Hello?" He barely had a chance to register that the voice on the other end of the line was unfamiliar, nasal and wanted to sell him aluminum windows when he heard the front door open. The receiver crashed against the table as he spun around. "Dammit, Kate!"

The door shut behind her. He caught a glimpse of her silhouette through the frosted glass. He started forward and then caught himself. He couldn't chase her down the walkway, like the villain in a bad melodrama. She'd said she needed time. He could give her that.

Kate had half expected Nick to follow her. She didn't know whether to be glad or sorry when he didn't. Par for the course, she thought as she slid behind the wheel of the truck and started the engine. She didn't seem to know what she felt about anything right now.

She drove with no particular destination in mind, but she was not surprised when she found herself pulling into the parking lot of one of her favorite parks. It was a neighborhood park, not particularly large but well kept, mostly by volunteer labor from the neighborhood it served. What she loved about it was the huge old sycamores that shaded it. The trees were much older than the surrounding houses, and she liked the idea that, when it came time to build, someone had cared enough to plan this park around the trees.

She didn't get out of the truck but rolled down the windows for ventilation. There were half a dozen boys playing on the basketball court and their shouts drifted to her on the hot, late afternoon air. She watched them run and jump and tried to remember what it had felt like to have that much energy.

For a long time, she was content to watch them, keeping her mind a careful blank, letting the tension ease from her. Joshua would be about their age, she thought suddenly. But the thought didn't bring the same fierce rush of pain it once had. The hurt had softened and there was a certain acceptance in it now.

She let her head fall back against the headrest and closed her eyes. Maybe Nick was right. Maybe she had been holding onto the anger and hurt for too long, hugging it to her. She thought of the times she'd seen her father over the past couple of weeks. Now that she knew he was leaving, she found it easier to see him clearly. And what she saw was a lonely, lonely man who'd spent his whole life chasing after a dream that he probably couldn't even define. She wondered if he realized how much the pursuit had cost him.

Kate opened her eyes and looked out at the soft green sweep of grass in front of the truck. What was she doing here? Running, just like her father. It was ironic that she'd tried so hard to avoid being anything like him, and yet she was following in his footsteps in this one essential way. Instead of dealing with things, she hid from them, just the way her father had always done.

Nick was right about a lot of things, she thought. He was right about why she'd agreed to marry Gareth. He'd been right about the way she'd let her father's actions influence her expectations of the people around her. Maybe he'd even been right about fate bringing them together again. And, God help her, he'd been right about how she felt about him.

She loved him.

There was a certain relief in admitting it. She loved Nick. And he loved her. This time, the thought brought warmth rather than panic. He loved her. He wanted to settle in Eden and build a life with her. Her hand settled on the gentle swell of her stomach. A life with her and their child, she corrected herself, and felt the warmth increase.

Why had that seemed so frightening? Because loving Nick meant risking everything. She wouldn't be able to live her life on the surface anymore. She'd be opening herself up, making herself vulnerable, trusting someone else with her emotions in a way she'd never been willing to do. It *was* frightening. But the alternative was even more frightening.

Kate sat up and reached for the key. What a fool she'd been to think that safety lay in closing herself off from loving Nick. The truth was, the only security was in his arms.

"I wish you'd stop walking back and forth like a duck in a shooting gallery," Harry said irritably. "You're making me seasick."

"I don't like it that she's been gone this long," Nick said. He stopped in the living room doorway and looked at the front door as if willing Kate to walk through it.

"She didn't tell you where she was going?"

"No." Hell, she hadn't even told him she was going at all, but he saw no point in telling Harry that.

Harry had arrived over an hour ago, carrying boxes of Chinese take-out. He'd found Nick prowling restlessly through the house, looking at the clock every five minutes and looking more like a tiger in a cage than anything as innocuous as a duck. The moo goo gai pan and Szechwan pork were congealing in their containers on the kitchen table.

"It's not all that late," Harry pointed out for the tenth time. He was ignored, also for the tenth time.

"She should have been back by now," Nick muttered, stalking to glare into the empty fireplace.

"She's a big girl and this isn't exactly the big city, you know. Maybe she had a flat tire or something."

"She was upset when she left," Nick admitted reluctantly. "We...argued. Sort of."

"About what?" The question was automatic, a habit ingrained by years of cross-examination. Always pull as much from the witness as possible.

"I told her I loved her."

Harry's brows climbed in surprise. "And this was a bad thing?"

"Not bad. Not exactly." Nick shoved his hands into his pockets and then pulled them out again. He paced from one end of the living room to the other, measuring off the distance between the fireplace and the bay window at the front of the house. He stood next to the window for a moment, frowning at the fading light.

"Not exactly?" Harry prompted from behind him.

"It wasn't exactly a bad thing." He turned from the window and paced to the fireplace. "It has to do with her father and putting down roots and...other things." He waved one hand to encompass the emotional complications of his relationship with his wife. "It's getting late," he muttered, glancing at his watch for the fifth time in as many minutes.

"It's barely eight o'clock—not exactly the witching hour." But Harry was frowning, too. It wasn't like Kate to disappear. She was nothing if not dependable. "Probably just car trouble."

"The truck went in for a tune-up a couple of weeks ago," Nick said.

"Tune-ups don't prevent flat tires," Harry pointed out. "If she was upset, maybe she went to see Brenda. Why don't you call and ask?"

Nick started to shake his head and then hesitated. Considering the strained nature of her relationship with Brenda, it didn't seem likely that she'd go there, but it was a possibility. He reached for the phone book to look up Brenda's number and the doorbell rang. He dropped the phone book with a thud and looked at Harry.

"Probably someone selling something," Harry said, but his eyes reflected the same fear that had grabbed Nick by the throat.

That fear took on form and reality when he opened the door and saw Gareth standing there. Behind him, he could see the distinctive outlines of a police cruiser. He looked at his brother and knew what he was going to say even before Gareth said it.

"There's been an accident, Nick. It's Kate."

Gareth drove with lights and sirens and damn the rules. Streetlights provided him with an occasional glimpse of his brother's face, and what he saw there chilled him to the bone. He remembered that look from the days after he'd dragged Nick away from the bodies of his wife and infant son. It was as if Nick was gone, leaving only a shell behind. Whatever had happened between them in recent months, he'd never wanted to see that look again.

"She was alive, Nick," he said fiercely as he slid expertly into a right turn without slowing. "I wouldn't lie to you about that."

"It's my fault." Nick's voice was calm, almost detached. Gareth remembered that voice, too. "We quarreled. She was upset. It's my fault."

"No." Gareth put all the force he could into the flat denial. "She didn't wreck the car because she was upset. We've got a witness who saw the whole thing. A truck coming the other way had a blowout and lost control. It was coming straight at her. She steered away from it and went over the embankmer. It was just one of those things." He thought he detected an almost imperceptible easing of Nick's tension, but he couldn't be sure. There was no time for more because they'd reached the accident.

At first glance, it looked more like a carnival than the site of a disaster. All the bright lights and noise gave the scene a macabre gaiety. Until you stepped into it and saw the grim purpose with which paramedics, police and firemen were moving amongst the equipment.

Since he was with Gareth, no one attempted to stop Nick as he made his way to the edge of the road. To his right, he could see the truck that had caused the accident. It was a medium-size truck, the sort people rented to move themselves across town. It lay on its side just off the edge of the road. He glanced at Gareth in automatic question.

"Driver's okay. He's banged up some. May have a broken arm but he's okay."

Nick nodded and dismissed the other driver as they stopped at the edge of the embankment. He looked down to where Kate's truck lay and felt the bottom drop out of his world. He'd told himself he was braced for what he was going to see, but nothing could have prepared him for the fifty-foot-long scar gouged out of the hillside where the truck must have slid and rolled its way down.

It lay, miraculously upright, at the bottom of the embankment. The fire department had set up lights around the wreck, and they showed the smashed vehicle with merciless clarity. It didn't seem possible that anyone could have survived that trip down the hillside.

"She's alive," Gareth said, as if reading his mind. "They wouldn't be working so frantically to get her out if she wasn't." He didn't wait for a response but turned and waved to one of the paramedics. "What's going on down there?"

She walked over to them. "You're related to her, aren't you?"

"I'm her brother-in-law. This is her husband." He gestured to Nick, who hadn't taken his eyes from the activity below.

"They're trying to get her out right now. Her legs are pinned under the dashboard and the doors are both crushed."

"How badly is she hurt?" Nick asked without looking at her.

She hesitated, her eyes flickering from Nick's profile to Gareth. He nodded. "We're not sure. One leg is fractured. No obvious head injuries. Possible broken ribs, contusions, scrapes. None of that is life-threatening."

"The baby?" Nick asked.

"There's no sign that she's miscarrying. We can't be sure until we get her out but we think the baby is all right."

When she stopped, Nick turned his head to look

at her, and she winced from the intensity of his eyes. "What else?"

"She's bleeding," she said slowly. "There's a four-inch-long gash on her right leg. We haven't been able to get to it well enough to see what kind of damage there is, and we haven't been able to stop the bleeding, only to slow it down."

Nicked nodded and looked at the wreck.

"How long is it going to be before you can get her out?" Gareth asked.

The paramedic shrugged helplessly. "Twenty minutes. Maybe a bit less, maybe a bit more. They had to shore up the lower side of the vehicle to keep it from sliding farther. Working conditions are awkward. I can't give you an exact time."

"She'll be dead before then, won't she?" Nick's tone was flat, emotionless. But there was nothing emotionless in his eyes when he looked at her. "Won't she?"

The woman shifted uneasily beneath the demand in his eyes. "I... We're doing everything we can, sir."

"I'm going down to her."

"I know how you feel, sir, but the best thing you can do for your wife is to stay out of the way and let us help her."

"I'm going down there." He looked at Gareth, his eyes flat and hard. "I can help her."

Gareth returned his look, his stomach knotting. He

knew what Nick meant, what he was going to try. He knew also what it would do to him if he failed, and for a moment he wanted to stop him, wanted to keep him from trying because the price of failure would be too high. He drew a deep breath and nodded. "Go ahead."

There was a flash of understanding in Nick's eyes, acknowledgement of his concern, and then he turned and started down the slope.

"I can't allow—" Gareth caught the paramedic's arm as she started after Nick.

"Let him go. I can't explain it to you, but he may be her only chance. Besides, the only way you're going to stop him is if you shoot him, and I'm not going to loan you my gun."

Nick slipped and slid down the embankment, following the path Kate's truck had cut through the scrub. Twice, he lost his footing. Each time, he slid several feet before he was able to grab a branch and slow his descent. He heard noise above him and knew Gareth was following him down but his attention—his whole being—was focused on the twisted wreckage at the bottom of the wash. Kate was in there and he had to get to her.

It seemed to take forever, though it was probably no more than a minute before he was standing beside the wreckage. It looked even worse at close range. The bed of the truck was twisted almost beyond recognition, and the cab was so badly crushed it seemed impossible that anything larger than a house cat could still be alive inside it.

Nick was vaguely aware of Gareth running interference for him when the rescue workers would have protested his presence. He wondered vaguely just what explanation he gave them, but it didn't seem important. Nothing was important except getting to Kate.

The angle of the slope forced him to drop to his knees to reach the window on the passenger side. She lay back against the seat, her eyes closed, her hair a pale frame for her face. He wanted to believe that it was the harsh lights that bleached the color from her skin but he knew that wasn't the case. He could smell the blood, could feel death hovering. They'd met before, battled before, and he had once come out the loser. But not this time, he swore. Not this time.

Forcing himself to ignore Kate's pallor and the bruises and cuts that marked her arms, he wedged his shoulders through the window until he was sprawled across the seat. When he touched her leg, he could feel the slickness of her blood beneath his fingertips. He forced himself to ignore that, too. It wasn't important. Nothing was important except that he— Yes, there it was. He felt the familiar warmth, the tingle of energy starting in his fingertips.

Always before, when he'd used his gift, he'd allowed the energy to flow through him as if he was nothing more than a conduit for it. This time, he grabbed hold of it, demanded it, controlled it, fed it with his own life force, built the power of it and then set his hands on Kate's leg and poured everything he was, everything he ever would be into bringing her back to him.

Kate was vaguely aware that something was not right. She'd been driving and then there had been lights coming toward her. She'd turned the wheel. She remembered that much, but after that things got hazy. Pain. She thought there had been pain. But if there had been, it was gone now. In fact, she didn't feel anything at all. She felt...peaceful.

She turned—or at least she thought she turned, though she couldn't feel her body moving—and there was a light ahead of her. It was white, but not a harsh, blinding white. It was soft and warm and so inviting. That's where she was going, she thought, and was surprised that she hadn't realized it sooner. Toward the light. That's where she was meant to be. She drifted toward it, content, at peace.

"Kate!" The voice rang in her head, hard and demanding.

She frowned fretfully and tried to move forward but the light wasn't getting any closer. In fact, it seemed to be a little farther away. She strove to get closer to it, but the voice was there again.

"Kate!" It pulled at her. She wanted to put her

hands over her ears but the voice was inside her head and she couldn't block it out. "Come back, Kate. Come back."

Through the shattered windshield, Gareth could see his brother's face. There was something otherworldly about him, as if Nick was no longer there at all. Energy shimmered around him, an almost visible radiance that lined his profile with a glow that had nothing to do with the stark white glare of the work lamps.

Gareth sensed that Nick was literally willing Kate to live, breathing the essence of his own life into her, determined to either save her or die with her.

Kate didn't want to go back. If she went back, there would be pain and noise and fear. She wanted to go forward, toward the soft, peaceful light. But when she tried to do that, there was suddenly a new light in front of her. This one was a deep, warm red— the color of passion and love blocking out the cool serenity of the other light.

She started to flinch, half afraid of what it represented, of the demands it made even as it promised warmth but then the light surrounded her, bathed her in a soft heat. And she was suddenly aware of how cold she'd been, how alone. She held out her arms in instinctive welcome and the light flared higher as if in triumph. It sank into her, warming her, completing her, filling an emptiness that she'd carried inside her whole life.

She'd come home.

"Come back, Kate." She knew the voice now. Nick. It was Nick calling her, pulling her back from the white light. She looked for it again but it was faint and far away. She felt no regrets. Now was not the time. This was where she belonged.

She turned away from the light and walked into the healing warmth of Nick's love.

Epilogue

The word *miracle* is easily used and rarely respected, but now and again, something happens that defies all logical explanation—a real miracle occurs.

The people who were there that night knew they'd witnessed the real thing—a miracle born of love and desperation. It was something that none of them would forget.

When Kate stirred and opened her eyes, Gareth felt the last of his bitterness over losing Kate drain away. He might have loved her, but she was the other half of Nick's soul.

Five months later, Steven Joshua Blackthorne came into the world, a miracle of another kind entirely.

There were other children, another boy and a girl with her mother's fair hair and her father's dark eyes.

Harry refused to sell Spider's Walk. Instead, he gave the deed to Nick and Kate as a wedding gift, and the big house rang once again with the sound of children laughing and playing. The gardens were restored to their former beauty, offering food for the soul and plenty of places to play hide-and-seek.

Gareth eventually figured out what Brenda had known all along, which was that they were meant for each other.

Kate spent the rest of her life in Eden, but she'd long since realized that roots weren't a matter of place but of mind. She loved having a settled home, but as long as she and Nick were together, she could be happy.

Nick had at last found his peace. Kate and the children were his own private miracle.

As for the other miracle in his life—the night of Kate's accident was the last time his gift ever appeared. And that was fine with him.

He'd had more than enough miracles in his life.

National Bestselling Author

MARY LYNN BAXTER

"Ms. Baxter's writing…strikes every chord within the female spirit."
—Sandra Brown

LONE STAR
Heat

SHE is Juliana Reed, a prominent broadcast journalist whose television show is about to be syndicated. Until the murder…

HE is Gates O'Brien, a high-ranking member of the Texas Rangers, determined to forget about his ex-wife. He's onto something bad….

Juliana and Gates are ex-spouses, unwillingly involved in an explosive circle of political corruption, blackmail and murder.

In order to survive, they must overcome the pain of the past…and the very demons that drove them apart.

Available in September 1997 at your favorite retail outlet.

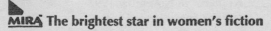

MIRA The brightest star in women's fiction   MMLBLSH

The SECRETS WITHIN

The most unforgettable Australian saga since
Colleen McCullough's *The Thorn Birds*

Eleanor—with invincible strength and ruthless
determination she built Australia's Hunter Valley
vineyards into an empire.

Tamara—the unloved child of ambition, a catalyst
in a plan to destroy her own mother.

Rory—driven by shattered illusions and desires, he
becomes a willing conspirator.

Louise—married to Rory, she will bargain with the
devil for a chance at ultimate power.

Irene—dark and deadly, she turns fanatical dreams
into reality.

Now Eleanor is dying, and in one final, vengeful
act she wages a war on a battlefield she created—
and with a family she was driven to control....

EMMA DARCY

Available in October 1997 at your
favorite retail outlet.

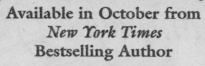